ASSORTED SISTERS

by

FLORENCE CRANNELL MEANS

illustrated by HELEN BLAIR

1947

HOUGHTON MIFFLIN COMPANY · BOSTON

THE RIVERSIDE PRESS CAMBRIDGE

Books by

FLORENCE CRANNELL MEANS

PENNY FOR LUCK

A BOWLFUL OF STARS

CANDLE IN THE MIST

RANCH AND RING

DUSKY DAY

TANGLED WATERS

THE SINGING WOOD

SHUTTERED WINDOWS

ADELLA MARY IN OLD NEW MEXICO

AT THE END OF NOWHERE

WHISPERING GIRL

SHADOW OVER WIDE RUIN

TERESITA OF THE VALLEY

THE MOVED - OUTERS

GREAT DAY IN THE MORNING

ASSORTED SISTERS

The Riverside Press
CAMBRIDGE · MASSACHUSETTS
PRINTED IN THE U.S.A.

With love to Hopiland, my East High,
and my Assorted Children, far and near.

ACKNOWLEDGMENT

The author wishes to express her appreciation to Mary Carolyn Davies for her permission to use selections from the poem 'Three.'

CONTENTS

1. The Family Comes to Friendship 1
2. The Good Old Days 17
3. Styles — In Skirts and Latin 30
4. A Spice of Mystery 40
5. A New Face 49
6. Mei-Lee's Junk Jewelry 63
7. The Chinese Center 72
8. Storm 82
9. Confession 96
10. Marita Shows Them 108
11. Common Ground 120
12. Joy Ride 134
13. Echoes 146
14. Consequences 158
15. Recruits 168
16. The Difficult Mr. Fong 182
17. Hovering Cloud 197
18. The House 207
19. Plots? 217
20. Such Things Don't Happen 231

I

The Family Comes to Friendship

MARY LOCKE turned sober gray eyes toward the impressive pillared façade of the settlement house. Her whimsical face was solemn under its mop of sun-faded brown hair. Father was the new superintendent of the settlement. Friendship House was the family's new home.

A new home, in a new city, meant a brand-new life to a girl of fifteen, especially if she had spent most of her life among a remote tribe of Indians. Friendship House seemed to make no pleasant promises. It glared as coldly as a building could.

Mary looked hastily away from it to the old station wagon which had brought the family from Arizona to Denver. It was boiling over with Lockes: her father and mother, her older brother, Rusty, and the Little Boys.

'Good grief,' Mary snorted, 'the Little Boys are simpally impossible.'

She caught at the car door to save herself as they hurtled past her and in on the station-wagon floor. They came up with added smudges of oil, dust, and melted chocolate, but also with what they had gone after. Jick tenderly pressed to his bosom a lump of modeling wax resembling a swan, and Bitsy clenched a limp gray lamb under his arm and rammed his thumb firmly into his mouth.

'Thank goodness the Board couldn't meet us,' Mrs. Locke said, grabbing at the mass of hats and coats that slid from her arm as she twitched up Bitsy's trousers. 'It's beyond me how the Little Boys always manage to look this way.'

Six-year-old Jick's milkweed-silk locks waved in a pale feathery crown and fell untidily over his angelic white brow. Three-year-old Bitsy's brown hair stood upended like a clothesbrush. Jick's shirt was half out and half in, while Bitsy had broken a suspender and lost a shoe. Both boys were lavishly coated with dust and chocolate.

Rusty, rummaging for the shoe and putting it on Bitsy's uninterested foot, said, 'Don't act so superior, Sis. We don't any of us look too nifty. Bitsy, where on earth is your shoelace?'

'Losted,' Bitsy said, still uninterested.

It was true that all the Lockes looked stale. Driving through the desert had been dusty business, and sleeping in the station wagon at night had not improved the family's appearance. The station wagon, given them years before, had been fitted with crankily ingenious beds. Mother said the beds were a blessing, with the hotels and motor camps so overcrowded. Father, who was less sensitive about finances, said it was certainly a blessing not to have to sleep sitting up, as they would have had to do if beds depended on their flat pocketbooks.

'I hope it's as grand inside as it is outside,' Mary said, gazing at Friendship House again.

'It isn't,' Father said cheerfully, turning to look with the others. 'Mr. Adams said it wasn't. He said he never could make out how such a county-courthouse effect on the outside could have so little room in it. Nor how so much money could accomplish such small results.'

The building was coldly imposing, with broad steps leading up to a columned entrance. A woman huddled against a pillar on the top step, completely absorbed in the play of a few children who swung and teetered on the playground. Yellowed papers had blown up against the wire fence and houses edged in toward it. There were forlorn little houses, with broken steps and windows, and grim big houses which had dropped from riches and one family to poverty and many families. Friendship House stared crossly away from them.

'This is going to be simpally awful,' Mary muttered to Rusty. 'What's the use trying to kid ourselves? We'll never in the world fit in a place like this, and with folks that will be just absolutely different from our Hopis and us.'

She tossed her sun-bleached mop of hair back from her face as if she were shaking the tears from her eyes. That small tanned face was shaped for mirth; the nose was tiptilted, and something about the gray eyes, their set and the fold of their lower lids, made them seem constantly on the edge of laughter. The wide mouth, too, with lips delicately cut and curling up at one corner, seemed always trembling into a smile. Now it managed to look doleful.

'Oh, come off, Sis,' Rusty snapped, his deep blue eyes

scowling at her. 'Don't nurse your blues. Let's get on
with it.'

Mrs. Locke was walking energetically up the front
walk, Mr. Locke striding after her and the Little Boys
trailing them, as Rusty and Mary fell into line. Mid-
way of the steps, Jick paused, with paternal solicitude,
to straighten the beak of his wax swan. The laboring
Bitsy came up against his brother's rear with a thump,
and fell backward into Mary.

The commotion startled the woman on the steps.
She shrank into herself and looked up at the family
with wide, blank eyes.

'How do you do?' Mother asked pleasantly.

The woman moved soundless lips.

A passing colored boy grinned up at the group, and
two little Spanish girls, skipping by, stopped and
stared.

'She don't talk no English, lady,' one of them volun-
teered. 'She just sits and watches the kids.'

With a smile and nod for the children and a reassuring
smile for the woman, Father turned the key, swung the
door wide, and waved the family inside.

The place echoed lonesomely. A dozen worn steps
led directly into a vast, stark room with lines and
circles painted on the floor and wire netting over the
windows.

'On beyond this gym,' Father said, with loud cheerfulness, leading the way, 'is a hall. Adams gave me a
diagram.' He flung open another door. 'Game room
on this side — chapel on the other side — and then a
kitchen, for Home Economics and for settlement-house

dinners. And there's a clinic in the basement, and class-rooms and showers —'

Just when a girl is growing up and wants a real home, Mary was thinking desperately.

Mother squeezed her arm understandingly. 'Oh, come, now,' she said. 'Our apartment may be entirely differ-ent. It's upstairs, isn't it, Father?'

The family climbed a space-consuming stair-well. Rusty said it was like the stair-well in a state capitol. At the top of it he opened the first door they came to, and they all found themselves in their apartment. Through the first room the Little Boys tiptoed and stumped, while the rest of the family followed in staring silence.

Suddenly Mary snickered, her lids folding and her mouth curling with laughter. 'We look as solemn as folks at a funeral viewing the remains,' she snorted.

'Compact living quarters,' Mother ejaculated.

'Well, and aren't they? Truer word was never spoke or writ,' Father observed dramatically.

The first room, perhaps eight feet square, was a living room, as evidenced by a dreary davenport, easy-chair and floor-lamp, of the type seen in second-rate waiting rooms. A minute kitchen adjoined it.

'You always wanted a modern kitchen,' teased Father, his eyes darting fun under his bristly brows: 'a kitchen without waste space.'

'I can stand in this one and reach every corner,' Mother said in awe, stepping across the threshold and demonstrating. 'And we're expected to eat at that little wafer of a table, sitting on those two benches.' Her voice had the do-or-die cheerfulness that rose from the depths of despair, like the smile on a daguerreotype.

'A family of Saint Bernards might feel this way in a toy dog's kennel,' Rusty said thoughtfully. 'That's one good thing I can say for it: I never felt so large before.' He straightened his slender five-feet-eight majestically.

'Maybe the bedrooms are bigger,' Mother said brightly, starting across the hall.

Father had got there ahead of her. 'Bedroom period,' he grunted.

It held a double bed, a dresser, and one chair. It held them with difficulty.

'And the bathroom,' Father called back, 'will at least keep the Little Boys from lining up to watch me every time I shave. You can only get in one at a time.'

'Why, where are the Little Boys?' Mother inquired suddenly. 'Jick! Bitsy! What are you doing? Stop it this minute and come here.'

'James! John!' Father roared in an irate voice which seemed very large for his size.

Above their heads sounded a patter of feet, a thump of solid little shoes on the stair, and then a bang-bang-bang and a howl. The family got out into the hall in time to pick Bitsy from the floor and his unlaced shoe from a far corner where his tumble had hurled it.

'We've got an attic!' Jick sang out, his spun-sugar hair on end and his blue eyes shining. 'An e-norm-ous attic!'

'We got a nackit!' echoed Bitsy, smearing his face with

dusty tears and waving his lamb dramatically as Father set him upright; 'a normouse sackit!'

'Well, that bears looking into,' Father said, starting up the stairs with the family once more trailing him; 'anything enormous in this apartment ——'

Mary came up last. As her face rose above the level of the dusty floor, she looked between her family's various feet and around the big, open space, cluttered with a few old sticks of furniture, a few boxes, a few old clothes hanging limply from two-by-fours.

'This really has possibilities,' Mother exclaimed, revolving slowly and measuring heights and windows with practiced eye. 'Since not one of us is over five feet eight.'

'Possibilities!' wailed Mary, in a high little shriek, as if she were a boy and her voice was changing. Mary's voice was soft and furry at the bottom, soft and slightly nasal in the middle, and soft and squeaky at the top.

Mother nodded vigorously. 'A big room for the three boys' — Rusty looked startled and indignant at being lumped with Jick and Bitsy — 'at that end, with that double dormer. Two rooms at this end' — she indicated the ends with her chin and lips, a trick learned from the Indians and startling on Mother's neat Saxon face — 'one for Mary and one for Father and me, with a half dormer for each. And a study for Father in between.'

'Without even a fraction of a window,' Father grunted, 'and with no cross-ventilation.'

'We'd not bring the partitions to the top, of course,' Mother replied. 'That space would help the ventilation. And the roof isn't insulated: that will help it some more.'

'And where do we get the money for these alterations, Felicity, my love?' Just as Mother seldom called Father by his first name except when under stress of emotion, so Father called Mother by hers only when he put on his ironic tone.

'A little wall-board,' Mother calculated, 'and some two-by-fours. And a little flooring; lucky most of it's floored. We could do the work ourselves. And the Board certainly ought to be glad to buy materials. You could almost say they got us here under false pretenses. Calling this living quarters indeed.'

'I'm positive I told them we had a family of four,' Father agreed.

Mother raised her eyebrows resignedly. 'That's it. That's probably just what you did tell them. Which four did you mean? The children, of course. I notice parents are zeros, these days.'

At that moment Jick slid the length of a strip of flooring and leaped the two-foot chasm to the next strip, and Bitsy, earnestly following, landed in the plaster, roaring.

'Why, he didn't break but just the tiniest hole!' Mary said wonderingly, lifting him out. 'All the same, that Board may think the false pretenses are on the other foot. Four in the family! And each of these *hombres* is the equal of two.'

But Mary's eyes were showing a trace of their habitual smile — the smile that came back if she didn't smooth it out by force — like a curl when you pull it straight and

then let go. Mother's voice had lost its brittle spright-
liness and was ordinary and businesslike again, and the
change gave life a brighter aspect. Mary dusted Bitsy's
plump trousers spankingly and pulled up his shoe and
set him down with an unwilling kiss on his solemn face.
She tiptoed over to the half-dormer that might be hers,
and looked out. She could see the Rockies, with snow
capping a majestic peak. Her eyes were jerked back
from purple mountains and gilded capitol dome. Jick
was giggling and Bitsy hoarsely bellowing.

'John Locke,' Mother ordered, 'stop tormenting your
little brother.'

'But I'm starved,' Jick argued.

'We all are,' Mother decided. 'Everything will look
better after a good meal.'

'Let's go to a restaurant this once,' Father suggested,
shaking his purse out on his palm, surveying the coins
and jingling them hastily back. 'Well, anyway, we've
got enough to buy things at a store and sort of picnic.'

'We've sort of picnicked for days now,' Mother
objected. 'Let's buy some honest potatoes and vegetables and make a stew.'

'And hamburgers!' clamored Jick, to whom hamburgers were above filet mignon with mushrooms.

'An' damburgers!' Bitsy echoed, jumping up and down
solidly on his short legs.

'And pop! Grape for me. Bitsy wants orange. And
Mother —— '

Father and Mary escaped in the middle of the list.

The nearest store was almost as dim and cluttered as
a trading post on the mesa. It had a few *riestras* of chili

peppers, blackening with age; strings of onions; bouquets of garlic. Dark-eyed Spanish were shopping there, and a Japanese woman and a Negro girl. Father and Mary purchased the potatoes — a quarter got only enough for one Locke meal — the carrots, onions and hamburger. They got bread that seemed exotic because of its unfamiliar wrapping; and oatmeal for breakfast; and raisins to put in the oatmeal so that the Little Boys would eat it. They crossed over to the drugstore, but found that it had run out of all soft drinks except ginger ale. So Father lugged the other things and Mary went bristling with tall bottles of ginger ale.

A car stopped in front of Friendship House just before Father and Mary got there, and a small, trim man backed out from the driver's seat, locked the car, gave a sharp glance at his near tires, and started toward the walk. The two Lockes stepped aside to let him pass, and he did so without glancing at them. Only as he inserted the key in the door did he seem to notice that they were behind him. He twisted around, darted a sharp look at their bundles, and another at their faces.

'I am Locke, the new director,' Father said inquiringly.

The small, trim gentleman's eyes edged back, distastefully, toward the ginger-ale bottles. 'Oh. Oh, I see. Biffin is my name. G. G. Biffin, president of the Board. We weren't expecting you till tomorrow. I came to see that everything was in order.'

He clicked the key around, creaked open the door, waited for them to enter. When the door squawked shut and his sharp, small steps followed the family up

the stairs, Mary had the guilty feeling of being escorted to the principal's office for a scolding.

In the small living room the small Mr. Biffin stood studying walls, floor, furniture, as if to see what damage they had thus far sustained.

'Excuse us while we set these down,' Mr. Locke said heartily, steering for the kitchen door. 'Mrs. Locke! Will you —— '

'Oh, there you are,' said Mother. 'If I can have those potatoes, I'll cut them small, so they'll cook fast. There isn't any skillet big enough, or we'd have them fried, this once. And look at the saucepans: like doll dishes.'

Mary giggled in spite of herself at the three pint-size pots briskly boiling on the small gas range, but Father shook his head and telegraphed with his brows as he thumped the supplies down on the small table. 'We have a caller, my dear,' he said, in the same hearty tone. 'The president of the Board. Come and greet Mr. Biffin.'

'I'll pare the potatoes, Mom.' Mary slipped into the apron her mother slipped out of, running a pointed tongue hungrily around her mouth. 'Leave the door open,' she whispered. 'I think this one is Scrooge.'

At that moment a small whirlwind blew into the kitchen and hurled itself on Mother from behind, shooting her without dignity into the living room. It was Bitsy, seeking refuge from a brother who had suddenly become a wolf, all teeth and claws.

Mother was proof against such accidents. She picked Bitsy out of her skirts, clasped the wolf firmly by a small, dirty hand, and smiled graciously at Mr. Biffin. 'These are our two youngest,' she said: 'John' — propelling the wolf forward — 'and James' — Bitsy wriggled back and hid his face between his mother's knees.

Mr. Biffin's face went empty with unbelief. 'Your two — youngest?' he stuttered.

'This is our daughter Mary,' Mr. Locke said firmly. 'Our eldest, Russell, junior' — involuntarily he gestured upward, as an even step measured the floor overhead — 'Rusty is investigating the attic as a continent we might flow out into.'

'But Mr. Adams gave us no idea,' Mr. Biffin protested. 'We thought even two children' — he concluded reprovingly.

'We were surprised, too,' Mother came back at him with her own deceptive, smooth brightness. 'These living quarters!'

Slicing another potato into the boiling water and jiggling up and down because it spattered her hand, Mary grinned. Mr. Biffin didn't know it, but no man was a match for that brittle, cheery sweetness.

'A director with a large family,' Mr. Biffin argued. 'A large family living in a settlement house —— '

'We are willing to partition off bedrooms in the attic,' Mrs. Locke conceded. 'Can you have the lumber and building-board for us at once? And about the beds. There is only one.'

'This davenport extends into a very fine bed for two,' Mr. Biffin said. Mary peeked around the door as he prodded it. It groaned and blew forth a languid puff of dust.

'We can move the one bed upstairs,' Mother went on, dismissing the davenport. 'Unfinished bunks will do nicely for the Little Boys. And unfinished single beds for Rusty and Mary. It will be a month before Rusty enters the university, so he can spare us time to put up partitions and paint beds.' Mother spoke firmly, her lips smiling. She looked every inch the lady, even in her travel-wrinkled dress. Mother had a remarkably finished, gentle face and head, not odd and quaint like Mary's. Only the set of Mother's chin gave you any warning.

Father came into the conversation at that point to help consolidate Mother's gains. 'Maybe you'd like to go up now and spy out the land, Brother Biffin,' he said in that deep, resonant voice of his. Immediately a medley of feet sounded on the attic stairs, Bitsy's, as always, lumbering in the rear.

Potatoes, carrots, and onions, sliced for quick cooking, were almost done, and Mary was mixing the hamburger with cereal and milk to stretch it, when at last the feet clattered and clipped and thumped down the stairs again, and, after a few more moments, the outer door clanged shut.

Mother briskly entered the kitchen, and scrubbed at the sink as if she were washing her hands of Mr. Biffin. Father leaned moodily against the door-frame. 'Incred-ible,' he said. 'The fellow is incredible. I thought that kind went out with bustles.'

'He looked at the ginger ale as if ——' Mary sputtered. 'Could he possibly think ginger ale was inTOXicating?'

'Avoid all appearance of evil,' Father rumbled, shaking his head. 'That was what the good brother was saying: Avoid all appearance of evil.'

'And the way he looked at the Little Boys,' Mother scolded. 'The lambs! As if it was criminal to have more than two children at the most.'

'I bet he hasn't got any. I expect' — Mary said cheerfully, trying to shape the oozing cakes of hamburger neatly, as Mother did, and the same size, so that the Little Boys would have no grounds for complaint — 'I expect this will be our Meanest Board Member.'

'Meanest Board Member?' echoed Rusty, coming from the bathroom with his reddish hair combed dark and crinkly. 'I should hope so. Was he ever furious over having to pay out money for lumber and stuff! And the way he checked my figures, as if he thought I was planning to go into the lumber business with what I pinched.'

'But you have to be fair, Bro,' Mother said. 'He was just trying to be accurate — and he's the kind that pares the cheese so thin you can read fine print through the rind. But there's probably some reason for his being like that; if we only knew the story.'

'Oh, Moth-ther!' said Mary, crowding six hamburgers on two small skillets after she had emptied the saucepans together to make room on the stove. 'He's just naturally mean.'

'Hush,' warned Father, 'here are the Pitchers with their big ears. I wish we'd got one of the pies at the grocery, Mary.'

'They'd taste like pasteboard and glue,' said Mother.

'But they would be pie,' Rusty put in, caressing his

lean stomach. 'Let's get one. Let's make it a party and forget Meanest Members — with Tragic Pasts.'

They got the pie, and they made it a party. The dining-nook benches admitted Father and Mother, Mary and Rusty, all tightly compressed. Jick sat on a stool at the drainboard, with one of Mother's best dish-towels for his tablecloth. Bitsy sat sidewise on a small hassock, with the commissariat as his table, the 'commissariat' being a battered blue bread-box in which the family carried food in the car. Bitsy rapidly shoveled hamburger into his mouth and over his front, his envious eyes on Jick, perched on the enchanting, tottery stool. Bitsy was to have the stool next morning at breakfast.

Food did make a difference.

'There's one thing to be said for a gentleman who shall be nameless,' Mother observed, sitting back and mentally loosening her belt. 'When that kind finally agrees to do something, he does it. Building material may be scarcer than hens' teeth, but I look to see the unfinished beds here tomorrow and the lumber and wall-board the first of the week. He'd do things promptly, or make it very unpleasant for everybody concerned.'

'Righteous,' agreed Father, doubtfully considering his small triangle of store pie. 'Self-righteous.'

'Not before the Little Boys, Father,' Mrs. Locke reminded him. 'Didn't I tell you the pie would be like this?'

'Like cardboard and glue,' Father admitted.

'And library paste,' Rusty put in.

But they ate it, all the same, and lingered at the table, comforted by feeling full.

Father said thoughtfully, 'What would you think of making a start by opening the gymnasium Tuesday, Mother?'

Mother nodded absently. 'I keep seeing that woman on the steps,' she said. 'There was something tragic about the way she sat there. There must be a story behind it.'

'Next week,' Mary interrupted with a small shiver, 'I start to school. I think I'll die.'

'Don't be so exaggerated,' Jick admonished her from his stool. 'I start to school, too, I guess, and you don't see me acting frantic about it.' Jick adored large words, and collected them like a magpie.

'Don't see Jick acking prandig about it.' Bitsy echoed his brother sternly, waving his fork and a last bit of pie at Mary.

She ignored them as one ignores mosquitoes that are always hovering. In spite of food, a cold desolation was settling down upon her as she thought of the strange new school. 'Next week a brand-new life,' she said; 'and it's going to be horrible.'

The Good Old Days

MARY'S HOMESICKNESS, banished for a few hours, swept back upon her with a rush that night.

Father and Rusty set up the complicated arrangement of beds in the station wagon. They slept there; the Little Boys on the opened-out davenport, which proved to be a chain of hills and valleys; and Mother and Mary in the one bed.

As she lay in the stuffy little room, stiff and still so as not to waken Mother, Mary thought with desperate longing of their big, rambling Hopi-masonry house under the brow of the Indian mesa. The weather-stripping Father had put in would be twanging like an Aeolian harp in the everlasting wind, but there would be few other sounds; no deafening rush of automobiles, no clang and rattle of streetcars.

That Hopi house! Wind came into it everywhere, driving sand as fine as flour. It drove into Mary's room, which was up under the eaves and had a little high dormer level with her chin, where she used to stand and watch the sun come over the edge of the desert, with nothing between it and Mary. Mary had set her collection of Indian baskets in the dormer, and when the wind was high those baskets always held enough dust to grow rosebushes.

She had thought it would be wonderful to live in a city, where she wouldn't waken, in winter, to find water frozen in her wash-pitcher. Yet hadn't it been fun to slip on her robe and run, shivering, down the boxed-in stairs into the delicious warmth? She had dressed behind the sitting-room stove, with breakfast cooking and smelling heavenly.

And the nights, with the stars over the desert brighter than anything on earth; and nothing else to see but the pale yellow windows of Hopis who had built near church and mission house. Nothing else but the far glow-worm of an automobile, slipping slowly across the vast black. And from above on the mesa the throb of Indian drums.

Again in memory Mary went through the farewells. Old blind Suta, riding down on his crop-eared burro, his feet almost touching the ground, bringing them his best hand-woven blanket. Long-haired men, their feet silent in small moccasins. Women with babies slung on their backs. Boys and girls. Carrie Kate, Mary's best friend, print dress starchy, hair like a crow's breast, blue in the sun.

They had brought gifts: baskets and pottery; bags of corn, newly dried on the ear, and delicious *nakaviki* and *piki*; and jewelry. Old Polemana, four feet wide and four feet high, had reached up to pat Mary's cheek, blubbering, ' *Eskwalli, eskwalli umpitu*, Thank you, thank you for coming.' She had shoved on Mary's wrist her own best turquoise bracelet, blue as the sky.

And John, the interpreter, grown grizzled and broad and slow like an old bear, had ridden little John — Jick — pickaback, as he used to do when Jick was a baby, trying to laugh while the wrinkles under his eyes shone wet.

And when at last they had climbed into the station wagon, poor Montmorency had broken into loud wailing. A man in years and a child in mind, Montmorency had been as faithful to the Lockes as a little dog. Now he stood with hands clenched at sides, sobbing after them the broken reproaches which the Hopis call 'scolding the dead.'

That death-wail raised the gooseflesh on Mary's tanned arms. It echoed in her ears like a black omen as they rattled away from mesa and mission and solemn Hopis. But Father said, his own blue eyes suspiciously shiny, 'Unselfish love is never a bad omen. It goes along with you like a sword and buckler.'

The Lockes took plenty of love from Hopiland. They had lived and worked there for years. Mary and Rusty had finished 'the grades' there.

Every morning they had climbed the winding trail to the Government day school on the shoulder of the mesa. Past the sacred spring, with its terraced vegetable gardens they had scampered, past the graveyard with its pottery bowls for feeding the dead.

People thought the Lockes eccentric to send their children to the Indian school. The Hopi children were at home in the Hopi language and ways, but retarded when it came to white schooling. Perhaps even Mr. and Mrs. Locke would not have persisted if it had not been for Shouting Luke, an old white man who tutored both Rusty and Mary from their seventh years on.

Shouting Luke was a character. From the watch-chain looped across his dim, spotted vest dangled a thin old Phi Beta Kappa key. From Yale. But soon after graduation Luke lost voice and health, drifted out to the desert and lived in a little Indian house below the mesa until his hair was white.

In Mr. and Mrs. Locke he had found echoes of his past, and Father said that he could smell Mother's Boston baked beans two miles away, even when the wind was in the wrong quarter.

Luke had begged to tutor the Locke children. He had taught them French and German early, with sound grammar but strikingly similar accents; and grounded them solidly in Greek and Latin. Thus Rusty and Mary had gone on into the Indian high school at Oraibi, sixteen miles away, with most of their actual learning done at the mission table, Luke whispering to them forcefully in his frayed voice.

The time had come when even Father felt that his children should come out into the normal life of America — if there was a normal life in America, he sometimes added gloomily. They must adjust themselves to their own generation.

That was easier said than done. The Lockes had sought the desert in the first place because of Father's asthma. He could not live and work in any but a high, dry climate. Apparently many other welfare workers, ministers, missionaries, also must have high, dry climates. At last, however, an opening had come: a social center in Denver.

For months Friendship House had been closed for lack of a superintendent. It was in a hurry and so was Father. He had gone down to 'the Railroad,' seventy-five miles across the desert, and had spent a day talking things over with a Board member on his way to the Coast. They had concluded arrangements then and there.

Father had been exhilarated by the interview. The Board member, William Adams, was young and enthusiastic. He could tell Father all about the minority groups in Denver, about the fine large colored population, for the most part thrifty and self-respecting; about the several thousand Japanese; about the Spanish-Americans and the discrimination they suffered. Mr. Adams applauded Father's foundation principle, that if you really believed in the fatherhood of God and the brotherhood of man, you had to be a brother yourself, and a friend. Father thought the name of the settlement, Friendship House, a happy portent.

William Adams was a fisherman, and Father loved fishing. William Adams described a trout stream that could be reached from Denver, a miraculous fly that he had invented and tied himself.

But William Adams failed to say how many windows there were in the 'compact living quarters,' or how big the windows were, or whether already curtained, or, indeed, anything at all about the apartment

Thus the Lockes had come to Denver. Thinking of it all, there in the close dark, Mary sniffled. Mother reached over and patted her.

'I know,' Mother said, 'but we'll get used to it.'

'I was thinking about Carrie Kate,' Mary whimpered, 'and Luke. And old Suta.'

'There are — folks — everywhere,' Mother answered. 'The Woman on the Steps. Funny we should meet her first of all. As if she stood for the people that need friends, right here in Denver.'

Mother did not forget the Woman on the Steps when morning came, though that day she and Father spent mostly bent over a tableful of papers, figuring out a tentative program for the center. They had Father's old records, from the Eastern center which they had directed before Father's asthma took them to Hopiland. They had the Board's books to give them an idea of what had been done here before Friendship House had closed its doors. They had the outlined program which Father had shown Mr. Adams that day in Arizona, and which Mr. Adams had heartily O.K.'d. Play school or nursery for small children in the mornings; clinics in the early afternoons; high-school age boys' and girls' clubs after school two days a week, junior age two, primary age one, and the game room open and supervised for those who were not in a club; evenings for young people's clubs and parents' activities, for socials, for other matters; Sunday for interracial church.

'Right here inside our own territory,' said Father, blue eyes shining with enthusiasm, 'we have Americans of Spanish, Japanese, Negro descent, and a few Chinese, as well as a scattering of most of the European nationalities. In the very nature of things all churches ought to be interracial. We can make this one a specimen. I see you have every hour of every day chuck full, Felicity, as always. No room to draw a deep breath.'

'Mornings aren't bad,' Mother argued. 'We can take

turns handling the play school. That will give the
other one time to get ready for afternoon and evening
and make calls.'

'Do you ever leave an hour for anything personal?'

'Monday,' Mrs. Locke said triumphantly.

'Yes, I know what Mondays will be like. Everything
we can't cram in anywhere else we'll cram into Mondays.'

'Monday,' Mother said more firmly, 'I mean to keep
for my home and my family. From now on. It's important for the children to have a home and school life
like other children's. And I don't think we ought to
let Rusty and Mary work in the center either, Rus, just
because they're our children. Only what they might do
if their father was an insurance man or a — a banker.'

Mary said impetuously: 'Oh, Mother, I'm glad you
feel that way. I've been thinking about it a lot, and
I'd love to spend most of my time with our kind of
people for once. Except like that woman on the steps,
Mother,' she broke off. 'I haven't seen her again, have
you? I asked some of the kids that play here, but they
couldn't tell me anything. Or wouldn't.'

Mother blinked at her above the ruled-off paper on
which she was carefully lettering classes. 'That vegetable man,' Mother suggested. 'He looks like the kind
that would know everybody for blocks around. We'll
ask him who she is and where she lives.'

Next morning she and Mary both ran out when they
heard the quaint cry growing louder. '*Sandias!* Water-
melons! *Melones! Frijoles verdes!* Green beans!' he wailed
dolefully.

His cry was the only sad thing about him. He drew
his old white horse back on its haunches with a grand
flourish, and beamed at them from under the faded blue
of his umbrella as if they were already favorite old cus-
tomers. He was gray-haired and rosy, and so fat that
he overflowed the high seat.

'Got the melon, lady, and for you the everbear straw-
berry,' he said, lifting his shoulders in congratulation
and turning about with soft groans and puffings. 'And
the leaves of the cauliflower, like you ask me yesterday
to save them for you: for free.'

Mother said: 'Thank you, Mr. Gallegos, that is kind
of you. The strawberries will be too dear for us. Is
there anything cheap today?'

Mr. Gallegos looked as if he were about to cry.
'Nothing never cheap no more, lady. But there are
bananas. One banan for each of you I can sell it to my
regular customer.' And he triumphantly pulled from
their hiding-place some of the rather rare fruit. 'Or if
you desire to use them this very now, these are best.
And cheapest.' He fished out some dark brown ones.
'And if you could can pears today' — he pursed his lips
and rounded his eyes inquiringly at her — 'I have this
basket. Cheap.' He shook a self-pitying head. 'A
lady, she say she must have them today. Ripe. And
today I hammer her door. No lady. — Scram, you kids!
Vamos!' he interrupted himself, for children had trooped
from all directions to climb on the wagon. Mr. Gallegos
shouted at them, but his face was one warm grin, and he
lifted out a large broken watermelon, oozing black seeds
and inviting juice, and put it into the nearest reaching

hands. 'Now you divide it up good and fair,' he warned them. Turning back to the Lockes, he said, 'Always, every day, I have the bad luck to break a watermelon. Funny, no?'

When the buying was done, Mary popped her question. 'Mr. Gallegos,' she asked shyly, looking up through her straw-tipped lashes as he settled himself in the high seat and gathered up his reins — 'Mr. Gallegos, have you noticed a woman sitting here on the steps of Friendship House?'

Mr. Gallegos was already shaking his head and making small clucking noises. 'That poor lady,' he said. 'She is so lonesome. She sit where she can see the kids. It is so sad.'

'But do you know where she lives?' Mother inquired, shading her eyes against the sun.

Mr. Gallegos pointed with his whip-handle. 'You know it that secondhand store down two blocks from this same corner?' he asked, benevolently nodding his own answer before Mary could nod hers. 'This lady — she is a Jew lady — she and her man they run that store. They come a while back from the Old Country, at the wartime. Terrible! And their *muchacho*, their boy, he *jorobado*, hunchback, maybe. Anyway sickly. Why you want to know?' he asked alertly, his eyes darting from one to the other.

Mother said: 'This is Friendship House. She looked as if she needed friends.'

Mr. Gallegos nodded rapidly, all his chins quivering. '*Si, si, si,*' he agreed. 'Good-bye, ladies. *Adios!*'

That evening the family went sauntering down the

street. 'The first star is out,' said Father. 'It's a good time for a call.'

'What's that about the first star?' Rusty called back. He had hurried Mary ahead, so that the Lockes should not look so much like a parade.

'Marks the end of the Jewish Sabbath,' said Father.

There were lights in the dusk of the secondhand store. When they went in, a small man in his shirtsleeves approached them, rubbing his hands and smiling as he asked, 'What I can do for you, please? A suit of clothes, maybe?' He scanned Father's, which sagged in places and shone in other places and had been inked where the edges wore through. 'I got it the fine, fine uniforms that can be remake and dye. Beautiful cloth, Hundert per cent pure wool.'

Father said, 'No, thank you. We just stopped in to say "How do you do." We're new neighbors of yours. At Friendship House up the street. Where your wife watches the children play.'

The little man's face was a hash of emotions; surprise, doubt, disappointment, even suspicion and fear. 'She don't do nobody no harm, the woman,' he said defensively, moving nearer the decrepit chair where she sat huddled.

Mary thought, Our imagination made her more than she is. Just a big, thin, untidy woman, with untidy, gray-streaked hair, and sagging as if there were nothing to hold her large frame together.

The man spoke to her in swift Yiddish, and her eyes came up quickly, with fear in them. The eyes were the whole of her.

And then from the dim depths of the store came the notes of a violin. Mrs. Locke turned her head, listening.

'Your son?' she asked. 'But — isn't that very good playing? I thought Mr. Gallegos said he was a little fellow.'

The father's face opened slightly. 'He is little,' he said huskily, 'but he play big.'

'It sounds like an awfully good fiddle, too,' Rusty broke in, enviously.

'Not like he have long ago,' the father mourned. 'That one we cannot take out — only our own three selves,' he added under his breath.

Mother spoke quickly. 'My son here is going to organize an orchestra,' she said. 'Boys and girls in the neighborhood. Would your boy like to come and join them?'

Rusty cast a resigned glance at Mother. Mary was sure this was the first he had heard of this plan. But he seconded Mother loyally. 'It would be great to have him help us out, Mr. — Mr. ——'

'Abramson,' the man said, and called in the next breath, 'Ben! *Komm hier!* Come you here a minute.'

The music ceased abruptly and uneven footsteps approached. The parents' eyes were upon the child as if nothing else existed. Mary looked from them to him. Perhaps not *jorobado*; but frail and small and rickety, with a large head and claw hands and no beauty except the eyes, like his mother's, and the mass of curling black hair.

Again the father's swift Yiddish poured out. With the words the mother looked toward the Lockes at last, as if her husband had waved a wand that made them visible.

The boy considered for a moment with repressed, unchildlike lips. Then he said politely, 'Thank you. I shall be glad to try. Once. When?'

'Thursday after school, Rusty?' Mother asked quickly. 'That should give us time to advertise it and get some instruments together. — At Friendship House, up the street.'

'Thursday,' the boy murmured. 'At Friendship.'

'And wouldn't your wife like to come to our English classes?' Mother asked Mr. Abramson.

'She is so busy,' he evaded. 'But we thank you.'

All this time the Little Boys had stood solemn and subdued for once, each grasping one of their father's hands. At first Mrs. Abramson had not seemed to notice them, but now she was gazing at them, and rocking her body to and fro as if in pain.

The Lockes said, 'Well, good-bye for the present,' and 'Good-bye, all,' and made their way out into the newly lighted street.

Mother said, when they were out of earshot, 'Mark my words, that woman has lost children.'

Rusty said gruffly: 'Mom, don't dramatize. She's touched, that's sure. But we'd have made a better start if we'd gone in asking for a secondhand chair. That's the talk they understand.'

'Mr. Abramson,' Mary said uneasily, 'he's just the type they call Sheeny. Rubbing his hands and smiling ——'

'It's the easiest thing in the world to use a rubber-stamp name like Sheeny,' Father warned her. 'The

American is a Shylock. The Spanish-American is a
mañana man — tomorrow man. The Hopi is a sharp
trader. Rubber stamps, stereotypes, are easy, but they're
bad medicine. There's always some truth behind them.
But you need to ask, how come? What's made the Jew
use every trick to save trade — and his own life?'

'You cooked up that orchestra mighty sudden, Mom,'
Rusty complained. 'What if I hadn't backed you up?'

'And how under the sun are you going to get that
English class into the program?' Father asked, laughing
indulgently.

'Not under the sun. Under the electric light,' Mother
answered absently. 'You know we ought to have
English classes.'

'Well, I can see our new life setting in with a bang,'
said Father.

3

Styles — In Skirts and Latin

YES, THE NEW LIFE set in with a bang.

On Monday morning Father drove Mary and Jick to their schools in the station wagon. Jick, for once remaining tidy ten entire minutes after he was scrubbed and dressed, climbed into the car. Gone was his usual nonchalance, his rowdy, sure gaiety. Mary squeezed his limp little hand, and he let her squeeze, looking straight ahead with unseeing blue eyes. His mouth was pathetic, Mary thought; closed with dignity, yet as sweetly helpless as when he was asleep. First day of school was an ordeal for Jick.

It was an ordeal for Mary, too. She deliberately narrowed her eyes into their usual laugh; deliberately chattered all the way to East High; but her voice went breathless more than once; broke oftener than usual on its funny high note.

Father let her out where other cars were gathered at the imposing entrance of East Denver High School, and she waved once and then did not look back again. Even above the confusion of sounds she knew that the station wagon had waited a minute. She could hear the peculiarly crotchety idling of its engine, and then its combined cough and cackle when it started away.

This is too much. · It is too long a jump from the mesas
and Oraibi High School, she was thinking, while her
heart thumped and banged within her, her breath
tangled, and her feet refused to work naturally. The
lofty pillars and statues at the entrance to the esplanade,
the great green trees of City Park stretching away beyond the rosy white-trimmed brick of the building, the
building itself, serene and mighty as a Sphinx, with its
great wings and central tower, unmoved by the noisy
throngs that besieged it, all were overpowering.

It was silly to feel so self-conscious, Mary told herself
fiercely, when no one was looking at her, not one single
person. She, Mary, might just as well have been empty
air.

And that was a funny feeling in itself. She had always
been Somebody. *That's Mary Locke, Reverend Locke's girl.
. . . This is the only daughter of our very able minister at the
Mesa church. . . . That's the only white girl around here who
can speak fluent Hopi — like enough the only white girl in
the world who can. . . .* Or even simply, *That's the white
girl, Mary Locke.*

At East High not one person even knew there was a
Mary Locke. Not one person cared. They clambered
out of cars and raced up the walks; they called to each
other; they looked over Mary, past her, through her ——

Mary stumbled in at the pillared entrance, trudged
with shaking knees across the resounding foyer. A girl
sat at a table by the grand stairway, a sign INFORMATION
before her, and Mary forced herself to approach and ask
for the office. When she had been directed and stood
before the general counter, the dean smiled at her from

an inner office, called her in and talked with her about her courses. During the next hour Mary felt herself in a great, rushing river, guided by someone whom the dean called a Seraph Sister, and whom Mary could see only fuzzily through the newness and the excitement. One thing she knew: the Seraph Sister was as tall as a movie star and as perfectly groomed, and she spoke to Mary gently, as to a child.

She showed Mary the locker assigned to her along with two other girls who had entered earlier. She gave her its combination. Mary left her hat on the shelf. She would not make the mistake of wearing a hat again. The Seraph Sister took her to the gym, where the teacher gave her another locker, and found a gym suit in her size, that she could buy. It was a blue one, bobbed off very short. The Seraph Sister took her to her first class, which was near her general locker, and left her there with a benign smile and wave of the hand.

The teacher of the first class lent Mary a book and gave her a seat. Mary was thankful that it was well back, so that she could watch her fellow students without being noticed.

Mary had felt fairly comfortable about her clothes; fairly sure that they would look like everyone else's. After all, the mesas were not quite a hundred miles from the railway. The fashion magazines came there regularly, and there was hardly a Hopi family, even on the tiptop of the mesa in a house centuries old, who did not have the latest mail-order catalogue from Sears-Roebuck or Montgomery-Ward. Every so often, too, movies were shown at high school, though Mary did take the movie clothes with a grain of salt.

But now she was astonished to find that there was a difference. Frowningly she looked down at herself, looked at the girls who trotted in, pranced in, shot in. It was hard to put a finger on the thing that made Mary look different from this Patsy Benton, for instance, or this Deirdre — Deirdre! — Kapps. Mary fixed her eyes on those two the minute they came striding and tripping in at the door.

Day — they all called Deirdre Day — was very tall, with slim, coltish legs and a shining coltish mane, and with the kind of face that would be distinguished in any period, and now was fashionable besides. Patsy was small and delicately molded, like a rosebud turned into a girl, and she had a floating halo of unbelievable fair hair.

The funny thing was that their clothes were much like Mary's. The differences lay in other things, some of which Mary had figured out before the close of that English class. Her hair was all wrong. It was so faded on top that she had tried to hide the strange, tawny streak by curling it tightly under. And her dresses were at least two inches too long. And she needed make-up. Make-up! Her heart sucked into her throat at the thought that she could do herself over; could come back to school another girl, like the rest, acceptable.

That day she kept very quiet, though she could have answered most of the questions asked, thanks to Shouting Luke's inexorable tutoring. Today she would do nothing to attract attention. Tomorrow, when she was made over, she would show them how smart she was: these girls, Day and Patsy and the rest; these boys.

For, naturally, there were boys. There had been boys in Hopiland, too, but with a wall between. Mary had had little acquaintance with them, except when they came to the mission to play games. Mother had always said, with the soft brightness which Mary dreaded, that Indian boys had a different attitude; that the nicer Hopi girls never climbed the wall between, either. So here the comradeship seemed startling and delightful, and the boys startling and delightful, too.

Mary sat very still until Latin, the last hour of the day. Everyone seemed sleepy, in that class, and completely uninterested in Caesar. Day patted a yawn and shook her head when the teacher inquired about ablative absolutes. Patsy, next her, murmured, 'Sorry!' in her light, smooth voice. And the translation! Mary sat with every nerve jumping with desire to prompt the beautiful boy who sagged exhaustedly against his seat, his shirt half in and half out, and stumbled through an easy sentence. It was frightful to know it so well as Mary did and not raise her hand.

Evidently the spark in her gray eyes, the twist of her lips, betrayed her. The teacher looked at a paper on her desk and smiled at Mary.

'Mary Locke, are you prepared to translate the next sentence?'

Slowly Mary rose, sliding the seat up behind her and standing in the shelter of the desk, because she could feel those extra inches of skirt like bands of fire across her knees. Fluently she translated, observing her schoolmates' backs. They stiffened slightly, in an intense silence. There! Mary thought triumphantly, maybe that will show them that Mary Locke isn't just a patch of empty air.

'And now will you read the passage in the Latin, Mary?' the teacher asked, her eyes warm and appreciative.

Easy as pie! Confidently Mary sailed in. But why the small ripple of surprise? Day looked back over her shoulder, her thin face blank; Patsy stared, sucking in her flower mouth.

Mary finished and thumped into her seat.

The teacher said, confidentially: 'Class, you have no idea how good that sounds to me. My father always pronounced his Latin that way. Eastern schools formerly used the English pronunciation. Did you come from the East, Mary?'

Mary shook her head, and her voice came breathlessly out of the top of its register. 'No, ma'am. From Arizona. But my teacher was a Yale man.'

This had spoiled everything. From their glances as they left the classroom, Mary read her schoolmates' thoughts: 'Little grandma, with her long dresses and frizzed hair and shiny nose! And with the style of Latin that went out with Teacher's ancestors.'

However had it happened that Father and Mother had not noticed Shouting Luke's old-fashioned English pronunciation of Latin? She both dreaded and longed to explode the news to the family.

But when she got home that night, after buying all her books at the secondhand bookstores to which she had been directed, she found everyone too busy to ask questions. Father, Mother, and Rusty were sawing and pounding in the attic, and the Little Boys were fully occupied getting into everyone's way.

So Mary made a pile of her new old textbooks, got notebook, tablet, and sharpened pencil, and settled herself on the lumpy davenport to study. Shouting Luke had taken her past her mathematics class and past her Latin and English classes; but General Education was new and puzzling; and she must acquire the Latin pronunciation of Latin without delay. She got hot all over at thought of Latin class, and set herself angrily to master the new rules. In no time at all Mother was calling the family to dinner.

The dinner table was always the Lockes' clearing-house for the day's news. Tonight everybody was ready to hear about school.

Mary said: 'East — well, Father, you saw what a beautiful big thing it is outside. It's just as grand inside. Big corridors with trophies and statues in niches, and sweeping stairs ——'

'Is there a good lunchroom, Sis?'

'A cafeteria, way upstairs. The food is wonderful. The teachers are nice, too.'

'And the young folks?' Father asked, shooting a blue glance at her under his bushy brows.

To her own surprise, Mary's face twisted, and she dropped her knife and fork with a clatter. 'Oh, it's horrible! It's horrible!' she wailed.

'My school's horrible, too,' Jick put in importantly, sliding his eyes around from where he sat at the 'commissariat,' to see what impression he was making. 'It's the most horrible, turrible, frightful old school. And,

Mummy, I got to have a pencil and a tablet, so I need to take a dime and a nickel tomorrow,' he added, his face shining with eagerness. 'And if I want milk at recess, I am to bring twenty cents a week. Or am I a poor child? If I'm a poor child, I don't haff to bring any money.'

Even Mary had to laugh through her tears. Everyone laughed except Bitsy, who sat on the stool at the drainboard, eating solemnly and without relish. Jick's schooling had chained Bitsy to the definitely inferior status from which he was always trying to climb, and he knew it.

When Mary had had time to straighten up her face, Mother asked carefully, 'Isn't it just that it's so new and so big, Sis?'

'It's because my dresses are too long and my hair's all wrong and Shouting Luke taught me the wrong brand of Latin,' Mary said, her smile twitching up in spite of her. No use mentioning the make-up. Father and Mother had never said, Thou shalt not; but Mary thought she knew exactly how they felt about it. It wasn't honest. If the Lord had wanted you pink and white, He'd have made you pink and white in the first place.

Mother blinked thoughtfully, and said, 'I wondered about the skirts. Let's see, Sis.'

Mary stood out in the center of the few inches of kitchen and revolved slowly.

'Nice and sensible and modest,' Father stated emphatically.

Mother reached back and plucked pins from a curtain; turned up the hem.

'Oh, more than that!' Mary begged, stooping to look.
'How do you expect me to pin it straight if you're
bending over double?' Mother asked. But she took out
the pins and turned up another inch without glancing
Father's way. 'It really does look nice,' she decided,
sitting back on her heels and squinting at it. 'It isn't
as if Sis were one of these great big girls.'

'The trouble with Mary,' said Rusty, craning from
his end of the dining nook, 'is that her legs are too short
and she's just a little bit underslung. But with her skirts
shorter, she's not too bad. Kind of on the cute side, like
a little kid.'

'Underslung!' Father roared. 'What a — a word to
apply to your sister, Russell! Mary is perfectly all right.'
He scowled protectively at his only girl. Mary had
the warm knowledge that she was something special in
her father's eyes, hard as he tried to conceal his pride.

'But I've always said' — he bit his cooky as if biting
an opponent — 'that everyone knows that a girl has
knees. Then why should she go to the trouble of dis-
playing them?'

'When a hundred girls show their knees and one girl
hides hers, the hidden ones get more attention than the
ones that are bare,' Mother said placidly.

'Yes, everybody thinks she must be knock-kneed or
spavined or something,' agreed Rusty.

Even Father grunted an unwilling laugh at that.

'Now the hair,' said Mother, puckering her brow.
'You can brush it more. I always told you that.'

Mary spent the evening hemming up skirts, brushing
her hair, and combing it this way and that to conceal

the straw-colored top layer. Her hair was naturally a medium brown like Mother's; but the desert sun had faded the top to a definite yellow, like slightly sunburned wheat. It looked so funny, she thought, frowning into the mirror: her face tanned brown as a Hopi; her eyes turned up at the corners and with those folded lower lids and her brown lashes going amber at the tips.

If only she were something definite, like Day or Patsy! Definitely tall or definitely and daintily small, instead of average height, or slightly below average, and inclined to plumpness. Or definite in feature, like Mother. The height she couldn't do a thing about, nor the elfish eyes, nose and mouth. But the color! The brown skin, the lightish lashes and brows, these she could change. All night she dreamed restlessly about what she meant to do with them.

4

A Spice of Mystery

MARY HAD TO POSTPONE her daring adventure, for Father took her to school the next morning. She couldn't let Father in on it. It was no crime, she kept telling herself, flushing hotly: it was not illegal. After all, it was just what ninety-nine girls out of a hundred did as a matter of course. By keeping it secret, Mary would only be avoiding unpleasantness, and a hurt to Father and Mother, who were too old-fashioned to understand. At the same time Mary knew perfectly well, knew from frequent experiences, that anything she had to argue with herself was — well, doubtful business; and that she would save herself trouble by taking it straight home for consultation.

Mary mentally bundled up all these arguments and shoved them away. What she was going to do she was going to do, in spite of Father and Mother.

Father said: 'What are you sighing about, Sis? You're "sighing like a furnace." And you forgot your hat.'

Mary was thinking, as she jumped out of the station wagon and walked up to the school entrance, what a difference it made inside her not to have on a hat. And to feel her skirts swishing around a few inches higher.

And to have most of the curl brushed out of her hair. And to look forward to tomorrow's revolution.

It turned out to be fortunate for Mary that she had not been able to start the revolution that day. It might have changed the course of her life, as they say a straw, placed just so, might change the course of a river.

The first class seemed only slightly different from yesterday's. The slight difference was that Day and Patsy, swinging in with that careless assurance of theirs, glanced quickly back at Mary and said something to each other. Mary felt herself flush. She fixed her eyes sternly on her open book, but she couldn't keep from looking up again, and there was Day, leaning across the aisle and chattering in an undertone to a boy called Zip, a boy who had not been in the Latin class.

Mary reminded herself that they could be discussing football, or a dance, or any one of a thousand things; but she watched them suspiciously through her thick lashes and her heart bumped when they turned their heads and looked back at her, grinning. 'Isn't she quaint?' Mary could imagine their saying. Only they wouldn't say 'quaint,' they'd say, 'Isn't she a scream?' And this Zip Forrester was something pretty special: tall and slouchy, with his shirt out, but with a way of looking at Day and Pat that probably made his careless clothes and slangy drawl captivating to the silly things.

All morning Mary caught people staring at her here and there. It was much worse to get that look of slightly wondering amusement than no look at all; worse to be stared at as if you were some odd sort of animal than to be stared past as if you were thin air. The morning strengthened her determination.

The morning also made it harder to take the first step. The first step was to squeeze out some money. Luckily Father had given her a month's allowance for lunch and carfare, saying that he'd better give it to her while he had it to give. She must cut her lunches to the minimum; and she was as hungry as any boy.

When her lunch hour came, she walked stiffly along the cafeteria counter, stealthily licking her lips, because her mouth watered so at sight of scalloped potatoes and brown gravy; at sight of spaghetti yellow with cheese; and thick wedges of banana cream pie with sirupy drops like congealed sunshine on the meringue.

She took a peanut-butter sandwich.

She had devoured the first half of the sandwich in ravenous bites before she remembered. Mother often told of an eating fad of her childhood; you chewed every mouthful till it simply disappeared. You didn't swallow it; it disappeared. That way of eating was called Fletcherizing, and it was supposed to cure all ills.

Mary had no ills to cure, but she thought Fletcherizing might take so long that it would cheat her clamorous stomach into feeling full. Besides, it would serve another purpose: it would put off the moment when she must brave the corridors crowded with noisy pairs and trios.

So Mary sat chewing and chewing, with tiny mouse-like nibbles and grindings, mostly surveying the table just beyond her plate, gravely, as if she were weighing serious problems. When the seriousness got stiff on her face, like beauty-clay she had once tried, she let her mouth curl up at one side and her eyes narrow as if she had recalled something too delightful and funny for words — in case anyone happened to be noticing her. Then her own sense of humor got the better of her and she giggled softly and looked up to see if anyone had caught her with that silly smile, like smiling and nodding at the telephone.

Someone had been watching her. A pair of eyes directly across the table veiled themselves slowly.

Mary forgot herself and looked with interest at the girl opposite. The girl had almost as little on her plate as Mary, and she, too, was eating slowly, daintily. Mary's heart warmed. This girl had a slight resemblance to Carrie Kate, her Hopi friend, though her skin was fairer — almost like porcelain, Mary thought, feeling weatherbeaten in contrast. The girl's hair was satin-black, like Carrie Kate's, her lashes as thick and dark, her face as expressionless. She lifted her eyes again, and dropped them slowly when she found Mary staring.

Mary giggled. 'Oh, do excuse me,' she said. 'I'm so lonesome. I've only just entered East, and I don't know a single soul. It's horrible. Besides, you do remind me of one of my Hopi friends. I guess I'm pretty homesick for them.'

'Hope-ee?' the other girl asked.

'They're a tribe of Indians. We've lived among them practically always. Oh, I know you're not Indian. But the ethnologists say the racial stock was the same to start with.'

'Yes, I have heard that. It is most interesting.'

'Oh, you came from China?' Mary asked, in surprise. The girl's English was beautifully correct, but the syllables were oddly divided, and there was a strangeness in the consonants, that made it like another language, certainly not the speech of the American-born Chinese. Mary, though used to strange pronunciations, had understood this girl only by sharp attention.

'Yes, I came from China. I, too, am alone,' the other girl said.

'Then we're two of a kind,' said Mary, narrowing her eyes happily. 'And you eat as slow as I do,' breathless laughter trilling through the words. 'Let's always eat together.'

'This American food,' the girl said, touching a large chicken wing with her fork; 'it is very nice, but it is very new to me, also. The cutting and holding with these silver tools — I am most clumsy about it. Our food is cut fine before it is brought to the table.'

Mary thought they had talked enough about eating, since she preferred not to explain why she herself was so slow. She nodded and said, 'My name is Mary Locke.'

'And mine — I am called Lee Foh-Mei. The Lee is the family name, so here I say, Foh-Mei Lee. Only I think perhaps I should call myself just Mei or Mary, here in America.'

'Two of a kind again!' Mary exclaimed, as if the coincidence were startling. 'But Mei-Lee is too lovely to change. And we'd be two Marys just the same.'

Mei-Lee nodded thoughtfully. 'I shall like that, I

think,' she said cautiously. 'It is strange, is it not? —
to be alone when so few are alone. Yonder is one
other who walks and sits by herself. All week I have
seen her. She is in gymnasium next period, and so also
am I. And you will think it most remarkable, but her
name also is a variety of Mary: Marita, she says it.'

'Well, did you ever!' Mary cried happily. 'I'm in
gym next period, too.'

She looked across the girls' side of the cafeteria where
Mei-Lee was looking — the cafeteria reminded her of
the Hopi church, with all the females on one side and
all the males on the other — and found the one other
person who sat alone. She was a slim girl, small as a
child, with hair blue-black like the Chinese girl's, and
done in a shining roll that made her face tiny and her
wide black eyes enormous. She held her head proudly
and drooped disdainful lids as she, too, ate with dainty
deliberateness. Mary thought with sudden insight,
'Why, she's lonely! That's why she acts so haughty.'

'Come along!' Mary said breathlessly to Mei-Lee.
'You're through, aren't you? Come on, then, and let's
get acquainted with this other Mary.'

Marita looked startled, almost affronted, when the
two girls, carrying their trays, stopped at her end of the
table. But Mary was used to Indian girls who hid behind their faces. She knew how to meet reserve. In a
matter of minutes the three were walking down the
stairs and through the corridors toward gym, tawny
brown head between shining black ones. Smiling at
each other, they gravitated together again when they
were dressed in their gym suits.

'We're Mei-Lee and Mary Locke,' Mary said. 'You haven't told us your whole name yet.'

'Marita de Herrera y Aragon,' the other responded.

'See! We're just three varieties of Mary!' Mary exulted.

Marita suddenly giggled. 'Mary was what I was really baptized,' she confessed with engaging sheepishness. 'Maria, in the Spanish. I am Spanish, pure Spanish,' she put in severely. 'But all the Americans called me MaRYEa — Ma-RYE-a! So I made a change: only the letter "t," which certainly is not much.'

Mary studied her and Mei-Lee admiringly and looked discontentedly down at herself. In her brief blue gym suit she was like a sturdy-legged child, while Marita in her scant yellow suit and Mei-Lee in her scarlet one were fragile and exquisite, delicately modeled dolls or ornamental figurines.

'But oughtn't you to have left your beads in your locker?' Mary suddenly asked Mei-Lee.

Silently Mei-Lee dropped her eyes to the beads. They were unlike any Mary had seen; grayish-green, carved like lace. There were more than a score of them, strung on a knotted silk cord which apparently bore some sort of pendant hidden in Mei-Lee's blouse.

Before Mei-Lee could have replied, the teacher's whistle cut across the gay murmur and confusion, leaving a sudden stillness.

At the end of the period the three girls rushed to the showers together. Irresistibly Mary's eyes were drawn to Mei-Lee's necklace. 'I was afraid the cord would break,' she apologized, though she could not think why she felt apologetic. 'Speed ball is pretty rough.'

'The cord is strong,' said Mei-Lee, 'and well-knotted. Always I leave it on. Always.'

'Like a talisman,' Mary said interestedly, leaning closer and lifting the beads to see them better.

With them she lifted the pendant. Mei-Lee's hand jerked upward as if to push it back and then she stood quiet and let Mary examine it. It was a cylinder, as much as four inches long and an inch in thickness, covered with brocade patterned in tiny, glistening figures, and the brocade in turn covered with transparent oiled silk.

'I suppose it's a Chinese kind of junk jewelry,' Mary concluded. 'I dearly love junk jewelry, but Father won't let me wear any.'

'Junk jewelry?' Mei-Lee asked, in a startled voice.

'That's what they sometimes call costume jewelry.'

'Junk jewelry,' Mei-Lee repeated musingly 'A good name, I think. Perhaps I am also junk jewelry myself.'

Mei-Lee's smooth, inscrutable face was twitching with real laughter; but, noticing Mary's puzzled expression, she smoothed out her amusement, and dropped the cylinder back inside her blouse. 'Both you girls wear the American Indian silver,' she observed, raising her voice above the laughter and chatter and the roar of the showers, as the girls captured adjacent shower-stalls. 'I like it very much.'

'How did you know they were Indian, our bracelets and things?' Mary asked Mei-Lee, when they were all dressed and on the way to their next classes.

'Oh, even in Pei-ping we see the American Indian: his silver; his blankets; his movies.'

'Pei-ping?' Marita inquired.

'I have visited Pei-ping,' Mei-Lee answered smoothly. Mary darted a quick glance at her. Mei-Lee's face was a mask again, astonishingly like those smooth, perfect oval faces in Oriental paintings. But she was nice, even if she was hiding something: something about Pei-ping; something about her necklace. Yes, Mary would bank on her being a really fine person. And a spice of mystery — goodness, that would add to her charm rather than take from it.

'Girls,' Mary said, her voice squeaking softly with urgency, 'can't you both walk home with me after school and meet my mother? And Father and Rusty and the Little Boys? Can't you? It's about a mile, but if you're used to walking ——'

She looked from one to the other expectantly, balancing her books on her hip.

Marita said: 'I'm sorry. On Mondays I must get home quickly — I have almost always an appointment.'

And Mei-Lee's face remained closed and unresponsive. 'It will not be possible for me, either, Mary.'

Mary went on to her next class feeling definitely snubbed.

5

A New Face

THE NEXT DAY Mary started for school
early. Not far from East she stopped at one of the gay,
luxurious drugstores which so astonished her, and made
her purchases. Though she bought small sizes wherever
she could, she used most of her month's allowance.
She would have to walk both ways, even in stormy
weather, and she must limit her eating as she had done
the day before. She thought longingly of bringing large
hearty lunches from home, but she dismissed the idea at
once. Surely these dashing young people at East would-
n't do anything so plebeian. Wouldn't it set her apart
at once from such girls as Day and Patsy? And setting
herself apart was the thing Mary most wished to avoid.

When she reached school, the corridors were still
empty and silent. Without waiting to go to her locker,
Mary made a dash for the nearest lavatory. She passed
only a few girls and boys, only a few teachers; but she
did come face to face with Mei-Lee, at her locker near
the lavatory. Mary spoke coolly, still smarting from
last night's snub. Besides, she did not want Mei-Lee
to delay her. She need not have feared delay. Mei-Lee
had on all her Oriental reserve, and spoke only a clipped
'Good morning.'

49

But everything was working well for Mary's project. The room was empty. A mirror ran the length of one wall, with a shelf running below it. Mary went to the farthest end, although that was also farthest from a window, spread her purchases on the shelf, drew a long breath, and set to work.

The pancake make-up spread on wonderfully. An exquisite pink-and-white face soon bloomed on the toasty-brown stem of Mary's neck. With solemn intensity she attacked the neck also. She sighed exultantly. A veritable apple-blossom skin.

This was like having Aladdin's lamp. What should she do to herself next? She recalled all she had read about the proper way to apply rouge, and blended a rosy flush into her brand-new skin. She penciled her mouth carefully with the lipstick, giving herself an ample upper lip in place of the thinly arched one that was her own. Next the eyebrow pencil made beautiful brows like dark scallops. And finally, her heart thumping as if she were running a race, she dragged the tiny mascara brush through her tawny lashes all the way to their amber tips.

She gazed into the mirror at this marvelous, this exciting new countenance. Aladdin's lamp, yes, and Cinderella's godmother: a fairy tale in which you were given a glamorous new face, new beauty. Now for a new life, the kind that she had at first dreamed she might find in Denver. No one could call her an unsophisticated little mouse now. No one could look at her as if she ——

Could look at her — subconsciously she had noticed

the opening of a door. Now she whirled around, feeling as if someone were standing there. It was Mei-Lee.

'Oh, I thought a girl named Mary Locke came in here,' Mei-Lee explained as Mary stared at her. Then Mei-Lei's calm changed, like a still pool into which a stone is plumped. She ran forward, frowning and shaking her head. 'Oh, no!' she protested. 'Oh, Mary Locke, no!'

Her heart churning, Mary turned back to the mirror. Now she could see things that were not quite ——

'I didn't get the lipstick under the edge,' she stammered, picking it up and leaning forward to apply it afresh. 'And I did get a little on my teeth. I know you're not supposed to get it on your teeth. And maybe the rouge should be — Maybe the rouge isn't just right ——'

'None of it is just right,' Mei-Lee said crisply. 'Look, Mary.' She took her by the hand and led her close to a window; handed her a mirror from her own handbag.

In the full light the effect was gaudy.

'If I dusted a little more powder over —— ?'

Mei-Lee shook her head. 'Already your nice little brown ears stick out as if they were pasted on the wrong girl.'

'Couldn't I powder them, too?'

'Wash it all off; all,' Mei-Lee directed, glancing over her shoulder at the door, beyond which feet were beginning to scuff and tap and voices to resound. She steered Mary toward a lavatory at the far end. 'Wash it all off quick.'

'But ——'

Mei-Lee was turning hot water into the bowl, wiping the porcelain fastidiously with a paper towel, letting in more water. 'Go on! Wash it off! They would say, Now where does she come from, that she knows no better than this?'

Rebelliously knotting her beloved dark scallops, Mary bent over the lavatory and washed. And washed. Mei-Lee watched with a competent frown, until at last Mary came up clean and bare of cosmetics.

'Such a fine, smooth tan,' Mei-Lee scolded. 'Why, even I have had time to observe how much the Americans admire a fine, smooth tan. You leave it just that way, Mary Locke.'

'But my nose is shiny,' Mary wailed.

'A *soupçon* of tan powder you may have,' Mei-Lee grudgingly granted. 'For your nose. And let me take your lipstick.'

With exquisite deftness Mei-Lee outlined Mary's quaint upper lip, finely drawn, with two little peaks in the middle and a curled corner; outlined her full lower lip and filled it in carefully, telling Mary, 'Smile! Smile big and wide so the creases aren't. Now close your mouth on a piece of tissue.

'Now your hair,' she went on, tilting her head this way and that and nodding. 'Where is your comb, Mary Locke?'

Mutely Mary fished it out and handed it to her. Mei-Lee removed the hairpins from Mary's hair, ran the comb through vigorously, pulled the tawny mass straight up till Mary's eyebrows flew with it, sighed in sheer exasperation.

'I suppose you had not even noticed,' she said wonderingly, 'how smart it is to have the striped hair.'

Mary stared blankly at her own reflection and Mei-
Lee's.

'Well, henceforth, observe. And you, who have this
— this dramatic great plume of gold, you turn it under
and hide it with ugly curls and rolls. Only look! Be-
hold!' Mei-Lee held it in place with a comb, while
Mary peered, bewildered, into the glass.

'And there you are,' said Mei-Lee, washing her hands
vehemently. 'Individual. Smart. Not like everyone
else, and yet in the — in the present mood. Don't be
afraid. I know. I have been watching these matters
ever since I have come to this America.'

'But — no mascara! No eyebrow pencil?' Mary stuttered obstinately. 'Why, you can hardly see my eyebrows and lashes.'

'Well, the brows,' Mei-Lee conceded. 'But carefully.'
She took the pencil from Mary's hand and darkened the
eyebrows.

'But you're leaving them just the same old shape!'

'I most certainly am. Though you do not deserve
them,' Mei-Lee retorted. 'Look at them. Only look.'

Reluctantly Mary smiled. Those eyebrows were exquisite, a pair of tiny wings, slanting upward and out-
ward from the bridge of her pert nose. 'But you would
take every speck of curl out of my hair?' she bleated.

Mei-Lee answered in a teacher's voice. 'You have a
curly little face,' she said, making curved gestures as if
to turn up her own straight nose, the corner of her own
straight mouth, the tips of her own arched brows.

'When your hair is fancy, it takes from the — the cunningness of the curly face.'

'And no rouge?'

Mei-Lee laughed at Mary's woebegone expression. 'You have also failed to observe how little rouge is being worn? But a *soupçon* only ——' She dabbed a speck of color on Mary's wide cheekbones and blended it out so vigorously that Mary suspected that the rubbing was what flushed her cheeks, rather than the rouge. 'And we are only just in time,' Mei-Lee exclaimed, as a door banged open and feet scudded in, bringing with them a full tide of noise.

Together the two girls hurried through the resounding halls and deposited Mary's excess baggage in her locker.

'How did you happen to come looking for me?' Mary asked suddenly. 'How did you happen to be here so early?' She was thinking, not too gratefully, Why did you look for me when you seemed so uninterested in seeing me at first?

'Always I come early, because Doctor Lau brings me in his automobile when he comes to his office. I am living with Doctor and Mrs. Lau,' Mei-Lee explained. 'And then I thought, Mary Locke looks strange and excited. And then, when you do not come out, I think perhaps you are fallen ill. And I am thankful that I went, for, do you know, if you had been like that' — she motioned in the direction of the lavatory — 'when you spoke to me yesterday, I would have answered politely, but there would have been an end of it.'

Mary stared at Mei-Lee, her mouth sagging and the blood flaring into her face. 'Surely it wasn't as bad as that,' she snapped.

Mei-Lee nodded with relish. 'Just so bad as that. Do not be offended,' she said; 'but I promise my mother, solemnly, I will make no friendships with strange people of whom she would not approve.'

Mary began to giggle. She giggled until her knees felt as if they had come unhinged, and she staggered as they came to her locker. It was certainly the first time her respectability had been questioned. The experience brought embarrassment and thrill at once.

And Mei-Lee; how different she was today! She had force and independence, that girl; and now a mothering way with Mary. Abruptly Mary asked, 'Can't you come home with me tonight? Mother so wants to know you.'

'Thank you. I will telephone to Mrs. Lau,' Mei-Lee agreed.

So in spite of its topsyturvy beginning, Tuesday was an improvement on Monday. Even classes were better. As with one accord Day and Patsy, after they seated themselves, looked back with amused expectancy at Mary. Mary forced her face to keep its usual look of budding a smile. Day's and Patsy's amusement faded to a slight bewilderment. Mary dropped her eyes and left them staring.

And that afternoon the three Marys walked to Friendship, though not until Mary had stopped in the lavatory and reluctantly washed off her lipstick, rouge, and eyebrow pencil.

It was marvelous to be walking with girl friends once more. Soon the three were chattering, pausing now and again to look into the windows of clothing shops, gift shops, along Colfax Avenue. Mary tried to hurry the others past the bakeries. Her stomach was one big, empty ache, and her mouth watered so that she had to keep swallowing when she saw a tray of chocolate eclairs, oozing cream, or a tray of big, feathery doughnuts, frosty with sugar. Even the smell from the opened doors was almost too much for her.

It was Mary who did most of the chattering, and she only vaguely noticed that neither Mei-Lee nor Marita offered much information about themselves. Marita had no mother, she said. She had lived with her grandmother till she was ready for junior high school and decided to come to Denver. Grande — Marita's voice softened — Grande was called Abuelita Persedis, Little Grandmother Persedis. Others called her Doña Persedis, as the fashion was in the Spanish villages of the Southwest. Doña Persedis! Title and name wore a black lace mantilla and a tortoise-shell comb. Mary's quick fancy pictured the fine lady, with her delicate ways, her autocratic manners.

She turned to Mei-Lee questioningly. Mei-Lee's mother, yes, and all the family, were in China, Mei-Lee said distantly.

Mary held back very little. She told about Hopiland; about Father's asthma; about how Rusty was familiarly called Bro and she Sis, because they were for years the only children. Rusty was twelve and Mary nine when Jick was born.

'Your brother Rusty — will be home?' Mei-Lee's voice sounded alarmed and her steps slowed.

'Why, I suppose so, but he'll be busy,' Mary answered,

eyeing her curiously. 'And he's all right, Rusty is. I mean for a boy he's all right. I have to admit,' she added with regret, 'that he is a boy.'

Marita's eyes flashed amused response. 'Aren't boys the limit?' she exclaimed. 'Abuelita used to say that when a boy got to be about twelve, nobody but the good God could really love him.' She shrugged. 'Me, I often doubt if even the good God can.'

Mary stopped short and clasped her hands. 'Oh, do you feel that way about boys, too?' she demanded, her words exploding like little firecrackers.

'To me they are of no conceivable interest,' Mei-Lee said primly.

Mary crowed. 'If that isn't the final coincidence! I bet you couldn't find three other girls like that in the whole of East High! Girls who have no use for boys in any way, shape, form, or manner. We ought to be a sort of club. We could call it Triplets, Ltd.'

'Why Ltd.?' Marita asked.

'Limited. No other girls. And no boys. Or we might be just The Three Sisters.'

'Assorted Sisters,' Mei-Lee suggested with a glitter of fun.

'Assorted Sisters it is!' Mary declared.

The mile from East had shortened surprisingly, with company and conversation, and the exclusive new club was turning in at Friendship House by the time it had come into being.

Jick and Bitsy fell upon Mary with cries of joy and unbelievably dirty hands when the three girls opened the door of the apartment.

'Where is Mother you have been into the sugar again,' Mary said all in one breath, making a face as her feet grated along the floor.

'She is up attic helping Bro,' Jick answered, steering away from the subject of sugar. 'She left me the respons-ility of Bitsy, and I have been reading to him. The story of David and Goliath.' He waved his hand importantly toward an open mail-order catalogue.

'Davit and Go-i-lah,' Bitsy contributed in his heavy little voice, nodding gravely.

'Will you come up and see what the Locke family is doing?' Mary invited her visitors, and together they climbed the steep stair to the bigness of the attic, fragrant with freshly cut wood.

Rusty came forward with more manners than Mary had thought he possessed. And of Mother she was proud, as always. Mother had on one of Father's coveralls, but she showed no sign of feeling informally clothed. She took the girls by the hands, saying, 'We're so glad our Mary has found friends. Now she will be happier.'

The words were commonplace; but Mother's smile was not. It enfolded them, mothered them; and both girls responded. Marita had a certain manner for grown people. Mary had noticed it when she spoke to teachers. It was much like Day's air, and Patsy's: that of being charmingly polite to people quite old and breakable, though all the time with the thoughts elsewhere. Now this manner dissolved, and Marita smiled lonesomely at Mother.

The three girls wandered around, inspecting the

progress of the work. The wall-board was rough and brown. 'Isn't it revolting?' Mary exclaimed, shuddering.

'I don't think so,' Mother said, lips and eyes thoughtful. 'Look, girls!' With each hand she held a Hopi *pota*, basket plaque, against the neutral surface. 'See. I can't imagine a more effective background for our Indian things. And Navajo blankets on the floor. And, Sis, how would you like to have that lovely soft old Hopi blanket of Suta's for your bedspread?'

Mei-Lee said, 'It does sound beautiful, Mrs. Locke.'

And Marita stared at the dormers and suggested, 'In a very smart house here in Denver they have used monkscloth in an Indian room, and embroidered it in wool — Indian designs.'

Mother nibbled her lower lip and blinked rapidly. 'Wonderful! Or if not monkscloth, then heavy unbleached muslin ——'

'Some of the best interior decorators here used unbleached muslin,' Marita said sagely. 'Cheesecloth, too.'

Mother clapped her hands in a gesture oddly like Mary's. 'Could you girls help me?' she cried. 'We want to start a high-school-age club; we haven't it organized yet. I thought of cooking and sewing, a sort of Home Ec Club. You wouldn't like to form the nucleus, you three, and help get it going?'

Mary thought, Mother probably began to plan this last night when I told her about the girls; and now she springs it as if it were a spur-of-the-moment idea. All three girls nodded consideringly.

'Fine! Let's have a cup of tea on it — or cocoa,'

Mother said gaily. 'Aren't you hungry after your arduous labors?'

Mary swallowed. 'I could eat Jick and Bitsy,' she declared.

'We can make some package gingerbread,' Mother proposed, 'and some cocoa — You girls get your hands washed and ——' She was peeling off her coveralls and hanging them on a nail where she could lay hand on them readily. She led the way to the bathroom for hand-washing, and on down another flight of stairs to Friendship House kitchen, on the first floor, the apartment kitchen being too small. Almost before they knew it, the girls were swathed in aprons, and Mother was showing them where the supplies were kept.

'And here is a tube pan,' Marita said. 'I find that it makes a lighter gingerbread ——'

Mother said, admiringly: 'Marita, anyone would know, just to watch you, that you were at home in a kitchen. Maybe it will be you who will do the teaching in our Home Ec Club. Mei-Lee, will you make the cocoa? We'll use half water, because we're a little short of milk.'

Mary stared covertly at the two girls. They had both responded strangely to Mother's suggestions. Marita's face had stiffened, resuming its haughty expression. And Mei-Lee's had gone blank. Mother had handed her a milk bottle, and she was clasping it helplessly in both slim hands.

'How — how do you get in?' she asked.

Mary took the bottle from her and pried out the top with a fork, and Mother laughed and said: 'Milk bottle tops can be stubborn. I suppose you didn't have this kind in China. You might get down the cocoa, Mei-Lee, if you can reach. Measure a teaspoonful into this saucepan for each person, and an equal amount of sugar, and just a grain or two of salt. Let's see' — she counted on her fingers — 'with Father and Rusty and the Little Boys, it's eight.'

Again Mei-Lee was looking helpless. The others tactfully left her alone, but Mary slid a glance at her and saw that Mei-Lee's hands were shaking as she measured cocoa and sugar into the pan. Marita mixed the gingerbread, looking down her nose at it, Mary thought, as if it were beneath her notice. She had it in the tube pan and the oven almost warm enough to put it in before Mei-Lee had even finished making a paste of the sugar and cocoa under Mother's lightly tossed directions. But at length the paste was cooked thick over a slow flame, and Mei-Lee began pouring the milk and water in, a little at a time, with fiercely concentrated care. Mary, arranging trays and getting out cups and saucers and plates, watched the cocoa-making with amazed amusement: in that one simple bit of cookery, Mei-Lee had managed to spill milk, sugar, and cocoa on table and floor, to blister her finger and scorch the cocoa.

Yet the tea-party was a success. Time went so gaily that Marita, after drinking a half cup of cocoa and eating a small piece of hot, moist, fragrant gingerbread, looked with a start at the clock and jumped up.

'Oh,' she ejaculated, 'I must hurry. I have to — I have an appointment at five.'

'Well, you'll come again soon?' Father urged heartily.

'Shall we try to plan the cooking days for Tuesdays
and the sewing for Fridays?' Mother asked, smiling up
at her. 'Several Spanish girls have said they would
join, and a Japanese girl, and ——'

Marita stood poised to run. 'Thank you, Mrs. Locke,
I think it will be delightful,' she said, her voice again
faintly cool. 'I'd love to learn more about — about all
those things.'

As Mary returned from seeing Marita to the door,
she was thinking that her new friends could behave more
like exiled princesses than anyone she'd known before.
And then she noticed still another expression on Mei-
Lee's face. At first Mary observed it only vaguely, a
startled, anxious, protesting look. Mary couldn't give
it her full attention because she was still hungry, and
was hoping to get another piece of the gingerbread
ahead of the Little Boys. But even in her mouth-water-
ing eagerness she could not be deaf to the tensity of
Mei-Lee's voice. Mary stood stockstill with a hand
poised over the cake plate, and stared.

'A Japanese girl?' Mei-Lee said. 'Mrs. Locke, did
you say a Japanese girl?'

6

Mei-Lee's Junk Jewelry

MARY STOOD STARING at Mei-Lee. Father looked up at her quickly. Mother's spoon moved slowly in her cup as if she had forgotten it. Jick's small paw darted in below Mary's hand and snatched the last piece of gingerbread.

'Yes, a Japanese girl,' Mrs. Locke answered Mei-Lee. 'She seems very nice. I hope she'll bring some of her friends. Ever so many Japanese-Americans relocated here after the evacuation.'

Mei-Lee was gazing down into her plate, crumbling her cake into small brown pellets, her face drained of the little color it had held. 'I know there are many in Denver,' she said tonelessly. 'Even after all this time it gives me a queer feeling when I meet them, on the street, at the high school.'

Mary sat down hard. 'But, Mei-Lee!' she protested. 'These aren't Japanese Japanese. They're Americans. You don't pick out the people with German ancestors and settle down to hate them all your life, do you? Well, then, don't be silly about this Yoshi.'

Mei-Lee smiled stiffly.

Father shook his head slightly at Mary. 'That's easy

for us to say, Sis; but probably Mei-Lee has come closer
to the thing than we ever have.'

'It's largely a matter of psychology: the emotions,'
Rusty put in with the condescension of eighteen years.

Bitsy was usually slow to make friends, but when he
saw their guest so white and silent, he planted himself
before her and held a cushiony palm under her nose, with
the crushed remnant of his gingerbread upon it. He
peered at her soberly and wheedled in his grave little
voice, 'Just see! Bitsy give you!'

Mei-Lee's mask broke at that. Her lips twisted into a
smile, and she took the gingerbread and hugged the
child. 'Thank you, Bitsy,' she said. 'I have a little
brother, too — I think I have,' she added in a brittle
voice.

'Couldn't you tell us?' Mother asked, her eyes wet.
'Often it helps, just to tell somebody who cares.'

Mei-Lee gave Bitsy another squeeze, and tucked half
the squashed cake into his willing mouth, the rest
heroically into her own. Then she folded her slim hands
lightly on the table edge, and swallowed cake and tears.
'If you would like to hear. But the story is long.'

'Oh, please, Mei-Lee,' begged Mary's soft, high
voice.

'We lived in — in a Chinese city,' Mei-Lee began.
'There were my grandmother, my father and mother, an
aunt who had been widowed, and her son and daughter;
also my sister, two years younger than I, and my baby
brother.' She paused, as if the thought of them stifled
her.

'Even a bigger family than ours,' Jick said soberly.

She flashed him a dewy smile. 'And with the serving women and the yard boys and the rickshaw boy ——' Her voice trailed off and began again, 'It was like a tiny village, with a high wall and a garden inside the court and everyone doing his tasks happily, beside the pool with the fish, under the trees ——'

'You must have been rich,' Jick interrupted.

Mei-Lee shook her head. 'Not any longer. The money had gone. Even the jewels had gone. But we were comfortable. We were happy. Of course echoes of trouble were always coming from outside: civil war; the Shanghai "incident" of the Japanese; the Communist and Nationalist friction. But it was as if nothing bad could get past our high walls, our moon gate. Even during the years I was away at school, we thought little of the rumors of war. Until ——' She stopped and blinked the tears back.

Bitsy had stood close beside her, small brown face intent. Now he put in a few slow words, like pebbles dropping into a pool: 'Were your fishies — gold-fishies? I and Jick — had gold-fishies. Once — I took mine for a walk,' he added regretfully.

'Yes, and he washed him with a toothbrush,' Jick added.

'Were your fishies — gold-fishies?' Bitsy repeated.

Mei-Lee nodded. 'Gold and silver,' she said huskily. 'My favorite was so-o big; and he had a tail and fins like silver. Fraying out, too, because he was old, old. I wonder if he ——' She caught herself and went on: 'My father told me I should never name my name nor even the name of our city. He could not think that it would be safe anywhere in the world. Because the Japanese hated our family with a long hate.'

'Why did they hate you?' Jick demanded indignantly, moving in close on the other side.

She answered him as if he were an adult: 'Well, you see my father had been against them when they went into Manchuria. He had been strong against them, and had used much of his money to try to keep them from taking Manchuria.'

Jick listened with his berry-red mouth a bit open and his blue eyes dark with interest.

'So, as the Japanese showed signs of taking our city, Father and Mother and Grandmother began to make their plans. Aunt wished to try to reach Shanghai with her children, and to take with her my youngest sister, who was then twelve. We had friends who were informed. They finally said there would be a train which would come to a certain point outside the city on a certain day. So Aunt dressed herself as an *amah*, and the children as village children: village boys, with my sister's beautiful hair cut short. I shall not forget how my mother looked, and my father, when they said good-bye to my sister. They could not go outside our gate with her, for there were always those who watched us. They bade her good-bye without a tear, and smiling. And then my mother stood still in the spot where my aunt and sister left her, till we drew her away by force ——

'They went to the place appointed, and waited there, those four. All day and all night they waited, though the weather was cold. This we learned later. Then they began to walk the long, hard way to Shanghai. My aunt made herself ugly and bowed; and soon she was limping in good earnest, so that she looked really old ——'

'Why?' Jick demanded, crowding closer and knitting puzzled brows. 'Why did she want to be ugly?'

Mei-Lee looked from him to Father and Mother.

Father told Jick, 'There were bad people, who might hurt them; and they weren't so likely to notice an old woman.'

Mei-Lee asked, 'Perhaps the little ones should not hear a story that has sadness and badness in it?'

But Mother said, with the firm directness which Mary always loved to hear: 'They live in a world that has much sadness and badness, Mei-Lee. We cannot let them believe that it is all soft and good. Of course we spare them the details ——'

Mei-Lee nodded understandingly. 'Of course. I go on, then.' She smiled at the two children, who pressed tighter and tighter against her, breathing noisily. 'It was a long, long way, going afoot. Sometimes they took shelter in the mud huts of the poor people. Sometimes, when Japanese soldiers were about, they hid all night in the tombs.' — Jick shivered. — 'They carried just enough money to buy coarse food. Without money they were safer. And at last word came to us that they were in Shanghai.'

Jick's face broke into a dazzling smile, and Bitsy, watching him, smiled too.

'Safe and sound,' whispered Mary.

Mei-Lee shook her head. 'No person had harmed

them. But my sister and my girl cousin, they were too young and frail for the long, cold trek. They sickened with lung sickness, and since I came here, I hear, very roundabout, that my sister, my little sister, has died.' The tears were welling up in her shining dark eyes. 'My little sister,' she repeated.

Jick's sensitive face twisted, and he burrowed his head into her lap and howled with sympathetic grief.

'There, there. There, there.' Mei-Lee patted the silver-gold head. 'He makes me think of my baby brother,' she said unevenly. 'Chou had just lost his first teeth when I came away. Like Jick.'

Jick came up in the narrow space between Mei-Lee and the table. 'But, anyway, you didn't die?' he inquired breathlessly.

Everyone laughed, happy to escape the somberness for a moment, and Mei-Lee patted her eyes and nose with her handkerchief, smiling at the peachlike face.

'Did your aunt walk you away, too?'

'No, I didn't walk. You'd never guess how I came away.' Mei-Lee made a wry, remembering face. 'Things had grown worse, and we knew that we were more closely watched, and that they had found out how some of us had made our escape. So — how can I tell you?' She paused, laughing a little. 'Well, one day when the garbage went out from the walls of our home, it was something besides garbage. Lucky I am not too big' — she looked down at her slim self — 'and could curl myself into the great, horrible pail. I can never forget. The strained, cramped position, the horrible smell and feeling, the bump-bump-bump.' She giggled unexpectedly, rubbing her elbows and shoulders as with a remembering hand.

'Breathing holes had been made for me. And it was two of our house servants who carried me, on their shoulder pole. You know, you've seen pictures of the pole, laid between the shoulders of two men, with the burden dangling between. Sometimes I could hear the men's breath, coming as fast and hard as yours' — she gave the Little Boys a hug — 'perhaps because they were passing someone they feared. Sometimes they would hum a tune, and I would know it was to comfort me. They did not empty me out till after dark, when no one could see.'

'Where did they empty you?' Jick demanded breathlessly.

'Into the sampan in the harbor. That's a small boat.'

'I thought it might be a junk,' said Mary, recalling Mei-Lee's remark about junk jewelry on the day they first met.

Mei-Lee laughed as if remembering. 'The junk came next. I don't know how my father managed it, but I was taken from the junk to a ship that was bound for America.'

Mary let go a long, audible breath, still staring at her friend.

'Never was anything in this world so good as my first bath,' Mei-Lee said, clapping her hands lightly and smiling down at the Little Boys, who clapped and giggled too. 'And the clean clothes, though they were queer clothes, and too large.'

'You could bring nothing with you, of course,' Father said.

Mei-Lee touched her beads. 'Nothing but these. These I wore under my clothes, with a rag twisted around them to keep them from foulness.' She made a charming little mouth at the children, who capered and laughed anew. 'These are all I have from my old life,' Mei-Lee added, sobering.

Mary still gazed, bits of pictures swimming before her eyes; pictures made from Mei-Lee's words and from books she had read about the life of the well-to-do in China; the gracious, ordered days; the formal courtesy; the scent of tea and of oleander blossoms; celestial blue tiles in a garden wall; silken garments.

'Your father and mother?' she whispered. 'Your grandmother and little brother?'

'I do not know,' Mei-Lee said. 'I have heard nothing. Nothing.'

Even the Little Boys were silent for a long minute. The busy, fussy tick of the clock moved into the stillness of Friendship House kitchen, and a meditative drip-drip at the sink.

Father was gazing down at his cup. He had emptied it, averse though he was to scorched food. Now he sprang up, knocking the chair over behind him. 'Never could stand a leaky faucet,' he muttered. Over his shoulder he said, hoarsely, 'Mei-Lee, you're a plucky girl, a downright plucky girl.'

Mei-Lee moved a deprecating hand. 'But you see — You do see, don't you? It's hard to get quite used to the Japanese faces. Yet I am sure you are right. We must not mix things up and say, Because their ancestors were Japanese ——'

Again there was a silence, while Father, murmuring to himself, pawed the cabinet drawer for a wrench.

'I will control myself,' said Mei-Lee. 'I will be in the club with this Japanese girl you speak of. Only for a little while please put Mary and Marita between us. Till I get a bit used to her.'

'A plucky girl,' Mr. Locke repeated resonantly, doing useless things to the faucet.

7

The Chinese Center

IT WAS FORTUNATE that Mei-Lee fortified her spirit, for Yoshi, the first Japanese girl, did bring others with her. There were Japanese in all the groups and classes. Friendship House had gone quickly into high gear. It held the conferences, clubs, craft classes and play school first planned, for neighbors from three to ninety; and into the crevices of the original program it squeezed a story hour and a youth conference, to say nothing of the English classes, which Mrs. Abramson never attended, and the orchestra, which Ben Abramson never failed to attend.

Dark-eyed Spanish children, curly-headed Negro children, Japanese children, pretty and neat as dolls, thronged halls and classrooms. In the next session of the Home Ec Club there were two Negro girls, one of them a student at East High. Mary had noticed her at school, this Carolina Collins. She was as proud-headed and long-eyed as an Egyptian sculpture, with a pale tan complexion and a piquant sprinkle of freckles across her nose.

Mei-Lee had looked around her hopefully, as the classroom filled up at the second meeting of the club: hopefully, then disappointedly. There was not another Chinese in the whole Friendship House group.

Denver's Chinese population was small: a few families and a few unattached men. Not so long ago the Chinese had filled a double row of houses, with an alley between which had been dubbed Hop Alley. Hop Alley had its joss house and its dim little shop where were sold spirit money and exotic foods and such drugs as deer-horn velvet and tiger's blood. There had been noisy and colorful celebration of Chinese New Year, in those days; and big men, Sun Yat-Sen among them, had spoken to their countrymen in the dim little shop. But now the row of dark, ill-ventilated houses had been torn down, and the few remaining families had scattered.

Mei-Lee lived with a childless Chinese couple, a well-to-do dentist and his wife, in a comfortable apartment house. Mother and Mary often speculated as to whether she was working for her board, and, if so, what she could possibly do to help Mrs. Lau. Apparently she had never handled broom or dishcloth, nor enjoyed close acquaintance with stove or sewing-machine. 'In some of the books those rich Chinese girls go through a regular apprenticeship at all sorts of housework,' Mary puzzled. 'Perhaps Chinese families are as different as American families,' Mother suggested. 'Well, I suppose Mei-Lee is learning something at Club, but her road is certainly a bumpy one.'

In the meantime, Mei-Lee was hungry for the companionship of her kind. She was so hungry for it that she even went along when Doctor and Mrs. Lau attended a Chinese funeral. Mary went with her.

The services were always held in this same mortuary, Mrs. Lau said, from the early days when thousands of Chinese had come to the state, to work in placer mines in the mountains, or on the adventurous new railroads which were opening up the West.

At this funeral the only white people were the mortuary staff, Mary, and one small, gray-haired woman, Miss Dorrance. As they drove out to the cemetery where all the Chinese were buried, Mrs. Lau told the girls Miss Dorrance's story. For years she had been mother, sister, friend, and guide to all the Denver colony. Into the worst parts of town, even at the dead of night, this soft-spoken, shy little woman with her tremulous smile would go: wherever, whenever, her people needed her.

Perhaps her love for them had been born with her, up in a gold-mining town where a Chinese girl baby was born next door to her and on the same day as she. The two had been friends all their lives; and after both had moved to Denver they had returned to the ghost town on their birthday, to celebrate it together.

'And during the war, all her long years of service were crowned with glory,' said Mrs. Lau. 'Chinese air cadets were trained at one of the camps; Chinese engineers are being trained here now. A Chinese Center was needed, and who but Miss Dorrance knew the Chinese well enough to conduct it? Thousands of Chinese boys have used the Center during these years.'

Mei-Lee's head jerked up and she widened hopeful eyes at Mrs. Lau. 'Why — why didn't you tell me?' she stammered. 'Can I visit that Center at once?'

'You would have to argue that with Miss Dorrance. She does not encourage the girls to come.'

'But some of those engineers — they might have been in my city. They might even know about my people.'

'Well, I suppose there is a chance of that.' Mrs. Lau spoke slowly, as if reluctantly. 'Perhaps you might try and see.'

They had reached the cemetery now, an old burying-ground at the edge of the city, beside the river. Mary stood silently watching as coins were distributed to the company, as paper money was burned at the grave. She knew when one must show no curiosity nor surprise, so she kept back her questions until they were driving home.

Mrs. Lau said, yes, all but the Christians bought the spirit money and burned it so that the dead might be provided for; and the coins were used to buy sweets, to take from the lips of the mourners the bitterness of sorrow. There was another ceremony, she said, that was sometimes still observed, even in this breezy Western city so far from old China. A small fire of paper was lighted on the threshold of the bereaved family, that they might step over it when they came home, and so warm their feet from the chill of the grave.

Mary nodded, her eyes shining. All this reminded her of Hopi rites to keep the darkness of death from the living.

Mei-Lee's eyes were shining, too, and her hands, usually so serenely still, folded and unfolded themselves in her lap.

'You are fidgeting!' Mrs. Lau said in surprise.

'I am so eager to go to that Center,' Mei-Lee admitted. 'I shall so like to see those young Chinese and learn whether they ——'

Mrs. Lau's forehead puckered slightly under her smart hat. 'You lonesome girl!' she said. 'Let us go to dinner at King Joy, so that you may see more of your people. You, too,' she added, smiling at Mary. 'We can drive past Friendship House and ask if Mary may go?' she asked her husband, who had driven in unbroken silence, without seeming to hear a word of the feminine chatter. He nodded absently, and went on nodding, as if he had forgotten to stop the machinery. All the while, distrait but amiable, he smiled.

The dinner was good, and though most of the waitresses were Spanish-American, with Chinese jackets for their sole Oriental flavor, the cashier was a pretty, chubby little Chinese girl; and through the open kitchen door darting Chinese cooks could be seen, busy at stoves and work-tables.

'But I thought it would be Chinese food,' Mei-Lee observed, when she had tasted her portion of the fleet of charmingly arranged dishes that were served them.

'American Chinese,' Mrs. Lau said, smiling. 'No Har Gow and Dim Sum here, nor Wife Cake and such specialties. And you notice this is Americanized Canton, too. Nothing like your North China cookery.'

'But how delicious!' urged Mary, her voice squeaking with earnestness. 'Oh, how very delicious!'

She looked speculatively at what was left on the serving dishes: the mosaic of vegetables covering the golden fried noodles, the savory pats of Chinese omelet left in their succulent brown gravy, the broken mound of fried rice, green with vegetables and pink with shrimp. She ate a little faster. Lunch had been one glass of milk today. Such skimpiness seemed even worse, since she was not using most of her dearly bought cosmetics. She could have had ten cents a day more for lunch if she had not bought the pancake and mascara.

That was Friday. The next Monday Mary and Mei-Lee went from school straight to the Chinese Center. Uncertain, they stood at the bottom of the closed stair that led from the street; then Mei-Lee gulped a deep breath and started up.

Miss Dorrance was sitting in a deep wing chair that made her look tinier and shyer than ever. She came out of it like a little gray bird ready to defend her brood against hunters or predatory animals. Mary felt a chuckle rising in her throat as Miss Dorrance glanced protectively toward the uniformed Chinese who was writing at a desk in the corner and had not yet seen the girls.

Mei-Lee caught the glance, and answered it hurriedly. 'Miss Dorrance,' she said, 'perhaps we should not have come. But I thought if I told you my story ——'

Miss Dorrance's kind eyes grew kinder as she sensed the girl's emotion. Smiling her tremulous little smile, she took Mei-Lee's hand and guided the girls to a group of chairs. They were across the room from the young flier, and Miss Dorrance fenced the girls in with her own chair; but the flier had become aware of them and was watching them in the mirror over the desk.

He was a trim, slim cadet, handsome in a lean fashion. Mary thought he resembled a youthful Chiang Kai-shek, with a glistening crop of black hair added. His eyes passed quickly from Mary to Mei-Lee, and stayed there, as Mei-Lee began to talk, hesitantly, to Miss Dorrance.

She should have heard from her family long before this, Mei-Lee told her. Even before postal service had been resumed, there should have been some way, and now, surely — Mei-Lee's voice quivered — surely if her parents were still ——

'Oh, but everything does take time,' Miss Dorrance broke in pitifully. 'We mustn't be too quick to think — the worst.'

Mei-Lee lowered her lids and her lashes glistened with moisture. In the mirror Mary could see the young flier's brow contract sympathetically. Mei-Lee gripped her lower lip between her teeth for an instant, and then spoke, again, unevenly.

'My father had made arrangements with one of the same family name in this country — my clan relation, you understand' — Miss Dorrance nodded her understanding, and so did Mary, for Hopis also had clan relations — 'and it was he who arranged for me to live here, far inland, with Doctor and Mrs. Lau. And now when I write this Mr. Fong to ask what he has heard, he answers that he has heard nothing. Nothing at all.'

'Mr. Fong?' Miss Dorrance asked.

Mary thought she understood the question. If he were a clan relation, why wasn't his name Lee?

Mei-Lee said: 'I took another name when I left my country. Mr. Fong had done likewise. My father was afraid I should be in danger if my true name were known. Now perhaps it no longer matters; but I have waited for my father to tell me what to do.'

'If you give me the city, and your name, I will talk to every boy who comes here,' Miss Dorrance promised compassionately. 'There are now sixty young engineers studying in Denver. They will go back and build roads and bridges and flood-control projects in China. I will tell them. You will forgive me, I know, if I seemed not to welcome you here.' She broke off with gentle dignity. 'It does not seem to me necessary to mix the sexes in a place like this.'

The young flier had sprung to his feet when Mei-Lee's voice had thickened with emotion. Now Miss Dorrance glanced up over her shoulder to see him towering there behind her, looking down over her head at the girls.

'I — I really am sorry,' Miss Dorrance went on, with the dignity of conviction. 'But, you see, unfortunate things have happened. The Chinese Government expressly ordered that the boys should make no engagements or marriages here. Yet somehow when young people — of the opposite sexes — get together, engagements and marriages almost always seem to happen.'

Both Mary and Mei-Lee looked in flushed discomfort toward the flier. Miss Dorrance reassured them.

'Lieutenant Hsu doesn't understand much English.'

Lieutenant Hsu, hearing his name, nodded and shook his head and smiled and frowned.

'One girl,' Miss Dorrance took up her explanation again, 'was so unwise as to announce her engagement. Well, that poor boy. He had his uniforms taken from him; even his watch: everything he had bought out of his officer's pay; and then he was taken back to China for court-martial. Right then I made up my mind that we would not run such risks.

'This is Lieutenant Hsu,' she said, more slowly, as if she had now done her best and must leave it to their good sense to be discreet. 'Lieutenant Hsu, Miss Mary Locke, whose father is head of a settlement house here. And Miss Mei-Lee ——'

'The real name is ——' Mei-Lee spoke swiftly, and dropped into Chinese, in spite of Miss Dorrance's look of quiet resistance. Mary could only listen with parted lips, catching now and again the name Fong, the name Lee, the name Pei-ping.

Only Lieutenant Hsu's dark eyes moved. They rested on the beads which showed at Mei-Lee's neck. She seemed to notice the glance, for she touched them with one pointed finger and said something, and he nodded and bowed and answered at length.

At his words, Mei-Lee's eager hopefulness seemed to deflate, to sag, till she stood still and drooping. She shook her head at Miss Dorrance and Mary. 'He does not know Pei-ping well. He knows nothing of my people. But he will ask the other Chinese at the hospital. He is on leave from the hospital,' she answered Mary's evident perplexity.

Again she addressed Miss Dorrance, even while her eyes turned wistfully toward Lieutenant Hsu. 'Please don't worry, Miss Dorrance. I will not come again to the Center.'

Quietly the girls trudged down the long closed stair,

almost colliding with three more young Chinese who came bursting in just as they reached the door.

'I don't know if I'd be so meek about not coming back here again,' Mary said rebelliously. 'That nice lieutenant was homesick, too.'

'But I am too young. My father would not — would not like any serious interest. Besides,' Mei-Lee went on demurely, as they walked down the street, 'while I was speaking with Lieutenant Hsu in our own language I told him where I am living. And I think he will be calling on Doctor and Mrs. Lau before long. Oh, I am quite sure he will be.'

8

Storm

ON MONDAYS, when Friendship House was closed, Father and Mother worked with Rusty on the attic apartment. They were forever trying to corral the Little Boys in one end of the barnlike place with pieces of wood and building-board for making edifices of their own. The Little Boys were skittish colts to corral.

'For goodness' sake!' Mother exclaimed, when Mary, just home from school, was helping her nail strips over the seams in the paneling. 'I haven't heard a peep out of the Little Boys for dear knows how long. Jick! Bitsy!'

Two small, innocent faces were thrust inquiringly out of their own doorway, but Mother and Mary, still suspicious, went to investigate.

'We were surprising you!' protested Jick, leaping up and down with the rage of frustrated genius. 'We wanted to astonish you.'

'You have. Even you; though I would have said nothing you could do would surprise us,' Mary said, after she and Mother had stood staring for a silent moment. 'Oh, Mother! When I had such lovely motifs picked out for their wall! Smart and amusing both.'

With crayons, with a black builder's pencil, with paints their elders were using for trim, the Little Boys had done a wild dado halfway round their cubicle.

'Where's the turpentine?' Mother said in a swooning voice. 'Let's see how much of it we can get out.'

'My teacher says I'm the best painting boy in my whole room,' Jick shouted, his face scarlet with fury.

'It's their room. Why not let them live with the mess?' Mary asked hardily.

'But what would people think?' Mother retorted.

Silence was not the only danger signal. Mary, hanging the unbleached muslin curtains at her windows while Father and Mother were looking after a boys' craft class and a story hour, became gradually conscious of an irregular spatter of tapping. She left the curtains trailing from their rod and ran stealthily toward the sound, which came from Father's study. Jick looked over his shoulder and smiled watchfully.

'I am putting up a shelf for my father's clock,' he announced blandly. 'My father says I am a great help to him.'

Already he had attached two large rough slabs, bracketwise, to the pristine expanse of wall-board opposite Father's desk. Bent nails and straight nails made a crazy constellation around them.

The wool-embroidered monkscloth curtains which Marita suggested had become by gradual decline stenciled muslin. Time and money were both lacking. Mary had taken the curtains as her project for Home Ec Club, and Mei-Lee and Marita both helped her, though Marita evidently disapproved of the substitution. The monks-

cloth would have toned in better with the wall-board,
she said; and you could usually find it in department-
store basements, reduced in price. But she sewed the
curtains up with dash and effectiveness, if not with perfect accuracy. And Mei-Lee's pointed fingers put on
the stenciled patterns to perfection. Mary's scrapbook of
Hopi designs, which she had kept for the past two years
at the mission, were invaluable, providing different
decorations for the four bedrooms. Four bedrooms, instead of the three which Mother had first planned.
Rusty had vowed through gritted teeth that he would
sleep on the ridgepole before he would share a room
with those two young imps of Satan.

'Son! If anyone should hear you!' Mother protested.

For once there was no argument about curtains at
Father's study windows. 'It's the only good point I
see in having no windows,' he sputtered. 'Curtains!
An invention of the Evil One. Leave them hanging and
they cut off your light. Loop them up and they grapple
with the shades every time you roll them up or down.
Tie them out of the way and your wife is indignant with
you. Some day I'm going to have a house without a
single curtain.'

'The idea! What would people say?' Mother responded automatically. She looked a little uncomfortable about his windowless den. Father had suggested
that the bedroom downstairs should be converted into
a study, but Mother insisted on using it for a dining
room. The Little Boys could not eat from drainboard
and bread-box forever. They would lose any table
manners they might conceivably have acquired; and,

besides, Bitsy had twice tipped over the stool and fallen with a bang on Jick, the bread-box, and Jick's dinner.

The attic apartment was not without charm. Mary even brooded over her room delightedly. She had painted the floor a warm gray like the adobe the Hopis used, though her mother warned her she would live to regret a painted floor. On the soft gray she spread an old Navajo blanket, white with the lightning design in red, gray, and black, the red faded to luscious rose-pink. It was soft from much washing, and had to be smoothed back in place every time anyone stepped on it; but it was a pleasure to the eye. Suta's blanket, on Mary's bed, was blue and black on creamy white; and Mary worked feverishly till dark, one Saturday afternoon, to mix exactly the right blue for the bedstead, only to find next morning that Bitsy had emptied in some chrome, so that the painting she had done by electric light showed in daytime unexpected swirls of yellow.

'You might like it when you got used to it,' Mother said placatingly, tipping her head this way and that. 'I've seen it done purposely. Everyone would think you meant to.'

'Yes, I've seen it, too,' Mary growled, 'and I've always de-spised it. I wanted smooth, smooth blue, and then flowers in every fadey color of the rainbow and edges rose-pink like the rug. Mother, you will let me get another can of blue?'

'Well ——' Mother agreed regretfully.

Mei-Lee helped Mary darn the Navajo blanket. Her *amah* had taught her to darn, she said, her eyes far away. The girls sat on the floor for hours mending and

talking, with the thump and thud and yell of children
in the gym far below them faint in their ears, and sometimes Mr. Locke's typewriter stuttering unevenly in
the study, so that the girls lowered their voices to keep
from bothering him. Or Mother calling, 'Jick! Bitsy!
Where have you got to now?' Or Jick and Bitsy trotting
in, a continual parade of two, Jick maybe boasting, 'I
hit a boy, wham! Mei-Lee and Mary, listen! In the
nose I hit him.' While Bitsy echoed, 'Inna nose he hit
him.'

Mei-Lee told more about her old life, that day. She
had no news. Lieutenant Hsu had several times paid his
respects to Doctor and Mrs. Lau, since the day the girls
had visited the Chinese Center. He had inquired among
the fliers in the hospital, and among the engineers.
'And not one thing does he learn.' Mei-Lee lifted
somber eyes from her over-and-over stitchery. 'Not a —
not a nothing at all. I cannot understand it, Mary.
Nothing and nothing and nothing.'

Mary did not know what to say. For once she
blessed Bitsy when he came stumping in, alone and
indignant. 'Jick gone with the other big boys,' he
complained in his deep voice. 'You tell Bitsy story.
About when you were a little boy.' And he plumped
himself down on Mei-Lee, where she sat on the floor.

She put aside her dangerous needle and thread, and
told him about her baby brother: how he used to watch
the fish in the garden pool and fall in, and climb the
plum tree and fall out, and climb the wall and fall off.

Bitsy's gravity broke into a chuckle. 'Just like Bitsy,'
he said.

'You'd be cunning in one of Chou's festal suits,' Mei-Lee told him. 'Fat little peach-colored trousers, tied in above his fat little shoes. And a fat little jade-green coat, buttoned with fancy frogs over his fat little stomach.' She illustrated, and Bitsy squirmed and giggled and covered his stomach with both hands. 'And a round black cap on his round black head, with a round button on top. But Chou would be as big as Jick now, if ——'

'Tell about the New Year parties,' Mary put in hastily, moistening an end of yarn to wriggle it through the eye of her needle.

Yes, the attic was a pleasant place during those first fall days and nights. But late in September came one of the early snowfalls common to Colorado, and a wave of crisp cold with it. The change came during the night. Mary, sleepily uncomfortable, considered drawing up the thick blanket folded across the foot of her bed, but was unable to rouse herself enough. She could hear Mother pad into the Little Boys' room, ease down their half of the dormer window, pause as if to see that they were covered. Then Mother was at Mary's bed, pulling up the luscious warmth of the blanket, while Mary nestled happily deeper, muttering unintelligibly.

Next morning she jerked on her clothes, shivering, and dashed down into the fragrant comfort of the kitchen. It was like running down from her room under the eaves at the mesa, she thought pleasurably. Father was not taking it so well. They could hear him striding to and fro over their heads, slamming shut the dresser drawers that always stuck. Mary, buttering toast with

practiced skimpiness, flashed a glance at Mother, who
was mixing a few eggs with a great many potatoes, to
make a filling breakfast for her famished crew. Mother
tightened her lips.

'Mr. Biffin was here last night,' she said. 'That man!
Your father fairly talked in his sleep. He held on to
himself nobly while Mr. Biffin was here.'

Mary spoke thoughtfully. 'It's been months and
months since Father has really ——'

'If only nothing comes up to upset him before he gets
his coffee,' Mother said. 'Your father does try, Mary.'
She seemed to be answering a certain tightness in Mary's
face. 'He tries terribly hard.'

She fell silent, for Father had banged a door and they
could hear strenuous splashing in the bathroom. Presently he gloomed into the kitchen, rubbing his hands as
if they were frozen, his heavy bathrobe over his clothes.

'And where are the boys?' he inquired with thin
patience. 'Let us go ahead. We will not wait for them
if they can't show the least interest in punctuality.'

'Bro!' Mother called, scurrying to the attic door.
'Jick and Bitsy! We're sitting down.'

Even the blessing Father snipped off as if he didn't
see much to be thankful about, though Mary was drawing deep breaths of the savory 'yellow-jackets,' calculating how large a helping each Locke would get.

Then there was a snicker at the door, and Mother,
pouring coffee, looked up, widened her eyes, shook her
head warningly. Too late. Irritably Father hitched
around, saying, 'Come in! Come in! Haven't you
boys kept us waiting long enough already?'

His brows drew down and his blue eyes snapped with wrath at what he saw. All three boys had on their bathrobes, their heads drawn down into the collars like turtles, their hands thrust deep in the pockets. All three were shivering violently. And to make sure no one should miss their imitation of Father, Rusty rumbled, 'Well, Wife, is breakfast ready for a starving man?' while Jick, bubbling with laughter, repeated the words after him, and Bitsy, prancing and giggling, was a jumbled echo.

Father sprang up and faced his sons. Mary could see his neck muscles tense and swell above the collar of his robe. She saw his hand rise. He couldn't strike Rusty, he couldn't: Rusty, a little taller than Father, his blue eyes now looking down defiantly into Father's. No, Father's hand went swiftly into his pocket as if for safety.

'No respect — no respect!' Father said, his voice thick with rage; and he thrust past Big Boy and Littles and, rapidly, to the attic stairs.

'Come in, boys,' Mother said in a controlled voice. 'Your breakfast is getting cold.'

Rusty sat down stiffly, and the Little Boys climbed into their chairs, their eyes seeking reassurance in Mother's face. Father's sudden, inconsequential angers had come so seldom of late that neither of the children remembered anything so upsetting. Jick's face had its soft, helpless look, and he gulped unconsciously. Bitsy was frankly bewildered.

'Did — my poppy — get nups at stummick?' he inquired in his hoarse little voice.

Mary seized on the funny phrase, her giggle high with nerves. 'Nups at — what, Bitsy? What did you say?'

'Nups at stummick,' he repeated patiently, his mouth already crammed with potato and egg. 'Like — when Bitsy — ate the too much bickit and mamma laig.'

'Upset stomach,' Mother interpreted absently. 'Marmalade.'

'Did he? Huh, did he?'

'Did he what? — Oh, your father is not feeling well,' Mother said, using her brightest tone. 'You mustn't tease him.'

Mary snorted indignantly into her cocoa. She felt sick and humiliated. Even food had slight appeal. She hurried through breakfast and pelted upstairs after her schoolbooks.

What would Father be doing, after that outburst? The study was perfectly still. Mary stepped back toward it as she started for the stairs. She could see Father's desk. And Father's arms, thrown out across the papers and books. And Father's rusty, graying thatch of hair down on his arms. Mary tiptoed softly downstairs. She thought about it all the way to school: Father, with his head down on his arms ——

Mary's heart softened, and hardened again. It was all right to be sorry, but he ought to say so. Father ought to say so. *They* had to say so, when they had been wrong.

The sky, usually so bright and clear, was heavily gray, the air sharp and thin. The few leaves that had fallen squashed underfoot, in a scatter of snow that melted as it touched the walk. A horrid, horrid morning, Mary thought.

The day progressed jerkily, part good, part bad. Mary's Latin teacher said that Mary didn't belong in Caesar. Had she had any Cicero? Mary admitted that she had.

'Does your next period happen to be vacant?' the teacher asked. It was. 'Then you may stop over and we'll try you out in Virgil.'

Somebody whistled, softly but audibly. It was the handsome, slouchy boy Mary had noticed the first day. He came out of his way, at the close of class, to pass Mary's desk.

'And such a slick chick, too!' he murmured, grinning down at her as he passed.

Mary was unaccountably pleased. Gordon Pitcairn, getting up out of the seat opposite her, muttered, 'Fresh punk!' and stared coldly after the other boy. Mary didn't mind that remark, either; Gordon was clever and not at all bad-looking, though not exciting like Zip Forrester or this Bud France.

Virgil was a triumph, too. Because of Shouting Luke's college-exam tutoring, Mary hadn't had to study much in her other subjects, and had had time to learn Latin pronunciation. She was beginning to feel at ease with it.

'We have been giving ourselves a review of grammar,' said the teacher, 'and are about to start in with translation. With so small a class ——' She sighed, as if the declining interest in the classic languages were a constant grief to her —— 'With so small a class we can try all sorts of experiments. How would you like to see what you can do reading and translating at sight, Mary?'

Mary smiled her slow, warm smile and stood up, thinking she must explain to the teacher that she and Virgil had already been introduced. '*Arma virumque cano*,' she read, savoring the swing and cadence.

Shouting Luke had been impatient to get her into the *Aeneid*, and had made it delightful to her. When she had given a good literal translation of a passage, he had read it to her from one of his old books, so that she could hear a poet's rendering. That had been only a few months ago, and in her mind now she could plainly see the big old green volume, with Shouting Luke's name in gold; a prize for Latin in his youth.

'I sing of arms and of the men,' Mary translated. Rainbow colors and tall-masted ships floated through her mind, and strong warriors and beautiful women ——

When she came out of Virgil, Gordon Pitcairn was leaning against the door, diligently making notes on a piece of paper, as if he had nothing else on his mind. But he looked up quickly as Mary passed. 'Oh, there you are!' he said. 'Where did you ever learn so much Latin, and you such a little girl?'

'Why, I'm fifteen!' contradicted Mary, devoutly wishing for Day's line, or Patsy's, and making up for the lack by wrinkling her nose at Gordon.

'I was wondering if I couldn't walk you home tonight — tote your books,' he said, a grin managing to break through his rather serious face.

Mary had a moment's temptation. But if there was anything she despised it was a girl who turned down her girl friends as soon as a boy deigned to notice her. 'I'm sorry,' she said. 'Some girls are going home with me tonight.'

She wrinkled her nose at him again, and curled up the corner of her mouth, and he accompanied her, one step behind, as far as her next classroom.

The unpleasant part of the school day was shoved along to the end. As usual, Mary stopped in the dressing room to wash off her lipstick and eyebrow pencil before going home, and, as always on Tuesdays and Thursdays, Mei-Lee and Marita went with her. Mei-Lee washed her hands fastidiously, and then stood watching Mary. Mary looked up from mopping her face with paper towels, and flushed at the steady gaze. Its lack of expression was expressive.

'I suppose you think I'm cheating,' Mary said stiffly.

Mei-Lee shrugged and said nothing.

Mary felt herself reddening. She hated to be criticized. 'Well, say what you're thinking,' she snapped.

'It's none of my affair,' Mei-Lee said coolly. 'It's only that it doesn't seem — like you ——'

Mary's temper boiled. She had just taken her books from the shelf, and she flung them against the wall, with the feeling that something had to crash outside or it would explode inside. The anger ebbed as quickly as it had risen, and she knelt and picked up the sprawled books, replacing the papers that had burst out of them. Marita helped her, looking amused. Mary felt flat and foolish.

She giggled weakly when they were out in the open. 'I've got the dickens of a temper, but I take after Father. Every once in a while he blows his top. That's what Rusty calls it. But he's wonderful, except for that.' Already she was ashamed that she had told about Father.

Marita nodded casually. 'Small men do get mad. Haven't you noticed that?'

Irrationally, Mary was indignant with Marita. Why should Marita speak so casually of Father? In such a superior tone? Or was she, Mary, annoyed because criticizing Father was another way of criticizing his daughter?

'Men are at a disadvantage when they're small,' Marita went on.

Yes, it was when Father's dignity was belittled — 'Father has overcome most of it,' she said defensively, frowning ahead of her. 'But it was unlucky for me that he had those fits of temper oftenest when I was just the age to be conditioned by them.'

'Our generation's funny,' Mei-Lee observed. 'We complain about the adults rationalizing, but we use every little bit of psychology we know to excuse what's wrong with us.'

Marita laughed lightly, still with that mature, superior tone. 'It all comes out the same. We manage to do what we want to, and we won't take the blame.'

Mary frowned. She almost wished she hadn't scrubbed off her make-up today. All the same, Father was to blame. If he would just this time, this one time, say he was sorry, she thought.

Her heart thudded with hope when they met Father on the stairs of Friendship. But he stood aside to let them pass, smiling as sunnily as if there had never been storm clouds.

That night William Adams, the Favorite Board Member, came to the Center with plans for a Monday fishing

trip in his fabulous trout stream.   All Father's eager boy-
ishness flamed up in response.

'I shouldn't wonder if I could make it, Adams,' he
began; and then he wilted.   'No,' he said dejectedly,
'it's impossible this time.   Though there's nothing I'd
enjoy more.'

Later that evening Father looked up from his book.
He had been reading it for fifteen minutes without turning a page.   'How would it be if we all went on a
bender Monday?' he proposed.   'After school, of course.
Take wieners and stuff and drive up Bear Creek where
those barbecue places are built along the stream ——'

'But why can't Father ever say he's sorry?' Mary
whispered rebelliously when her mother came into the
room to say good night.   'Mother, if he'd only once ——'

Mother rumpled Mary's hair indulgently.   In the dim
light that shone from the study, over the low partition,
Mother was looking at her daughter amusedly, as if
Mary were about Bitsy's age.   'And Father punishing
himself by giving up a fishing trip!' Mother said, speaking as if Father were her child, too.   'With you, Sis,
words mean so much.   Don't you know you can say
you're sorry other ways than by saying it?'

9

Confession

THE NEXT AFTERNOON Mary did not wash off her make-up. Yesterday's tempest seemed to have blown away some sheltering camouflage in her mind. She looked small and shabby to herself.

Meeting Mei-Lee and Marita in the hall outside the dressing room, she said sheepishly, 'I've got to hurry home tonight. I shan't stop to ——'

The other girls made no comment. Mei-Lee smiled at a point far down the corridor, and Marita put up her hand to hide a giggle. They talked of other matters as the three walked to the corner where Mei-Lee and Marita took the bus.

When she had left them there, Mary did not hurry, but trudged along doggedly, wondering how things would work out. Let's see: according to the day's program both Father and Mother would be busy with clubs and classes, and Mary would not see them till dinnertime. She could still wash off the incriminating evidence.

But when she reached Friendship, she did not wash off the evidence. Her face feeling stiff under its light layer of cosmetics, she studied for a while. Then she

amused Jick and Bitsy, whom Mother sent upstairs to
see if their sister was there to look after them.

Jick said, 'Sis, you look so beautiful!' Jick already
had an eye for color. Mary, posing before the small
living-room mirror, put two red roses behind her ears,
as Patsy had done that day.

'Now how do I look, infants?' she asked.

'Brootiful,' Bitsy assured her. 'Like a namboolance
with two red lights.'

Mary laughed, but she was thinking, Well, if Jick
noticed the difference, there's no chance the folks will
miss it. She thought, No wonder people say their hearts
sink: mine feels as if it had dropped into my shoes. It
feels as if I'd swallowed a whole fruitcake.

She settled the Little Boys with a catalogue and some
crayons and started dinner. Her dinners had always
been perfunctory, when she had got them at all. It was
galling that Marita should handle foods as an artist
handles paints, and Mary turn out nothing more interesting than boiled potatoes, hamburger, cakes, canned
peas. She could imagine Marita saying loftily, 'If you'd
scallop the potatoes — or do them *au gratin* — And
hamburger can be rather civilized if you make a meat-
loaf and dress it with a sauce ——'

'Just for that I won't make a meat-loaf, Marita
Paulita Vicente de Herrera y Aragon!' Mary said aloud,
laughing at herself for being irritated by Marita's superior manner. But if she hurried, she could use the
hamburger for tamale pie, for there was corn meal and
there were canned tomatoes. The family loved tamale
pie, just warm with chili so the Little Boys could eat it,

savory with onion, tomato, and a hint of garlic, and spiced with Mexican *oregano* and *comino*, marjoram and cummin. Mother had learned the dish from Shouting Luke, and had written down the recipe. Mary would open a can of butter beans to make the meal seem more like Hopi fare; and there was enough of the Hopi dried-peach sauce left from yesterday, peaches richer flavored than any others in the world.

It was strange how lonesome the Lockes were, some-times, for Hopiland. They used to think they were tired of the isolation and impatient with the people. The Indians were so slow to take new ideas, so set in their ways. But now, seen from afar, Hopiland was the most fascinating place on earth. Mary thought wist-fully that Denver had only three advantages she would find it hard to give up. First was the freedom from mud. In the wet season in Hopiland galoshes were a necessity for every step, galoshes that grew big as bushel baskets with the adobe clay they collected. Second was freedom from wind. Always the wind squealed around the Hopi houses and the mission, and drove the fine sand into eyes and nose and mouth. And third were Mei-Lee and Marita, with Day and Patsy, Zip, Bud, and Gordon in the background to complete the picture.

When at last Father and Mother came up from down-stairs, Mary had the table set and dinner ready to bring in, steaming and fragrant, and the Littles washed and tidy. Father and Mother were talking so busily that they did not even look at Mary.

'Why, this is a real treat, Sis,' said Mother, sighing and settling herself in her chair as if her back were tired.

'Smells like home — I mean like Hopiland,' Father contributed, dipping the serving spoon into the big brown casserole with boyish zest. 'I don't suppose anyone's hungry tonight, though.'

Jick wriggled importantly. 'I don't like tamale pie one bit,' he cried, archly imitating one of his father's jokes.

'Don' like mollypie one bite,' growled Bitsy, watching his leader out of the tail of his eye.

'Boy oh boy!' said Rusty, who had just got home and washed his hands at the kitchen sink.

All this time Mary sat hunched together waiting for the Moment when they would notice her.

'The man I was talking to,' said Father, slowing up slightly after he had taken the first edge from his hunger, 'was from Juvenile Court. He was asking whether we'd had any trouble with gangs of young rowdies. I told him that outside of breaking a few windows and ——'

He stopped short, and Mary thought, This is it. She took another forkful of tamale pie and choked on it. After all, she reminded herself defiantly, this is not the Dark Ages. She lifted her eyes to Father's face.

Father was not looking at her. He was smiling ruefully at Jick. 'Son,' he said, 'did you really have to tell the man that your daddy got so awful mad that he stomped upstairs and wouldn't eat any breakfast?'

Jick interrupted his eating to gaze wide-eyed at Father.

'And that your daddy was just about to wham the tar out of your big brother that goes to college?'

'Pete's sake!' Rusty protested.

'I thought you were, Daddy.   Going to wham the
tar out of Rusty.   I was terrified,' Jick said in a small
voice.

'Rus, do you mean Jick told a perfect stranger all
that?' Mother demanded.

Father said, 'The Little Boys escorted him to the door
and I overheard their entertaining flow of reminiscence.'

Mother said, 'Well, this time I really do think Jick
should be soundly spanked and put to bed.'

Jick turned round eyes to her and back to Father.

'No, Mother' — Jick gave a quivering sigh — 'We
want our young ones to be forthright.   I guess they'll
have to learn the limits of decency themselves.   Well,
what has the family to report today?   Anything new and
startling?'

Mother said: 'Yes, Mrs. Abramson.   Mr. Abramson
telephoned and asked if I could come and see her.   Of
course I went; Mrs. Noda took over the class I had just
then.

'He is so tender with her.   As if she were a queen.
And I was right: they did lose children.   In the terrible
times in Germany.'

'I suppose they were very grand and wealthy people
in Germany,' Rusty said ironically.

Mother said, 'He didn't mention who they were, or
what; only the children, all lost but Benjy.'

'Was there anything you could do for Mrs. Abramson?' Father asked.

'Not much.   But she's so lonely.   I made toast, and
I had taken along some marmalade, and I fixed her a
tray.'   Mother laughed to herself.   'I started to wash

up the dishes, but Mr. Abramson came out in a flurry and stopped me. I guess I was doing something improper. It seems there are special cloths and dishpan for the milk dishes, and they must be kept separate from the meat utensils, and so on. Kosher observance. Just the same, I think they liked having a neighbor fussing round. They're floundering so, as if they'd been swept ashore by a great flood, and hadn't got their footing yet.'

Mary's heart was hitching along uncomfortably, awaiting the moment when someone should notice her, and thinking how long people could sit at the same table without really looking at each other. At last the dreaded instant came. Rusty lifted his eyes from contented contemplation of his refilled plate, and whistled.

'And what is the meaning of that remark, may I ask?' Father inquired, his eyebrows tangling with question.

'Gosh,' Rusty answered, shooting out a rude forefinger at Mary. 'Look at Sis.'

Everyone looked. 'Well,' Father observed dryly, 'how long has this been going on?'

'Why, Mary!' Mother said mildly, her round firm chin roundly firmer.

Mary said squeakily, 'You mean ——?' and touched her lips with an inquiring forefinger.

'I don't suppose it's the change of climate that gives your lip that fevered scarlet and your cheek that damask bloom?' Father said sarcastically. 'Yes, and your eyebrows — My daughter had blondish eyebrows; I distinctly remember them: a shade lighter than her nice, honest tan.'

Mary laid her knife and fork together at the edge of

her plate, as if life depended on their being exactly parallel. She lifted her glance to Father's snapping blue eyes.

'I think our Mary looks more pretty this way,' Jick piped up, waving his silver earnestly in her direction.

'You can keep still or leave the table, John,' said Father.

Jick crowded back in his chair and kept still.

'They all do it,' Mary said thinly.

Mother seconded her quickly. 'It's true. It has become the accepted thing, Father. A face bare of powder and rouge is more conspicuous nowadays ——'

'A touch of rouge,' Father admitted grudgingly, 'I can comprehend, though without approval: a person might be flushed from excitement or the sun. But this lipstick — nobody in normal health has a chronic case of chapped mouth. I thought Mary had more backbone. Next thing I'll hear she's taken to smoking, because cigarettes are the accepted thing at high school.'

'Not at East,' Mary assured him with pride. 'At least not in East. The Student Council is death on smoking.'

Father was not mollified. He snorted like an engine getting up steam. 'I can remember,' he growled, 'when no respectable woman painted her face ——'

'You can remember,' Mother put in surprisingly, 'when no respectable woman listened to the radio. Or rode an airplane.'

Father shifted his eyes from Mary to Mother. 'Now what the Sam Hill? What do you mean by that, Mother?'

'I mean that times change,' Mother said briskly. 'I

think Mary has used her make-up very nicely — if she had to use it at all at her age,' she added more primly. 'Still, I believe I could improve on it in some particulars. If you'll go and wash it all off, Sis, we'll have a demonstration for the gentlemen.'

Mother folded her napkin precisely, rose precisely, and herded a shaky-kneed Mary out of the room before her, while the rest of the family sat staring.

'Don't rub your cheeks so hard you get them nice and pink,' Mother murmured.

'You said — *don't?*' Mary stuttered. 'Shall I get my powder and things?'

Mother shook her head crisply.

When Mary returned, her face denuded, Mother was setting a small box on the table, pushing her plate out of its way. It was a familiar box. Mary had always vaguely associated it with ointments and antiseptics.

'You see,' Mother said, laughing lightly, 'here she is Before Taking. Now — just a film of this cream, which is practically Mary's own color, and which is protective to the skin, really medicinal ——' Mother nodded her head sagely, working in the cream deftly as she talked, while Mary swallowed, moistened her lips, controlled her amazement. 'Next a touch of rouge — a trifle more yellowish than yours, Sis, and placed a speck nearer the nose because you are broad at the cheekbones. A more brownish lipstick, too; but you did put yours on nicely, I noticed. And if you'll watch, Father — and Rusty — you'll see that a brown eyebrow pencil doesn't mar the subtle effect of our Mary's two little wings. There, now! Here is After Taking.'

Mother leaned back and waved triumphantly at the finished product. At the same time she handed Mary a small mirror from the box, so that she could see, too. Mary was almost too puzzled to look at herself, but she had to admit that the new make-up was even better than the one Mei-Lee had achieved.

But — Mother! Mother was talking fast and breathlessly, the way Mary sometimes talked to divert attention. And there were red spots under Mother's sparkling eyes.

'Confess!' Mother was saying gaily. 'Confess that Mary's face is in good taste and quite as pleasing. Even more pleasing when one has become accustomed to seeing most faces made up.'

'Swell paint job,' Rusty said, as if hypnotized.

'But why?' Father had worked himself up to a roar. 'Why paint the rose? Why gild the lily? If the Creator had wanted Mary's eyebrows dark, wouldn't He have made them that way?'

'If He had wanted your face clean-shaven, wouldn't He have kept it that way for you? You might as well say that,' Mother retorted. 'Why shave? Why cut your hair? Why trim your nails?' Mother waved dramatic hands.

'To make us neater!' Father shouted.

'Well, doesn't Mary look neater?' Mother asked, tilting her head to survey her work.

'But look, Ma Locke — that make-up kit?' Rusty sputtered, as if he had just come up for air. 'Where did you get a make-up kit, the likes of you?'

Father's brows jerked together and he stared at the

box. 'Folks were always sending the silliest things to the mission,' he suggested, eyeing Mother uneasily.

Mother drew a deep breath. 'But not these!' she said with that brittle gaiety of hers. 'I've picked these with great care. That's why they suit Mary so well. Our features aren't much alike, but our coloring is.'

The two men stammered in unbelieving duet: 'But — Why, Mother, you don't mean?'

Mother nodded brightly. 'Whenever I feel tired and dragged out, I put on some health. I have felt that I owed it to my family, if not also to the world at large.' There was a stunned silence. 'For ten years now I've been using rouge. Like a lady.'

Mother sounded relieved, Mary thought with her head whirling; just as she herself had always felt after a confession.

Father shook his head as if he were groggy from a sudden blow. 'Who am I, a mere man?' he rumbled ironically. 'But one thing, daughter: if you must use these — these wiles and snares — then use them as your mother has, so subtly that even the spouse of her bosom, the husband of her youth, never once guessed the truth.'

'Spouse of her bosom,' Jick murmured, tasting the new phrase.

'And now,' Father said briskly, as if gladly putting behind him this baffling situation, 'there are more important issues than paint and powder. This man from Juvenile Court tells me that the wave of lawlessness has not been checked. These young *pachucos* — but perhaps no more the *pachucos* than any other American boys ——'

'They've talked to us about it at East,' Mary broke in. 'We're nearer the downtown area than most of the high schools ——' Mary tried to keep her tone fittingly sober, but it soared gaily in spite of her. That crushing burden gone from her shoulders!

She felt queer, besides, as if she were looking at Father and Mother through new glasses. They weren't just Father and Mother, they were folks, Russell and Felicity, who still had some of the same human feelings as Mary and Rusty. It was a frightening realization, but a nice one, too. It put you more on your own, and yet on a more sharing basis ——

Father brought her back to the present conversation. 'This is not laughable, Sis,' he said. 'There have been serious incidents; people badly hurt. Awhile back a Spanish-American boy prowling around a school dormitory was shot and killed by a young hothead who had warned him away without any effect. Others have been seriously injured. American boys have ganged up on Spanish-American boys, and the Spanish-American boys have reciprocated with interest — and with knives.'

'But if all this is known,' Mother expostulated, 'why hasn't the law taken a hand?'

Father shook his head, thrusting out an expressive lower lip. 'Some say it's political interests: a bloc of Spanish-American voters, maybe. Whatever the cause may be, the thing is glossed over, cases not prosecuted, boys let loose on probation to do the same things over again. But the thing I want to make perfectly clear is this: you young people must stay off the streets after nightfall.'

Rusty frowned. 'I can't do that, Dad. I'm no kid. And I even have an evening class out on the campus. You surely wouldn't expect a guy my age to keep under cover because of some fresh high-school punks?'

'Well, you heard what I said,' Father retorted. 'You can at least avoid any unnecessary evening trips. The danger has become serious.'

10

Marita Shows Them

MARY HAD A FEELING about parental warn-
ings, a feeling doubtless left over from childhood. A
danger you had been soundly warned against could never
overtake you: the warning was a kind of vaccination
that made you immune. Mother's usual good-bye —
'Now, Bro — Sis — Jick — be careful!' was the same
kind of vaccine.

This time it didn't quite work. Only the next week,
Rusty, returning late from the campus, came upon a
gang in the shadows of Friendship House, a gang that
looked as if it were making plans.

Rusty was telling the story a half-hour later. 'They
were those *pachucos* you see in the papers,' he said. 'And
when they saw me, one of them let fly with a rock. I
took after them — what else could I do, Dad? — and
grabbed hold of one. I remembered a trick a Hopi kid
taught me, and had him out cold in half a sec. But then
some of his buddies came at me, and there was a knife,
and for a few minutes I had my hands plenty full.'

Rusty's picture was on the front page of the morning
News, picturesque in a head bandage, for the opening
stone of the battle had wounded him slightly. Not only

Mei-Lee and Marita, but Day and Patsy, rushed at Mary that morning, asking information; and Zip Forrester said, 'Hi, kid, that your brother? Guess we'll have to gang up on those bozos.' Bud France drawled, 'So it's the fighting Lockes!' And Gordon Pitcairn met her at the door of Virgil, saying, 'I hope it was nothing serious, Mary ——'

A pretty little girl with spun-copper hair demanded: 'You at Friendship House? Well, why haven't you joined Girl Reserves? We've got a keen gang here at East.' And Day and Patsy overtook the three Marys on their way to the cafeteria and said, 'It's too nice a day to stay indoors in that madhouse. Won't you three perambulate with us?'

'Where would we get anything to eat?' Mary wanted to know.

Day waved a lunch-box. 'I brought mine. But you can buy hot-dogs and doughnuts and things right across the street. And pie that's out of this world.'

They sauntered up and down the street in the bright fall sunshine, meeting and passing other saunterers, and Mary slowly nibbled an ice-cream cone — double dip — and cast hungry glances at Day's hearty sandwiches and cake and fruit. Here she had been afraid of being snubbed if she brought lunch from home! She had been slowly starving; and all the time Day, the top-notcher, elegant and finished and suave, Day brought a lunch, it seemed, or ate in the cafeteria, or picked up a hamburger or a piece of pie at one of the neighborhood stores; whatever she wanted to do. You could be awfully silly in your judgment of people, Mary thought.

'You re-ally like the pies?' Marita inquired languidly of Day. 'I think they use lard. Baur's pastry is the only bakery pastry you can be sure of.'

'Mary, how old is your brother?' Patsy interrupted. 'Is he as good-looking as his picture?'

'Did it hurt him much? Those awful Mexican boys —' Day began.

Mary felt well enough acquainted to dart a swift sidewise kick at her shin.

'Don't mind me,' said Marita, noticing the kick. 'If I had my way, I'd put them all in jail.'

As they started to Home Ec Club that night, Mary and Mei-Lee carefully avoided mention of Marita's national group. That was difficult, for a certain Cris Maes was lolling, as he so often was, against one of the pillars at the entrance to the esplanade when they came out, and this time Marita excused herself and stopped to speak to him. Mary looked back uneasily. Cris was undeniably handsome, with his waving, varnished-looking hair long on his neck and growing in exaggerated locks before his ears. He was grinning down at Marita and carelessly shaking his head.

'She's certainly laying down the law about something,' Mary observed. 'Maybe she's asking him if he knows anything about any of these gangs.'

Catching up with the girls, Marita was smolderingly silent. At the corner nearest Friendship she stopped short. 'Now look,' she said darkly, 'I want you girls to get this straight. You don't have to handle me with gloves, just because some Spanish-American boys are mixed up in this mess.'

'There have been plenty of non-Spanish,' Mary's high little voice expostulated.

Marita stamped a small foot. 'There you go, always trying to smooth it over. I tell you I'm as mad at those *pachucos* as you are. But I'm even madder at their families. So many of them don't pay any attention to where their kids go or what they do. The boys, that is. You can bet most of them keep track of their girls. And I'm mad at the politics of this town. Oh, maybe it's no worse than other towns. But they ought to step on those crazy kids. Hard. For their own sakes and for the ones of us that are trying to get ahead. It blackens us all.'

Mary spoke uncomfortably, from the husky low end of her voice. 'Rusty says brothers of these same boys got Purple Hearts and Bronze Stars and all sorts of decorations in the war. Marita, why do you suppose — I mean, how do you suppose these fellows got this way?'

Marita lifted slow eyes, her face smoothing and cooling. 'I don't have to suppose. I know. Anyway, a big part of it.'

'Well, what?' Mary demanded. 'We better be going on or we'll be late to Club. — But what do you mean, Marita?'

The three moved on slowly, scuffing through the leaves that had fallen under the few trees on the stark street.

'It's hard to explain,' Marita answered. 'If you don't see it you don't really understand. I suppose I could show you.'

'How do you mean?'

'Well, I know a little sick baby. If you would like to go with me and visit its mother — It isn't a contagious disease: something about its heart. A Spanish family. No, not Spanish,' she amended haughtily — 'Mexican.'

Mary thought how funny people were. Some of the 'plain Americans' looked down on the Spanish-Americans; and the Spanish looked down on the Mexicans; and she had heard Mexicans say that they detested the Spanish. Yes, folks were funny. But she said hastily: 'I'd love to go. Wouldn't you, Mei-Lee? And would it be all right for Mother to come along? She hasn't been able to start calling yet.'

Father took the four of them in the station wagon the next Monday after school. That day Rusty got home early enough to mind the Little Boys; and if they went in the car Marita could get around in time for her usual Monday appointment.

The house was an old store building, and Mary's heart began to crimp with pity as soon as they pushed open the back door. Its peeling paint and smoky paper were so drab. Its doorway was blown full of rags and papers and accumulated dirt that had never met a broom. Its windows were broken, and even its door was cracked. From a splintery odorous hallway with closed doors along it rose a steep stair.

The odors reminded Mary of the ancient Hopi villages, but the Hopi villages were frankly primitive about plumbing. This was a city tenement.

They climbed the stairs, all avoiding the hand-rail, and Marita tapped at a door. Presently a girl opened it. For a moment she seemed to oppose them; then she stood aside to let them enter, and nervously tipped clothes and shoes from chairs so that they might sit down.

'Rosa,' Marita said, 'we came to ask about the baby. These are friends of mine. From Friendship House.'

Mary thought, Rosa doesn't look much older than we do; and with half a chance she would be lovely. Rosa glanced down rather unhappily at her soiled dress, and smoothed back her rough, uneven hair as she acknowledged the introductions.

'I was up all night with her,' she said haltingly. 'There is something bad wrong with her. She is what you call a blue baby.' She lifted from the bed a whimpering little bundle at which she gazed tenderly.

With the cooing cry of the born mother, Mrs. Locke took the baby from Rosa's thin arms and cradled it gently. 'Such a sweet little love,' she said, her brows drawn with pity as she studied the blue-tinged lips and nails.

'They said perhaps — the hospital ——' Rosa faltered.

'Do bring her to the Clinic at Friendship,' Mother urged warmly. 'The doctor is fine with babies. He'll tell you all anyone can.'

Mary was scrutinizing the rooms without seeming to, as she had learned how to do when in strange places. Here almost the entire floor space was taken by two beds, a stove, a table, a dresser, and the chairs which the callers now occupied. The other room, smaller, was equally crowded by its two beds.

'How are your mother and brothers, Rosa?' Marita asked. 'They're still living here, aren't they?'

As if in answer a woman entered, panting from the long stair, and a boy in his early teens raced in after her. The room was stuffy, and now it seemed as if there were literally not air enough for so many. So Mrs. Locke rose and gave the baby back to its mother.

'They're doing wonderful things for blue babies nowadays,' Mother said. 'I hope you will bring the little darling to Friendship. The doctor could probably tell whether her condition is the kind that can be helped by surgery. — And here's a little present for her,' she said with another of her mothering smiles. 'You didn't tell us her name.'

'Mary Consuelo.'

'Oh, lovely!'

Mother really loves folks, Mary thought with new realization.

With good-byes all around, the four filed out of the stuffy room and down the long stair, while little faces, wide-eyed and curious, appeared at narrowly opened doors.

Marita murmured to Mary, 'How could your mother bear to pick up that baby? I won't touch them when they're dirty like that.'

Mother overheard. 'Babies are babies,' she said, as if that were reason enough. 'And it can't be easy to keep clean here. I didn't see any running water in Rosa's rooms.'

'Where can the bathrooms be?' Mei-Lee asked.

'In this building? There aren't any bathrooms,' Marita answered.

'No bathrooms?'

Marita shook her head. 'They use one next door. But people keep clean if they want to bad enough. Only you can't get the smells out, no matter how hard you scrub. I know, because I have some relatives — very distant — living here.' She hesitated at the foot of the stairs. 'I'd like you to see their apartment. Then you'd see what I mean.' She turned her hand and looked at her watch. 'We could take just a minute.'

A childish voice answered her tap: 'Who is it, please?'

'It's I, Marita Aragon. With some friends.'

'Oh, Marita!' A key rattled in the lock and the door creaked open on two eager young faces. 'Oh, Marita! *Buenas tardes!* Good afternoon!'

'These are children of Abuelita's god-daughter,' Marita explained. 'That makes them relations of mine. Serafina and Asuncion Ortiz. Girls, these are my very good friends.' As the little girls shrank back timidly, she spoke to them in fast-flowing Spanish, ' *Estas son mis amigas bonisimas, muchachitas!* We cannot stay,' she added; 'I'm due home this minute. But tell your mamma I was here, *queridas*, dears. She is well, I hope.'

Mary was again busy taking in all she could see. The high-shouldered room was as crowded as Rosa's, for it was clear that the mother and two girls, at least, lived, ate, cooked, slept in it. But it was as clean as soap and scrubbing could make it, and brightly papered. The beds had crocheted spreads, and the cretonne-curtained windows were banked with thrifty geraniums, begonias, foliage plants, in tin cans and old kettles painted red and blue. From wall to wall were stretched clotheslines from which hung sheets, pillowcases, towels, still wet.

'Those beautiful little girls!' gasped Mary, hurrying out behind Marita and Mei-Lee. 'Only the younger one — Asuncion did you say? — why, you can practically see through her, she's so thin.'

'Why are they locked in?' Mei-Lee asked.

'It wouldn't be safe without. Their mother works at a restaurant from noon to midnight. And they came only a few months ago from the southern part of the state, so they do not know many people who might stay with the girls. — But now I must hurry like everything ——'

They were standing by the station wagon, and Father had thrown open the door.

'We'll take you home,' Mother offered. 'You have time for that, haven't you, Father?'

Poised to hasten away, Marita hesitated. Mary thought, She never has told us where she lived. Perhaps this is why. If anything so exquisite as Asuncion and Serafina can be hidden behind these filthy, scarred walls, maybe even the proud Marita — And how she'd hate to let us know.

Marita's hesitation passed quickly. 'Thank you,' she said to Mother. 'The address is ——' And she gave a street and number that made Mary stare in surprise.

As they rode, Mother sat with her arm along the seat-back, turning toward the three girls. 'Marita,' she said, 'you made your point without a word. The reason for much of this adolescent lawlessness and violence — why, it was right there, in that house and all the others like it.'

'Just about what I was thinking while I waited for you,' Father boomed. 'Rusty would say those lads are compensating; making up for the deadly drabness and lack of fun by making their own excitement and color ——'

'And trying to make up for being despised,' Marita's smoldering voice put in. 'You don't know what it's like to be despised; you can't imagine it. And when people think you're low, the easiest thing is to let yourself *be* low. You say to yourself, Well, no matter how hard I try, half of them will class me as a dirty Mex, so what's the use? Why not get a little fun where I can? Only sometimes' — Marita's voice thickened and shook till they could hardly make out her words — 'sometimes it gets worse than that. You get to feeling, I can't stand it . . . I can't stand it!'

Mary and Mei-Lee glanced at each other and away again. Marita's eyes were swimming with tears and her proud, closed face had lost its slick finish. She looked like a little girl who had found things almost too hard to be borne.

'But, Marita,' Mary argued, her own lip quivering in sympathy, 'when it's like that, I don't see how you can say what you did the other day. That those gangs ought to be stepped on. I should think it was all our fault — somehow ——'

The station wagon had emerged from the lower end of town and was chugging along a parkway bordered by charming, modern houses, set back in tended velvet lawns. The station wagon looked apologetic here. It was not really old, but prematurely aged, for the desert hates automobiles and goes to work on them the minute it meets them, skinning their bodies, pitting their windshields, stripping their brakes, spraining their gas-lines.

The people in the station wagon were not thinking of the contrast: their minds were busy with Marita. Mother still sat with her arm along the seat-back and her shoulders turned toward the girls, but her eyes rested unseeingly on the pavement ahead. Father's eyebrows worked up and down and he scowled ferociously as he drove; and Father's most ferocious scowl was a sign of his warmest sympathy.

Marita was the first to recall the group to normality. 'There's where Day lives,' she said, her voice only slightly uneven, and her wave of the hand nonchalant.

Mary drew in a sharp breath. Marita was indicating a huge modern house, all enormous glittering windows and sun-decks and walls of glass brick. 'It looks like Day,' said Mary. 'It's so groomed and perfect. Does Patsy live near here, too?'

Marita said: 'Oh, Patsy's house is as different as it can be. A funny little old house, but cute. Patsy's folks are poor as church mice.'

Mary looked incredulous, though she had found that Marita was an encyclopedia of information, and knew odds and ends about even the teachers. 'But Patsy always looks like a million dollars!' she expostulated.

'She makes all her own clothes,' Marita explained briefly. 'It's the house next the corner on your right, Mr. Locke.'

The station wagon shivered at the curb before a

spruce, smart stucco house with scalloped green awn-
ings; with a tile roof, with leafless vines draping its
high walls.

'So this is your home, Marita,' Mother said.

Mary thought, We are all a little surprised, but why?
Marita fits well enough, her hair so shining and so
smart, and her clever, boyish coat and expensive-looking
oxfords and all. Only somehow I didn't quite think —
And the boy that waits around to get a word with her:
he doesn't fit in this at all.

Marita jumped out lightly and turned toward them.
'No, it isn't exactly my home,' she said, her chin lifted.
'It's where I work. For Mr. and Mrs. Park, who live
here. I've worked for them ever since I entered junior
high.'

11

Common Ground

MOTHER was the first to recover. 'Marita, how — how enterprising of you!' she cried, before Marita, eyes veiled and chin haughtier than ever, had swung away. 'And what a pleasant place to live!'

'Maybe it's mean of me,' Mary put in breathlessly, 'but I'm sort of relieved, Marita. I was thinking how ashamed you must have been to ride with us in this old plowhorse of a car.'

'See you tomorrow — lunchtime if not sooner!' cried Mei-Lee, waving a gay hand as the station wagon coughed and hitched away from the curb and Marita looked back at them, still coolly, over her shoulder.

Mother said, in a worried murmur, 'Surely the child didn't suppose we'd look down on her ——?'

'People get such silly notions about people,' Mary said, thinking what silly notions she herself had had. 'And do you suppose this — about Marita's working — sort of explains her superior little ways? Sometimes I've been mad enough to pop, because she always knew a little more about everything than anyone else.'

'Defense mechanism?' said Mei-Lee. 'Mmm, maybe. But, anyway, isn't it nice?'

'Isn't what nice?' Mary demanded.

'This American democracy. Perhaps Marita's relations live in dreadful places. Like the house where Rosa is, and the beautiful little girls. Yet Marita can grow up looking and talking and acting much like the girls who are richest and most privileged at our East High. And she learns gracious American manners, at a home like the one where she works. And what is to prevent her from becoming whatever she pleases?'

'Cristobal Maes could prevent,' Mary said darkly. 'But I get what you mean, Mei-Lee. Still, Marita's folks may have been very different from Rosa's. Doña Persedis sounds like an aristocrat.'

'You really do find America more democratic than China?' asked Father, looking back at her and taking a corner so fast that he scraped the curb with a sickening screech.

Mother said, 'Oh, Father, please!'

'China is democratic in its way,' Mei-Lee replied. 'Always men can work their way from the peasantry to the upper classes. Not like Japan, where classes are fixed at birth. In China they can climb if they want either of two things enough to work for them.'

'Two things?' Mary asked.

'Learning or land.'

Mary was following her own thoughts. 'Now high school is democratic, and it isn't,' she said. 'In class it is. And poor kids can get to be head boys and head girls. So can Jewish boys and girls, and colored ones, and — and Orientals. They can be active in school offices and clubs and things, if they're outstanding enough, smart and all that. But what about the social life? And don't you ever get fed up with having them gawk at you, Mei-Lee?'

Mei-Lee shrugged. 'You'd get stared at, too, if you were in Pei-ping.'

Father let the girls out downtown. Day and Patsy had planned to go to a sweater sale, and Mary and Mei-Lee hoped to get there in time to meet them; but when they reached the store, the sweaters were well picked over, and none of the East High crowd were in sight. So Mary and Mei-Lee sauntered pleasurably down the street, window-shopping for possible winter coats and dresses and shoes, or more likely for impossible ones. Before one window Mei-Lee stopped and stood as if rooted, watching a glass-blower produce fantastically charming little animals.

'The candy man —' she breathed. 'At home the candy man blows things the same way. Whatever you ask for, a lamb or a bird, or a boat or a flower. Out of candy.'

'You make me hungry,' Mary complained. 'Now all those glass thing-a-majigs look like candy to me, and I want to gobble every one of them. I tell you, let's go on another block and look in Baur's window. Besides, if the kids are still downtown you can count on their landing at Baur's; they always do.'

Mary's eyes took on a spiritual shine as she gazed in hungrily at the famous confectioner's frosted cakes, flaky pies, luscious chocolates, all set off with satin ribbons and gay dolls and bright-hued dishes.

'It's the first of the month,' she said ecstatically,

'and from now on I'll be carrying most of my lunches from home. So I mean to have a nut sundae this minute. With slathers of butterscotch sirup' — she swallowed convulsively — 'and pecans and whipped cream and a cherry. Come along, Mei-Lee, it's my treat.'

Mei-Lee's attention was elsewhere. 'There come Day and Patsy now with some of their Pep Club crowd,' she said. Her tone changed. 'And Caro.'

Mary looked up. Carolina Collins was the pretty little colored girl whom Father called Nephritite, because she looked so like the decorative statuary head of that Egyptian princess.

'I suppose they wouldn't walk with her on a bet,' Mei-Lee murmured. 'I see what you mean about democracy. Hm. Democracy.' The word was a challenge.

Mary grew hot and then cold. Strange that anything so simple should be so — so drastic. Her heart swooped downward as it had done once when she was small and Rusty had dared her to keep her foot on the steel of the railway track when the approaching train was making it sing. She spoke rather too loudly, because she was afraid her voice would go back on her.

'You kids stopping here?' she asked. 'Day? Caro?'

The other girls swept on past, Day and Patsy with friendly negative headshakes and waves of the hand, the rest with eyes straight ahead.

'Come on, Caro,' Mary persisted. 'It's my treat.'

Carolina looked at the bright windows, and her eyes hid her thoughts so completely that there might have been no thoughts there. 'Thank you, but I couldn't,'

she said, without expression. She smiled at them stiffly
and went on.

Mary said, 'I don't care about a sundae after all.'

'No,' Mei-Lee agreed.

'She knew they might look crosswise at her if she
went in,' Mary said soberly, watching Caro march
away. 'Oh, yes, there's a law in the state. You've got
to serve anyone who asks to be served. But a law can't
force a waitress to be nice about it. And, besides, Caro
maybe thought I didn't mean it. Or was only trying
to be noble.'

'Maybe you were,' Mei-Lee suggested.

Mary stared at her thoughtfully. 'But, oh, it's so —
so horrible to have people look at you the way those
girls did. Or not look at you at all.' Mary's voice
shook. 'And they're in Pep Club, Mei-Lee. And I
thought we might go in for Pep Club.'

'I never could see why you didn't associate yourself
with Girl Reserves or some of the other groups that
aim at uplift,' Mei-Lee said, in the English that was still
stilted at times. 'When you begin to get acquainted at
East, you find there are any number of them.'

'I get plenty of uplift at home,' Mary said hoarsely.
'And I'm sick of being tagged a good girl. I'm sick of
being a kind of goody-goody freak. If your father's a
welfare worker or a minister, they always catalogue you
that way. I want to be just me, and have fun.'

Next morning Mary responded coolly to Day's and
Pat's greetings, but Day was not easily snubbed. She
plunged at once into the topic foremost in their minds.

'You — you spoke of being interested in Pep Club,'

she said hurriedly. 'But Pep Club really isn't so much.
I think maybe it's running down, don't you, Pat?
Anyway, some of the girls are plain dumb.'

Mary felt her wrath boiling. 'You mean they don't
care to be seen with girls who consort with the colored,'
she said thickly. 'Well, Day Kapps, let me tell you
how I ——'

Mei-Lee laid a firm, quiet hand on Mary's trembling
arm.

Day said: 'Mary, it wasn't the kids; really it wasn't.
I took the kids down to the Old Courthouse Square and
sat them on a bench and made them see the light. But
then they go home and their fathers and mothers ——'

'Oh, well,' Mei-Lee said lightly, amusedly, 'our country people still call the white folks foreign devils.'

The throb in Mary's temples was quieting. She even
made herself smile at Day. 'We wouldn't want to be
in a club with kids who were ashamed of us,' she said.

And that afternoon at Home Ec Club, Mary was too
busy comforting Caro to think much about her own
hurts. Today Carolina's hazel-gray eyes could not hide
her thoughts. She stared steadily at the flour she was
measuring for muffins. 'You needn't think you have
to — to fraternize with me,' she said grimly. 'Don't
imagine that I didn't see the Pep Club girls give you the
cold shoulder. It hurt me as bad as it did you, so where's
the gain?'

'Day says it wasn't the kids ——'

'I know. Like last year when they were arranging the
grads for commencement. The kids were decent enough
about having the whole crowd mixed up together.

They really seemed to think it was good sense, or plain democracy or something. But not their fathers and mothers. Oh, my, no! A lot of the kids came back, after telling about it at home, and had the same song and dance; grandpa and grandma would turn in their graves if their little white lambs were actually seated next to ——'

'It's — slow work getting folks educated,' Mary said uncomfortably.

'And if each generation forgets what it has learned just as soon as it grows up ——' Caro said with a gasp of suffering like a sob.

Mary could think of no solace. Caro had to endure this stabbing misery over and over and over. And why? What had she done to deserve it?

'Caro,' Mary said when Club was over, 'it's only half-past four. Marita and Mei-Lee are planning to make panoche and read aloud. Won't you make it a foursome?'

Caro did.

The reading continued through the whole winter. They had chosen a long novel, *Great Expectations*. If today's tempo was too swift for reading Dickens to one's self, reading him aloud was still delightful. Especially when they were munching. Once a week, twice a week, the girls gathered. Sometimes they pooled their still scarce sugar, added corn sirup, and made candy or popcorn balls; sometimes they got wieners and buns for hot-dogs; sometimes they bought packages of cinnamon rolls, or a whole cake, deep in frosting. The Little Boys haunted them and got a share of the goodies, and occasionally Rusty sauntered in and draped himself across the foot of his sister's bed, reaching negligently for the refreshments, irritatingly sure of his welcome as a superior male.

The reading times were good times. As Mary sometimes commented with unconscious wistfulness, they were good times that would have been impossible if the girls had had their days all cluttered up with school clubs and other activities. And here, gradually, the barrier between Carolina and the others seemed to break down.

Mary read, '"Whom have we here?" asked the gentleman, stopping and looking at me. "A boy," said Estella.'

'Do you notice,' asked Mary, looking up from the book, 'how sort of universal a good novel is? I mean a really good novel. Now we none of us ever had any contact with a life like Pip's' — she waved the volume, with one finger shut in it to hold the place — 'but we feel perfectly at home with Pip and Jo, just the same.'

'As I've heard you say, "folks is folks,"' Mei-Lee commented, swaying placidly in the room's one rocker.

Mary, sitting cross-legged on the rosy old blanket on the floor, thoughtfully regarded her. From Mei-Lee her gaze went to Caro, under the window embroidering something for Christmas, and to Marita, lying across the bed, blinking sleepily at the rafters.

'Do you suppose our thoughts are very different?' Mary asked, almost as if she were thinking aloud. 'I suppose we all had pretty different beginnings. Now my earliest memories — really clear memories — are of things in Hopiland. A storm on the mesa is one of the most vivid ones. You girls ought to see and hear a storm on the mesa. The rain rushes down with a noise like a — like a hundred railway trains, and goes plunging over the edge in a brand-new waterfall.

'About the same time I remember going to the sweetest of all the Hopi houses, the one we always called the House on Top, because it was four houses up, and I used to think it looked as if it had been built on a cloud. It was just above Carrie Kate's place. You know who Carrie Kate is: my best Hopi friend.' Mary's voice dropped its reminiscent tone and sharpened querulously. 'Darn Carrie Kate, she won't write to me. Indians are funny that way: they just won't keep up a correspondence.' Mary frowned indignantly, and then relaxed as she selected a thick square of creamy candy and began to nibble around the edge. 'You're next, Caro,' she said. 'What's your first memory?'

Carolina said slowly: 'Grandma, I think. Mother's grandmother, really; did you ever notice how often the storybook kind of grandparents are really great-grandparents?

'We went to see Grandpa and Grandma down in Arkansas the first Christmas I can remember. Grandpa kept bees, and we had honey on the hot cakes Grandma made. And she had a way of sitting in front of the open fire after breakfast and wrapping her apron around me. I was a kind of chilly little spider, and I can still feel that apron and the warmth of the fire, and hear the stories she told while she toasted me there.'

'That's swell,' Mary commented, still nibbling.

Mei-Lee rocked and gazed out the window into a

cottonwood tree whose last golden leaves twinkled in the late sun. 'My grandmother comes into mine, too,' she said. 'She was very precise, and strict, but she kept little goodies for us; and she had carved ivories that she treasured, wrapped in silk in her chest, and she would take them out and let us touch them, carefully ——'

When the silence had stretched too long, Mary broke it. 'I had a great-grandmother, too,' she said, standing on her shoulders and paddling the air vigorously with her feet, so that her voice came jerkily till she gave up the exercise and flopped back at ease on the floor. 'She was Father's grandmother, and she was a great old girl. She was little; all the Lockes are shrimps, I guess; and quick on her feet even when she got as old as the hills. And she was interested in everybody. Father says she used to get up in the night to see how many of her neighbors still had their lights on. And warm-hearted! — she never could turn away the measliest-looking tramp. But she had a tongue that could fairly take the skin off.' Mary began to giggle. 'She wasn't a bit like your grandmother, Marita, with the trailing skirts and the mantilla; nor like Mei-Lee's. There was a scandal about mine: she scrubbed snuff. That was what they called it: scrubbing snuff.'

Marita was still for a moment, with the kind of stillness that is louder than sound. Suddenly she sat up, her face flushed. 'Abuelita never would have recognized my picture of her,' she said. 'It wasn't exactly made up, but — well, those skirts: they were long; but not the trailing, trainy kind. They were just old-

fashioned full black skirts, swishing around her ankles.
And it wasn't a mantilla she wore: it was a *rebozo* or
tapalo, yards of black scarf or shawl, wrapped around
her head and shoulders.   It was nice the way she
wrapped it, like the draperies on a statue; and just so,
because if it was worn one way it showed that the person was unmarried, and if it was twisted a different way
it meant she was married, or maybe widowed — I can
see her as plain as I can you, her little face framed in the
tapalo like something carved out of bone or ivory; and
even when she was old, her eyes were the biggest, black-
est things.   The deep, hollow sockets seemed to make
them bigger.

'And her house: I suppose I let you think it was elegant, too.   I wish you could have seen it.   It was a
New Mexico adobe, with a flat roof and pole-and-brush
ceilings, and clay floors that were higher in some rooms
than in others, so that you stepped up, stepped down,
all over the place.   And those floors were completely
covered with little rugs, rag rugs mostly, overlapping
and even two deep.   And those big, heavenly blue
morning-glories climbed all over the outside; and there
was an outdoor oven like a storybook beehive; and a
well with a roof ——

'I was Grandmother's child even before my parents
died.   We Spanish-Americans have a custom of giving
a child or two to the grandparents.   So I lived with her
till she died, when I was eleven ——'

'Glory, it sounds won-der-ful,' said Mary, twisting
around to lie with her legs up on the bed.   'I'd trade two
ladies with tortoise-shell combs and fans for a real one
like that.'

'I think she was wonderful,' Marita agreed solemnly.
'So independent. Why, she lived decently on practically
nothing. She knew so much about food, and what to
feed sick people. And she was the grandest cook I ever
hope to know. Her parched corn-meal gruel, when I
was getting a cold — and the *chicos* — and her *frijoles*
with green chili. And for Christmas she always made
empañadas, little pies. And her *buñuelos* with honey and
piñon nuts: it makes my mouth water to think of them,
even. And I wish I could think of the green stuff she
used to put over the beans to make them more digestible;
I never knew an English name for it.'

'I drool,' Mary said elegantly. 'Well, grandmothers
seem to be definitely common ground.' She was thinking that she had never known Marita to forget herself
and let down her guard so completely, except during the
few minutes on the way home from Rosa's house, in the
station wagon. 'And eternity,' Mary went on.

Mei-Lee stopped rocking and lifted questioning brows.

'Yeh, eternity. Marita and I feel the same way
about eternity. It's too big for us,' Mary said, giggling
at the mildness of her own estimate. 'We both get the
heeby-jeebies, thinking how on earth can there be
something without a beginning or an end. It makes me
feel sick, and Marita says it does her, too.' Mary
pressed both hands to her stomach with an expression of
acute agony.

'It's the sky that affects me that way,' Mei-Lee contributed. 'Space; on and on. And where's a beginning
and end to that? I want to scream.'

'And such a terrible mess of little bitty stars, and then

come to find out, they're bigger than this earth,' Mary said meditatively. 'It makes you feel too small.'

'It's something else that gets on my nerves,' said Carolina, lifting wide eyes from her work. 'Our physics teacher told about the electrons swinging around in every particle of — of anything; whole solar systems in a common pin. Enough energy to run New York City, don't they say? It's all the atom stuff that bothers me. I don't know — you get to thinking ——'

'And God,' Mary added solemnly. 'I don't see how anybody could have created God, of course. But if they didn't, where did He get started? And when?'

Marita shifted uncomfortably. 'I like the way Asuncion thinks about Him better,' she said. 'You know — Asuncion, the little skinny one. That kid said to me, "God is so sweet I don't know what name to call him by." How's that for a little thing like Asuncion? And another time she said, "Marita, don't you think God takes special care of the sick and the poor?" Golly!'

A deep silence was shattered by the entrance of the Little Boys, who made for the candy dish.

Mary leaped up and held it out of their reach. 'It is too near dinnertime,' she said righteously, and then, illogically, 'Not unless Bitsy sings for us. Bitsy, sing "Row, row, row your boat!"'

Bitsy lifted one shoulder and self-consciously pillowed his cheek on it, rolling his eyes toward the candy.

'No song, no candy.'

'Now, Bitsy,' Jick adjured him in an elderly tone, 'if you don't sing, you can't have a turn on my wagon.

Come on, Bitsy,' he prompted, 'it's easy: "Row, row ——".' '

Bitsy straightened up.

> 'Row, row, row your boat —
> Jelly down the street' [he roared],
> 'Mary, Mary, Mary, Mary,
> Lifa balla dree.'

Giggling, the girls applauded him, and he and Jick got the last pieces of fudge.

12

Joy Ride

ALTHOUGH the three Marys had opened their triangle to Carolina, to Day and Patsy, the trio remained a unit within the currents of the big school, a miniature club for comfort and support of one another. They had tried to find a name that fitted them, hunting through anthologies and encyclopedias of quotations for 'something snazzy,' as Marita put it.

Mary found verses by Mary Carolyn Davies which seemed to suit them to a T: she read couplets from it in a voice that rose high with her pleasure:

'Three men, together riding,
Can win new worlds at their will

Three can laugh and doom a king,
Three can make the planets sing.'

'I'm not so keen about — what was it? Dooming a king? But she sure said a mouthful when she said "Three can laugh." One alone can do a lot of things, but you've got to get together if you want to laugh ——'

They tried calling themselves Three Laughers, but it fell too far short of saying what the poem said. They tried T.T.R.: Three Together Riding; but it didn't catch on. Finally they fell back on their first choice and called themselves ASSORTED SISTERS when they called themselves anything.

But though they still clung together, the Assorted Sisters found themselves less and less afraid of East's size and lofty repute; less and less shut out by the fact that many of the boys and girls had started school together in the first grade, and talked sentimentally of Dora Moore School and Morey Junior High. Even in East three could laugh.

Day and Patsy were their friends, and the five often promenaded together on sunshiny days, eating their lunches. Gordon and Zip and Bud and a Spanish boy named Ammie were always hailing them. 'Why don't you show some school spirit?' Zip would drawl. 'Why don't you come to the games? Why don't you show up on Rec Night? Hey, Mary, aren't you in circulation?'

'Well, why don't you?' Day asked, too. 'Recreation Nights are fun, kids. They always have an entertainment to get it started. And then there are games in the girls' gym, and dancing for those who want it in the boys' gym.'

'Well, let's!' Mary squeaked, stopping short and looking from Mei-Lee to Marita. 'Nobody's going to bite us. They start early enough so we could get there alone, and I think I could persuade Rusty to call for us and see us home.'

'I don't mind trying it,' Marita agreed languidly.

'Very well,' said Mei-Lee. 'It would be for me a new experience.'

Marita spent most of that first Recreation Night

dancing, and Mei-Lee in watching Mary play table tennis. She was good at the game, for it had been one
of the attractions at the Mission social room, and she
had had plenty of practice. For Mary the hours flew by
on swift wings.

Zip Forrester was one of the gayest features of the
evening, though Mary had to admit that he played a
poor, uncertain game of table tennis. He was slouchy,
in the negligent manner of the day, and his attentions to
Mary were careless and slouchy, too. He reminded her
of Dan, most careless and reckless of Louisa May Alcott's
heroes, and Mary's secret favorite. She did wish,
though, that Zip would not chew gum so vigorously,
and that he would not use so much 'stickum' on his
thick black hair. On Zip's person decent soap smells
fought with stale cigarette smells and clove gum smells
and that occasional strong whiff of whatever it was
that he seemed to use on his hair to slick it back.

Mary's heart skipped a beat when he slouched over
to her toward the end of the evening and asked if he
couldn't take her home. This was the sort of lighthearted gaiety she had missed; easy, full of fun and
laughter and forgetting for a while the more serious
side of life. Regretfully she shook her head.

'We three girls came together. We go home together,
too.'

Zip eyed the other Marys and then Mary Locke.
'You're nuts,' he said; 'but I guess we could gang up
and take the crowd. Tell you: Gordy's got a big car.
Gordy'll be tickled to do us a favor. You needn't think
I haven't noticed him carrying the torch for you.'

Gordon Pitcairn was easily found, for he had been shadowing Mary all evening. He was not only willing to use his car, but eager.

'That's settled, then,' said Zip. 'You three girls, and Tod Peters and Jim Bates and Jim's date and me.'

Gordon cleared his throat. 'And me,' he put in.

'Girls,' Mary appealed squeakily, 'is that all right with you?'

Mei-Lee scanned Zip dubiously. 'What about your brother, Mary?'

'Oh, I'll telephone Rusty. He'll be home. Quiz to-morrow.' Not giving the other Marys time to object, she dragged them away to a telephone booth.

'Bro,' she said breathlessly, when she got him on the wire. 'Good news! you don't have to call for us! We've all got a lift home. — Well, sure I know them. What do you think I am? — Boys *and* girls. — It's Gordon Pitcairn's car.' She glanced behind her to be sure who was in earshot, her foot tapping impatiently — 'He's that kind of goody-goody one I've told you about, so you see it's all right. Good-bye, then.'

'I notice you didn't give him much chance to consult your parents about it,' Mei-Lee said dryly, as Mary emerged.

Mary flushed. 'Well, for crying out loud! I'm not in kindergarten, Mei-Lee. And who could possibly object?'

Mei-Lee lifted her brows, but when they had got their coats she and Marita went along with the crowd and out into the night.

Ammie Trujillo dashed out after them and stopped Marita on the walk, his thin face knotted with anger.

'Marita, I'd sure be obliged to you if you'd put me straight,' he exclaimed. 'You hold me off with this stuff about not going out with fellows. What do you call that bunch of jerks? Girls? Pitcairn's the only one I'd trust as far as I could throw him.'

Marita shrugged haughty shoulders. 'This is entirely different, Ambrosio Trujillo. We're all going together and you know it.'

Ammie hardly bothered to lower his voice, 'Look, Marita, I could get all three of you into my jalopy and have you home a lot safer and surer.'

Marita's laugh was a disdainful chime. 'Safer, does he say? In that pile of junk? Run along, Ammie.'

Glaring at her, he marched away to his despised jalopy, drawn up among the ranks of parked student cars: stripped roadsters, gaudily painted Model T's, respectable family sedans.

Mary's heart beat high as they sauntered along toward Gordon's car. This was it: sharp, bright stars, shining through leafless trees, streaming lights and soft darkness, silly, lighthearted banter. Pretty goofy, this other girl, Sandra Somebody, but young and gay.

At the car Sandra stood giggling with Jim Bates. 'You'll have to fit us in with a shoehorn,' she said to Zip.

'Easy as falling off a log,' Zip retorted. 'Two-story, what did you expect? I'll take Mary up in front. Come on, Mary,' and he started to lift her, his hands under her arms.

'Quit that, Zip Forrester,' Mary commanded, kicking backward at him till he dropped her. 'I always hated pawing. I'll get in back and hold Marita or Mei-Lee if there's holding to be done.'

'Prissy!' Zip scoffed, making another grab for her.

Mary jerked open the rear door and jumped in, the other two girls following her.

'Oh, have it your own way. You'll change your mind,' Zip sneered. 'Get in back, Gordy, and I'll drive. They're scared of me.'

Gordon hesitated, but Zip gave him a shove that sent him sprawling into the back seat. The other four crowded into the front.

Mary spoke up, her voice muffled by Marita, who sat on her lap: 'I'm at Twenty-Fifth and Blank. Marita is out Seventeenth, and Mei-Lee is down near the Capitol. If you want to take them home first, it's all right with me.'

She felt delightfully daring. She had showed Zip that she wasn't a prig, and yet she'd managed neatly in the matter of seating arrangements, and she was confident that she could continue to master the situation.

Zip only grinned at her and gave her a little, rebuking slap, as he reached back for Gordon's car key. He inserted the key in the ignition, and then muttered inaudibly and paused. The funny smell Mary had noticed all evening floated back to her again, more pungent than before. The boys and Sandra, one after another, tipped back their heads. The car purred into action.

Mary's gaiety went out like a candle flame, and she sat breathless. Hair-pomade! You little idiot! she was telling herself.

Of course she had heard that some high-school boys and girls carried flasks; but she had never before seen it happen. She sat holding her breath till Marita squirmed round and inquired, 'Uncomfortable, Mary? You're all hunched up and stiff as a poker.'

Mary let out her breath. 'Marita,' she whispered, 'they're *drinking*.'

Marita nodded. 'The fools, to drink when they're driving. I thought I got a whiff, back there in the gym. — Hey, Zip, where you heading? This isn't the way to any of our houses.'

Zip waved a hilarious hand and the car lurched side-wise. He righted it, as Gordon groaned and leaned forward. They came out into a through street and Zip stepped on the accelerator.

Off to her right above the mountains Mary could see the familiar Belt of Orion: that meant they were headed south. None of their houses were south of East High. 'Zip Forrester!' Mary shouted determinedly.

Zip waved again and started singing, Jim and Tod and Sandra joining him. They were singing 'Home on the Range,' and their voices, loose and uncontrolled, sounded like those Mary had sometimes heard passing Friendship House in the dead of night. And the car was speeding now, and shooting heedlessly through red lights.

Mary recalled fleetingly the cars she had seen tearing along city streets, boys and girls laughing and shouting, reckless of consequences. Now it was happening to her. No, she thought, it can't possibly be. Won't I feel like a goon if I get killed in a smash-up tonight! And the headlines:

EAST DENVER STUDENTS IN FATAL CRASH

East High would be smirched; and Friendship House — oh, Friendship House, just when it was getting a good start! And Father and Mother and even the Littles ——

The car shot into Washington Park, at the south end of the city, the front seat still singing. Gordon tapped Zip's shoulder, croaking, 'Forrester, I demand — I demand ——' But Zip slapped at the hand, making the car careen across the drive toward the lake.

Mary squeaked, 'Zip Forrester, if we pass a policeman, I am going to scream for help.'

Zip said, 'We won't pass any policemen, Sister,' and his three companions shrieked with laughter as if he had said something brilliantly witty.

It was Marita who took command. Marita was not so shocked as Mary and Mei-Lee, but she realized the danger even more acutely. She whispered to them, 'Be ready to get out, quick!' and then leaned forward and spoke into Zip's ear. What she said was not startling, but there was a deadliness in her voice that was like a bare blade, and it lashed out, sharp and unashamed: 'Zip, if you don't stop this car and let us out you're going to wish you had.'

The car ground to a stop, and the three girls tumbled out, shaking with excitement.

'Gordon ——' Mary begged.

But the car swung into motion again, with Gordon twisting about to call to them: 'Can't leave the car — the three of you — you'll make it home all right ——' while Zip speeded up and left the three girls standing desolate under a park light.

'Well, this is a pretty kettle of fish!' Mary ejaculated,

gazing after the tail-lights as they roared off into the dark.

'But if I was ever thankful to be walking instead of riding!' said Marita, shaking herself daintily and pulling down her bunched-up coat. 'The car-line is just beyond the lake. If it isn't just like the luck: me with spike heels.'

'Have you an extra carfare?' Mary asked tremulously.

There was a moment's silence. 'I have one of those tokens,' said Mei-Lee.

'I didn't bother,' Mary said, 'because of Bro's calling for us.'

Marita was rummaging her pockets, her slim legs braced. 'Me either,' she said flatly.

'I *wish* you wouldn't say eyether and neyether,' Mary burst out petulantly. 'And PEEanist and restaurAHNT and such things. You act so superior about them, and they aren't as good usage as the plain ordinary way.'

Marita twisted her mouth in astonishment. 'Well, I'll be ——' she said simply. 'Out here in the dark miles from home and you jump on me for my pronunciation!'

Mary laughed weakly. 'I've always wanted to say it,' she explained, 'and now it just swelled up and burst.'

'How far is it home, really?' Mei-Lee asked out of a giggle.

'Four or five miles.'

'Let's hurry. Let's get started,' Mary urged, looking fearfully round her at the bigness of the park. Lights shone on the black waters and wound along the driveways. An occasional automobile passed, and a streetcar banged cheerfully along beyond the lake, all brightly lighted and with a few people sitting in its security, not even knowing how lucky they were. Mary thought of all the times she had been out later than she was supposed to be, and of how guilty and lonesome and frightened and eager she was as she hurried home, getting her excuses ready on the way. Tonight all those childhood feelings were rolled into one.

'And, oh, girls!' she cried, her voice stifled by terror. 'There's a car, a horrid-looking car!'

Still almost invisible in the night, the car was chugging and rattling along the way they had come, and the girls clasped hands and hurried on, feeling completely defenseless. 'I wish I had a long hatpin,' Marita muttered.

The car had almost reached them ——

This is one of those horrible dreams — here it comes, passing us — no, slowing, stopping — I'll scream, but who is there to hear me?

Here Mary's panicky thoughts found voice. 'Run, run!' she babbled, dragging at the other two girls. But Marita held back.

'Ammie Trujillo!' she shrieked. 'Am I ever glad! But if you say I told you so, I'll never speak to you as long as I live.'

She pulled the other girls with her to the chattering, groaning jalopy, wrenched the door open, climbed in, Mary and Mei-Lee wedging themselves in beside her and on her.

'They'd been hitting the bottle,' Marita said tersely.

'If they don't crash before they get home, it will be a wonder.'

Ammie said nothing. When they passed under a light, Mary could see that his jaw was angrily set as he swung round the lake and back north up the parkway. Mary relaxed and relaxed, though she had hardly room for relaxing. The tears started to her eyes, and she gave a long, shuddering sigh.

At that Ammie glanced sidewise and spoke, though gruffly. 'Hang onto that door, Mei-Lee. It pops open. I suppose you and Mary didn't have sense enough to know what you were letting yourselves in for; but Marita ——'

'You get tired of being sensible,' Marita said loftily. 'Besides,' she added, 'these infants needed someone who knew the ropes. Gordon's all right, but he's a weak sister.'

'What are your addresses?' Ambrosio asked. 'Oh, Friendship House I can find. I'll drop you there first, Mary.'

Mary clambered out, cramped and still shaking, ran on weak legs up to the entrance and rang the bell. As soon as Rusty had opened the door for her, the jalopy clattered away. Rusty stared after it and then stood aside to let Mary pass, frowning at her heavily, his eyes as stormy as Father's.

Even the frown was beautiful to Mary. The bleak, worn stair was beautiful, and the hollow echo when the door slammed shut, enclosing her, safe and whole, in the blessed security.

She was safe! She was safe! Nothing had happened.

She jumped awake a half-dozen times that night, snuggling under her own Hopi blanket, hugging her own pillow, hearing her own father and mother snore peacefully in the next cubicle. The loveliest snores!

Nothing warned her, that night, of the shock that awaited her at breakfasttime.

13

Echoes

BY MORNING Mary was sleeping soundly, and Mother had to call her twice before she could pull herself out of the deep, sweet comfort of her bed. Happily she raced to get ready for breakfast, hustling out of her way the Little Boys, who were earnestly making puffs of gray lather and distributing it over the whole bathroom, already well-puddled by their ablutions.

Mary's eyes were heavy, but her heart was light. And she had decided one thing before she first went to sleep (in the middle of her prayers): she was going to tell Father and Mother the whole story. This time she wouldn't put it off and go around for days with that miserable prickly feeling inside.

Breakfast had already begun when she dashed in, glowing from her shower. Everyone but Rusty was at the table, and she could hear him bang the front door and start slowly up, probably with the morning paper. She did not delay her confession for his coming, but blinked, cleared her throat, and began with a rush, moving her table silver attentively this way and that.

'You know, you're looking at an awfully lucky girl,

Mom and Pop,' she said, 'and I hope you won't say you hope I've learned a lesson, because I've done learned it already. But good.'

'What's this?' Father demanded, stirring two tea-spoons of sugar into his coffee and fixing suspicious blue eyes on her.

'It's like this,' Mary answered. 'Marita and Mei-Lee and I came home in Gordon Pitcairn's car. That is to say, we started home in it. You know Gordon Pitcairn is that very fine, serious-minded boy I've talked about.' Mary was talking fast, to put the best possible face on the affair before she sprung the real story. 'But it was really Zip Forrester who asked us. There were four girls and four boys and we never dreamed that Zip For-rester ——'

Father had laid down his spoon and Mother hadn't pretended to eat. They knew from experience that Mary's torrent of gay speech was portentous. Only the Littles were as yet unaffected. Jick spooned in cereal rapidly, and Bitsy followed suit, watching for his brother's raisins out of the tail of his eye.

A long whistle sounded from the doorway. Rusty was standing there, looking cynically at his sister over the tabloid newspaper. 'Gordon Pitcairn, did I hear you say? Zip Forrester?'

Mary jumped. She moistened her lips and nodded, speechless.

'Well, my young sister was moving in swift circles; and I do mean swift.' Rusty turned the paper so that the family could see the big black headlines:

EAST DENVER STUDENTS IN AUTO SMASH

Below the words were a picture of a jumbled mass that looked like something from a junkyard, and photographs of Gordon and Zip.

'Was — anyone — hurt?' Mary whispered, her heart beating great, slow hammer blows and her mouth hot and salt as if she had been running uphill.

'Sure. Guy in the other car,' grunted Rusty, twisting the paper about and reading silently to the end of the page; turning to the next part while Mary's heart went on thudding.

Then came a clamor of question and expostulation, and Rusty's voice reading aloud. Mary thought dizzily, Now any minute we shall hear, 'Other passengers in the car had been Mary Locke, whose father is head of Friendship House, and Marita Aragon, and Mei Lee ——' She still stared at Rusty in miserable expectancy, when he stopped reading and looked at her accusingly.

'It didn't mention — us girls?' she stammered.

'Do you mean to say you were there? When the accident took place?' roared Father. 'Let's get the straight of this, Mary.'

Mary began at the beginning and left nothing out.

Father snorted loudly and took a drink of his coffee, unconsciously scowling at it for growing cool.

Mother said, 'Well, at least the boys were gentlemen enough not to mention your having been with them.'

'Gentlemen!' — Rusty was scornful. 'They'd feel like heels if it got around that they left the girls to walk home from Washington Park. And how about this Pitcairn? Looks as if he's having to take more blame than belongs to him. And his dad's car smashed up into the bargain.'

Mary grew hot all over. Gordon would never have surrendered his car to Zip if he hadn't wanted to make an impression on Mary. But, after all, she argued to herself, he was a free agent and would have to take the consequences of his own foolishness. And Mr. Pitcairn's car was sure to be covered by insurance; the Pitcairns were substantial people.

'You said the other car was in the middle of the road?' she asked hopefully.

Rusty nodded. 'Lucky for Pitcairn, since its driver was pretty badly banged up.'

In meek silence Mary ate a completely tasteless breakfast, and hurried to school, eager to see the other Marys, eager to know more of what had happened, and yet afraid to.

She found more than the usual number of chattering groups in the corridors. But no one looked strangely at the Assorted Sisters. No one stopped talking when they approached, nor acted in any way as if the Marys were involved. Apparently the boys had continued to keep silent about them.

Zip and Gordon were nowhere to be seen, nor Sandra. Gordon's absence was explained when Patsy Gordon, passing the Marys at their locker, called casually, 'Hi, Mary Locke! Your Gordon Pitcairn got canned. Did you know it?'

'Oh, no!' Mary wailed softly. 'Why, it wasn't Gordon ——' She stopped, for Marita had pinched her bruisingly.

'But my goodness!' Mary protested angrily. 'We'll have to go tell Mr. Graham. When Gordon wasn't

even in the driver's seat — when he'd tried his best
to get Zip to let him ——'

'Tried his best!' Mei-Lee said scathingly.

'Poor fish,' Marita agreed.

'And you have to think what is fair!'

'Perhaps you should think also of your father and
mother and their work,' Mei-Lee suggested; 'and even
of the rest of us,' she added, her fine brows contracted.

'And I suppose it was all my fault,' Mary muttered.
'You two wouldn't have gone, nor Gordon, if it hadn't
been for me.'

'Of course not,' Marita said uncomfortingly.

'But we went,' Mei-Lee put in. 'Come, now, Marita:
didn't you think it would be fun yourself? I did.'

Marita refused to admit anything. 'Anyway,' she
said, 'you oughtn't to spill it without talking it over
with your folks first. You owe them that much.'

Mary pulled her curly mouth straighter. 'If they say
yes, I'll go to the office by myself. You two can stay
out of it. I'll just tell Mr. Graham that Gordy wasn't
driving when I left.'

'Shucks,' said Marita, 'we're all in for it if you are.
No, Mei-Lee?'

'"Three together riding,"' Mei-Lee said with a
chuckle.

Father and Mother had late classes that afternoon,
and Mary got dinner, the weight at the pit of her
stomach growing heavier and heavier. The Little Boys'
chatter she answered at random.

'Do they mine money out of the ground?' Jick inquired.

Mary nodded absently.

'But why does a nickel, that's so big, only buy one ice-cream cone, and a dime, that's littler'n a penny, buy two?'

As Mary tried to focus on the question, Rusty came leaping up the stairs. Gloomily triumphant, he thrust the pink expanse of the *Post* into her face.

There it was, all over again.

'But the driver of the other car — they say he's in fair condition.'

'Compound fracture of one leg and one arm and possible internal injuries. And "fair condition" usually means definitely poor,' commented Rusty.

Mary groaned, a comic-sounding tremolo groan, but deeply felt.

'And your friend Pitcairn gets kicked out. Hard luck; but it serves the guy right. He was as big a sap as my dear sis.'

'Put that thing away till after dinner,' Mary begged. 'I've got to talk it over with Dad and Mom — what to do about telling Mr. Graham the facts — but can't we have dinner first? Dad won't eat after we get to the smash-up, and Mother started his favorite Swiss steak in the oven this noon.'

'Anything to put it off,' Rusty grumbled; but he cooperated with her loyally, helping to steer the talk away from the accident until the last mouthful of dessert had disappeared.

Mother was easy to steer, for she was all excitement over a report by the Clinic doctor: he believed there was hope for Mary Consuelo, the 'blue baby' they had first met when Marita took them to visit Rosa, her young mother. The physician believed that the baby's valvular defect was the type that had been helped by remarkable new operations in the East. 'Now,' said Mother, her face glowing, 'if only we can find a way to send Rosa and Mary Consuelo to those surgeons!'

The meal finally drew to a close. Jick and Bitsy had pursued the last raisins in their rice puddings and captured them, and Mary cleared her throat and began.

'I've got to talk to you, Father and Mother,' she said solemnly. 'It's dreadfully important.' She clasped her hands in her lap and told them about Gordon's expulsion.

Father scarcely let her finish. His face purple with wrath, he banged the table till the dishes rattled. 'You see!' he roared. 'You see what a little thoughtlessness can do! Your generation! No sense of responsibility! No sense of fitness! No sense!'

'It won't be good for Friendship House to have your name dragged in, Mary,' Mother worried, her full, sweet chin doubling slightly, as it did when she was intensely serious. 'What will people say? Of course you had nothing to do with the accident, but all the same ——'

'But all the same Mary can't let someone take the rap for what he didn't do,' Father went roaring on, 'no matter how much embarrassment it may cost her. Or us.'

'Of course not,' Mother said soothingly, refusing to be roared down. 'I was thinking more about the effect on the work ——'

Father glared round the table, taking in even the

Littles, who met his eyes as if hypnotized. 'If complete honesty,' he said, 'is not the foundation, the whole thing may as well go to pot. And good riddance to bad rubbish.'

'What's that mean: good ribbons to bad rubbidge?' Bitsy piped up out of his awed silence.

Mother laughed tremulously. 'It means your daddy's upset. But you're right, Rus. Of course you're right. There's nothing else for Mary to do.'

Marita and Mei-Lee were waiting for Mary when she reached school. Mei-Lee's face was as smooth, as impassive, as usual. Marita's was tight-shut and frowning, but that was apparently because Ammie Trujillo stood close at her side. He stayed, stubbornly, even after Mary joined them.

'Ammie,' she said, smiling at him with special warmth because she thought Marita too cross for politeness, 'I shudder to think what we'd have done without you, the other night.'

Ammie flushed, and his good, direct eyes turned with a shade of triumph to Marita.

'We'd have got blisters on our heels. So what?' Marita said coldly. 'Don't get him all puffed up, Mary. He already thinks he's got a lease, or that he's been engaged as a permanent nursemaid. I can't move without tripping over him,' she complained, drooping her extravagant black lashes.

'Well, you need a nursemaid,' Ammie retorted.

Marita turned a deliberate shoulder on him. 'What I'm dying to know is what your father and mother said, Mary.'

'What would you expect? They said there was no choice.' Mary spoke with pride. Though it was nice to feel that your father and mother were real people and not just Parents, it was just as nice to know that you could depend on them when you needed to.

'You mean you're going to Graham?' Ammie demanded.

'Sure we're going to Mr. Graham.'

'Then count me in,' said Ammie. 'I saw the start and the finish of your part of it. I'm going along when you tell him.'

'Oh, you are no such thing!' Marita flared.

But Mary surveyed Ammie thoughtfully. 'I don't know but it's a good idea. And if Zip Forrester is here today, I think we ought to let him know what's doing.' The goose-pimples rose on Mary's arms as she spoke. It wouldn't be easy to tell Zip.

It wasn't.

They found him in his first-hour classroom, lounging across his desk and Day's, chewing gum with his mouth open, tossing back his heavy hair and laughing loudly. His arm was in a sling, and he was a hero.

'Old Gordy looked like he was going to burst out crying,' he was saying when Mary came to the door. 'Oh, hi, Mary!'

Feeling powerful under all her cold discomfort, Mary beckoned him to the hall with a careless flip of the head which she must have borrowed unconsciously from Day.

'S'long, kids!' Zip said, something artificial in his laugh as he sauntered out to the group that stood awaiting him.

Mary, standing straight and still, told him what they were about to do.

Zip swallowed visibly. 'My gosh,' he complained. 'That's a fine way to do us. We keep you three sissies strictly out of it. And it all happened because of you, besides, Mary Locke.'

Mary flushed miserably. 'I know,' she said, 'and I'm terribly sorry. But all the same I can't let Gordon take the rap when it wasn't his fault.' She made herself stare at Zip until she felt her eyes going out of focus; and she stood so straight that her knees buckled.

Zip shifted his feet unhappily, looking something like Jick when things got beyond him. 'I've been trying to figure what to do about Gord,' he mumbled. 'You see Gord agreed to it, sort of — letting them think he was at the wheel. I haven't got a driver's license — And besides ——'

'And besides, your breath would have been a dead give-away,' Marita said sharply. 'Well, kids, let's go. I don't hanker to have this thing hanging over me all morning.'

'If you're set on being so pigheaded, I might as well go along,' Zip said sourly.

'It would sure look better for you,' Marita agreed.

The principal heard them through attentively. This changed the situation, he said. As he spoke, he went over to a battery of files and pulled out two folders which he carried back to his desk. Mary could see, by craning and peering unobtrusively, that one folder was marked FORRESTER and the other PITCAIRN.

'In view of these revelations Pitcairn will be reinstated,' Mr. Graham said, scanning the papers in the Pitcairn folder. 'He had had a perfectly clear record up to date. If it had not been for the seriousness of the affair — and the finding of the liquor bottle ——' He opened the other folder.

Zip's eyes flicked toward it quickly, and away again.

'As for you, Rollo Forrester, your record is a different matter,' Mr. Graham said, shaking his head. 'And your victim is at Saint Luke's, still in a doubtful condition. We shall have to take the matter under advisement.'

Zip had resumed his gum, chewing with stiff champings of his bared teeth while he gazed fixedly at the window.

'Will our names have to be in the papers?' Mary stammered.

'I don't think you need worry much about what the papers can say about you.'

'But we don't want our names in at all!' Mary exclaimed.

The principal's brows shot up in half-humorous surprise. 'You haven't done anything wrong; only a little foolish, Mary. And it was right-minded and public-spirited of you to try to straighten things out. East sets high value on that kind of citizenship. As to your getting into the papers, I can't promise. If you had broken a law you would be kept nameless because you're minors; but in this case — too bad; but it certainly can't do you much harm.'

Perhaps not, Mary thought doubtfully. Mei-Lee looked as doubtful as Mary felt.

They trooped out of the office into halls that had

grown silent and empty because classes had begun. Mary and Zip separated from the others to go to their first recitation, and Mary hurried ahead. She had no desire for more talk with Zip.

Zip overtook her at the door. 'You think you're so smart!' he hissed. 'Why, you're just a nosy little goody-goody!' He chewed his gum viciously, as if he wished it were Mary he was biting.

Mary glared up at him, unable to think up a reply stinging enough for the occasion. Scarlet-faced and breathless, she went in, gave the teacher her excuse slip and sat down. At any rate, this was over. It was over.

14

Consequences

It was not entirely over, the Affair of the Joy Ride. For one thing, Gordon Pitcairn returned to school next day and was so grateful to Mary that he tagged after her as Ammie tagged after Marita.

'Mary, you're — you're tops!' he stammered, his fair face flushed with feeling.

'Well, Gordon, I think you were pretty much of a sap,' Mary retorted flatly.

'But it looks as if it would come out all right. The guy we hit is doing better this morning. Looks like our worries were almost over.'

'Well, maybe,' said Mei-Lee.

Mei-Lee was more silent than usual as she walked home with Mary that afternoon. She was invited to dinner, and she was planning to make North China dumplings. They were the size of marbles, she said, and filled with chopped meats and greens. She had seen the cook make them at home, and she had been experimenting in the Laus' kitchen. But now she seemed to have lost interest in her project.

'Is it the car mix-up?' Mary asked. 'Why are you so worried about it?'

'Let's get the *Post* and see if our names are in it,'
Mei-Lee said, shrugging. 'I dare not imagine what my
family would say if I were to get my name in the paper.'

Mary glanced at her and quickly away again. Mei-
Lee's family! Father, Mother, the Laus, Miss Dorrance
— none of them believed that Mei-Lee's family had sur-
vived the war. They could surely have made contact
with Mei-Lee before this if they had. 'We'll get a
paper at the corner drug,' Mary said.

They held the bulky paper between them and turned
the pages with difficulty as they made their jerky way
down the street. At last Mei-Lee gave a little cry and
stood still.

'Miss Mei Lee ——' she read.

'Miss Mary Locke, daughter of the superintendent of
Friendship House' — Mary read on squeakily — 'Miss
Marie Aragon — had been taken home in Gordon Pit-
cairn's car after a school gathering — now reveal that
young Pitcairn had been restrained from driving —
Rollo Forrester at the wheel when accident occurred —
I can't get over Zip's name being Rollo, can you?'

Mei-Lee laughed absently, unconvincingly.

'Really, there's nothing much to this, Mei-Lee,' Mary
said, glancing sidewise at her friend's somber face.

Mei-Lee only shook her head, murmuring, 'No ——'

So Mary set herself to be gay. She giggled over the
Little Boys, as she corraled them with picture books in
the breakfast nook. She giggled over the scarcity of
supplies in the refrigerator.

'It would be fun if you didn't have to stop every single
time you planned a meal, and ask yourself, What's

filling? What's cheap?' she said, her young-boy voice making the complaint funny. 'Beans, beans, beans, because they swell so. Oatmeal for breakfast, with raisins to make the Littles eat it. Lots of dressing to stretch a tag-end of pork. It's like our clothes, an endless struggle.'

'Your family always looks nice,' Mei-Lee demurred, beating dumpling batter with a large wooden spoon.

'You're just talking. And if Mother didn't sew so well,' Mary rattled on, 'and if I weren't pretty fair at it, too, we'd look still worse. Whenever Father or Mother get a new suit or dress, you can look at it and say, Well, you're going to be in this family for a long, long time! Because it will be made over and made over till it ends up on the Little Boys.'

Mei-Lee dropped her spoon and hid her face against the wall. 'Oh, Mary,' she said chokily, 'you're such a lucky girl.'

Mary's eyes misted. She knew what Mei-Lee meant; anyone with a family was lucky. Bitsy and Jick did not understand, but Jick's mercurial temperament dissolved in contortions of his flower-soft face, and he flew to comfort Mei-Lee. For once the slow and solemn Bitsy got ahead of him. Bitsy had plumped down on the floor and emerged from the dining-nook corral on all fours, to fling himself on Mei-Lee with one of his own special 'braces.'

Mary waylaid Father, Mother, and Rusty, when they came in, to inform them that Mei-Lee was on the verge of tears. The whole family exerted itself to bring the visitor gaily into the inner circle of family jokes and family vocabulary, so that she should feel that she belonged. After dinner Rusty washed dishes and Mei-Lee wiped and Mary put away. Mother read to the Little Boys on the davenport, and Father rambled in and out.

'Board Meeting tonight,' he announced, reaching into the refrigerator. 'I've heard that a swallow of milk will take the onions from the breath. I don't doubt Biffin — Mr. Biffin — is allergic to onions.'

'But why a Board Meeting tonight?' Mary inquired, looking sharply to see whether Rusty had cleaned the sink. 'This isn't the regular time for it.'

Father shook his head as he tossed down a half-glass of milk. 'Mr. Biffin said there were delicate matters to be brought up, and that Mr. Adams is in town, which he seldom is. So Mrs. Noda is taking over Mother's Craft Class and one of my boys is pinch-hitting in mine.'

Mary swallowed and ran her tongue around her lips. It was silly to suppose that even Mr. Biffin would take serious offense at that item in the paper; but this was a coincidence.

'You know,' Mother called in from the living room, 'we may have been too severe in our estimate of — of a certain gentleman.' Mary glanced through the door. Jick was listening intently. 'He lost his wife and daughter back in the flu epidemic of 1918.'

'Lucky for the wife and daughter, I'd say,' Rusty observed irreverently, hanging up a dripping dishcloth which Mary snatched and wrung out self-righteously.

'Rusty! He might have been an entirely different man if Mrs. — if his wife had lived.'

'Mrs. Biffin,' said Jick, still absorbed in the conversation. 'Mr. Biffin's wife would have to be Mrs. Biffin, wouldn't she?'

'My soul, what is the use?' asked Mother.

'You Little Boys hyper up to bed now,' Father said severely.

'I want to see Biffin,' Bitsy said in a hollow voice.

'You want to go to bed,' Mother told him with finality. 'And say *Mr.* Biffin if you don't also want a good spank.'

'But not me,' Jick announced. 'I'm too old now. I want to listen at them talk. I want to show them the airplane I drew at school and my teacher said ——'

Father tapped the table. 'If once,' he said in a tired voice — 'if just once you Little Boys could go to bed without a civil war ——'

'Oh, hurry, hurry, hurry!' Mary was begging her fellow dishwashers. 'I want Mei-Lee to see what a Board Meeting is like. We can slip in on a back seat, Mei-Lee.'

'Oh, no,' Mei-Lee objected, with a shyness that only now and then showed through.

'Well, then, we can prop open the sliding window — you know, the service window from the community kitchen. They use it when they have dinner in the chapel. That way we have a reserved seat and no one sees us. Mother and Dad don't mind.'

'Dull as dishwater,' Rusty warned, hanging up a draining pan that dripped like the dishcloth.

'For goodness' sake, wipe out that pan!' Mary scolded 'And you might take us to a movie, if you're so solicitous.'

'Got to go out on the campus.' Rusty excused himself hastily. 'No, that's the straight goods, Sis.'

Mary snickered irritatingly. 'What's her other name?' she asked. 'Well, come along, Mei-Lee. We've got to hurry if we're to get fixed in our ringside seats.'

Barely a quorum of the Board appeared at this hurriedly called meeting. There were two cushiony, comfortable women who looked as if they wanted everyone in the world to be well fed in mind, spirit, and body — the motherly complex; an alert, trim woman; two business men whose prosperous tweed chests seemed to have coasted down to their laps; two ministers, clean-cut and genial; Mr. Adams and Mr. Biffin.

'Wouldn't you just know Mr. Biffin would be president of the Board?' Mary whispered, as the girls perched themselves on stools, drawn up to the slit at the bottom of the service window. 'The others are all O.K. except for a few ciphers.'

Mr. Biffin had risen and faced the group. 'We should have had a bigger attendance tonight,' he rebuked them, twiddling his spectacles by one bow. 'We have an important and delicate matter to discuss.'

Mary waited uneasily.

'The attendance in the various activities of Friendship House,' Mr. Biffin continued, 'did not start out in any spectacular way. But this has always been an unresponsive district, and I may say that the Board has been well satisfied with the substantial beginnings. I will say, Brother Locke, that we were gratified, all things considered; yes, gratified.'

'Well, who would ever have suspected it?' Mary breathed.

'We had had our doubts. I don't mind telling you we had had our doubts. Not having been precisely informed as to the size of the family ——' Mr. Biffin shot a reproachful glance at Mr. Adams, who had not precisely informed them, and at Father, who had been so inconsiderate as to have the large family. 'But the work promised well; it promised well. Now, however, what meets our eye? A sharp decline in attendance. And why?'

'Flu,' said Father.

Mr. Biffin waved the flu away. 'A sharp decline even in the number treated at the Clinic,' he declared triumphantly.

Mr. Adams, sitting forward and gazing at Mr. Biffin curiously, as at an extraordinarily large wasp, inquired, 'And what is your explanation of the phenomenon, Biffin?'

Mr. Biffin ignored the query, merely waving his spectacles in Mr. Adams's direction. 'And on analyzing the situation as we would analyze any efficiently run business,' he went on reproachfully, 'what do we find? This is what we find.'

He put on his glasses, fished in his pocket for his wallet, fished in the wallet for a memorandum, put the wallet back, trained his eyes on the memorandum. All the while Mary and Mei-Lee crouched breathless at their peephole.

'September attendance,' Mr. Biffin read slowly and impressively, '25 per cent Negro, 20 per cent Spanish,

25 per cent Caucasian, 10 per cent Japanese — and
20 per cent miscellaneous,' he added, after a moment's
flustered calculation. 'Now!' He took off his spectacles, waved them up and down, and put them on
again. 'Now listen closely: October; 20 per cent Negro,
10 per cent Spanish, 10 per cent Caucasian, 40 per cent
Japanese. You see what is occurring,' he said pro-
foundly, folding the paper and using it for a pointer
instead of his glasses. 'You see what is going on here.'

One of the ministers said, 'Looks as if the Japanese-
Americans were the cooperative ones.'

Mr. Biffin glared at him. 'And during this past
week,' he said solemnly — 'during — this — past —
week, there has been practically no one but Japanese in
attendance. The other groups, the groups we first lo-
cated here to serve, they are crowded out.'

'Crowded out nothing!' Mr. Adams objected. 'Somebody's been doing some dirty work and stampeding
them — been talking a lot of rot to them, I don't doubt,
un-American, un-Christian rot.'

'But, Adams, the result!' Mr. Biffin vibrated with
passion. 'The people for whom this Center was planned
and built, by sacrifice and — and blood and tears —
these people are not being served.'

'What do you propose?' Father asked quietly.

Mr. Biffin wheeled on him. 'What do I propose?
Brother Locke, it cuts me to the heart to propose it;
but I believe we must not encourage the Japanese.'

'Oh, no!' Mei-Lee whispered indignantly.

The Board members were talking in a jumbled chorus,
and Mr. Biffin rapped severely for order.

'What would you suggest, Biffin? Putting up a sign, No Japs Allowed?' Mr. Adams asked ironically.

'It hardly seems an occasion for levity, Brother Adams. I am sure Brother and Sister Locke, with their long experience, can figure out a delicate and Christian way ——'

'As how?' Mr. Adams asked flatly, uncrossing and recrossing his long legs.

'Why — on the spur of the moment I should say that classes might be reorganized, with some for Spanish-Americans, some for Negroes, some for Japanese. They would get the idea without our needing to be crude.'

Again a clash of voices, most of them protesting.

'The greatest need of the greatest number,' Mr. Biffin twittered.

'Oh, that tears it!' Mary murmured from beyond the window.

Father had leaped to his feet. '"But God chose the weak things of the world,"' he thundered, '"that he might put to shame the things that are strong. . . . And God chose . . . the things that are despised . . . and the things that are not, that he might bring to naught the things that are." Mr. Biffin, Board members, if this is your will, I offer you my resignation.'

In the deep silence, Mei-Lee clasped Mary's hand so tight that it hurt. Mary stared into the brightness of the chapel room and the lights expanded and blurred until the Board members were people in a dream. Chills chased each other up and down Mary's backbone. This might mean moving on. Where? And beginning all over again to adjust to this strange world.

All the same, Father was splendid. And there was Mother, standing beside him.

'I agree thoroughly with my husband,' Mother said.

Mr. Biffin threw out his hands. 'Brother Locke! Sister Locke! Let us not act hastily. I am sure this can be handled.'

'The Board will please act on the matter,' Father said icily. 'At once. Am I to stay and work according to my conscience? Or am I to go?'

'Will someone make a motion?' Mr. Biffin said, defeated.

Mei-Lee tightened her grip on Mary's hand, and Mary shivered convulsively, there in the chilly darkness.

Mr. Adams sprang up. 'I move we ask Mr. and Mrs. Locke — and their valuable family — to stay and work out these problems according to their own devoted judgment.'

Mr. Biffin said stiffly, 'Brother Adams, would you care to make an amendment to your motion? That we ask Brother Locke to stay through this year on the terms you specify?'

Another silence. Another murmur. Then one of the ministers spoke smilingly. 'Let us add the amendment. After all, it only gives Mr. and Mrs. Locke a fuller opportunity to show the splendid quality of their leadership.'

'Very well, I so move,' William Adams said grudgingly.

'All in favor, signify by a show of hands,' Mr. Biffin said. 'All opposed — It is unanimously so ordered.'

An audible sigh followed the vote, but it was lost in a clatter which jerked the eyes of the Board to the service window. In her excitement Mary had given a triumphant wriggle which sent her stool skidding on the linoleum and deposited her with a crash on the floor.

15

Recruits

THERE IT WAS AGAIN! Under the mingled flowers and prickers on the surface, there was the rock-ribbed strength of the Hopi mesas. In the chill of the attic apartments Mary curled up that night and basked in the sense of her father's and mother's integrity.

When I have children, she thought, yawning luxuriously, I hope they can bank on me like that. Know that I'm a — a person, human and all, but a person they can count on, too. Nothing else, she thought, could give a kid such a sense of security.

Still, day made many of the prickers visible again. Mr. Biffin's amendment put Father and Mother to the test. If the Negroes and Caucasians in the Clinic, the classes, the clubs, kept dwindling before the tide of quiet, neat Japanese — what then? The question appeared to worry Mei-Lee even more than it did Mary.

'You kids act as if you had butterflies today,' Marita observed at lunchtime, the next day. 'As if you'd eaten something that didn't agree with you,' she explained to the two pairs of questioning eyes.

'"Nups at stummick"?' Mary asked. 'We're on trial for our life, Marita. Next fall might see the Lockes fur, fur away.'

Marita stood still with her tray, clogging the whole line at the girls' steam table. 'Give!' she implored. 'Make with the explanations.'

Mary shoved her gently with her own tray. 'Go along, or we'll be lynched or brought up before the Student Council. We'll tell you while we're eating.'

At the table, sitting close and talking in undertones, they told her about the growing boycott of Friendship, and about last night's action of the Board.

'The heck,' Marita said simply, and began to eat absently, her fine black brows knotted.

There had been a shadow lately between Marita and the other Marys. Ammie's pestering had made her sulky, and when Marita was sulky she was a thundercloud. Moreover, Mary and Mei-Lee suspected that she had been having carefully concealed dates with Cris Maes. But today any shadows were forgotten. Marita was all warmth and eagerness.

'I can herd some of the Spanish into line,' she said, her eyes sparkling. 'Some of the Mexicans, too.' Marita consistently kept the distinction before the Sisters.

'The kids, maybe,' Mary assented, her whimsical face at its soberest. 'But Biffin — Mr. Biffin — really doesn't think kids count for much.'

'Oh, I can manage some of the grown-ups, too,' Marita promised loftily. 'Some of them are so dumb. I have to telephone for them, and see the Juvenile Court when their kids get in trouble and tend to their relief warrants for them. They just better listen to me — or else. And the ones that are smart — well, it oughtn't

to be hard to make them see that this is just a matter
of a few folks trying to make trouble. And I'll talk to
Mr. Gallegos, your vegetable man. He has influence.
There's a bunch of folks I might influence through him.'

Mary couldn't help saying reproachfully, 'I thought
you'd mostly been influencing this Cris Maes.'

Marita ate the remainder of her blueberry pie and
daintily wiped her mouth. 'Oh, Cris,' she said imper-
turbably. 'I've known Cris since I was knee-high to a
grasshopper. His brother's mother-in-law was a god-
father of my first cousin Joe Duarte's wife.'

'My, what a close relation!' Mary exclaimed.

'Isn't Ammie related to you, too?' Mei-Lee asked.

Marita refused to be baited. 'Oh, probably. We
haven't gone into that. Cris is so much more fun.
And better-looking.'

'I like Ammie's looks,' Mary protested, in her growli-
est tone. 'And I like the way he looks at you. You
make me sick, Marita. I had an aunt who had two
suitors. One of them was an inch shorter than she was,
so she took the taller one, and he landed in the peni-
tentiary.'

Marita patted a yawn.

Mei-Lee got up, her tray half full. 'You talk to the
Spanish group,' she said, dismissing the chitchat about
Cris and Ammie, 'and I'll talk to somebody, too.'

Mary said, 'Good gracious, have I started something?'
and devoted herself hurriedly to her bowl of chili.

It was easy to lose a person in the noisy, bright-colored
swirl of the school corridors, but Mary and Marita, on
their way to class, did see Mei-Lee down the hall.

'Well, would you just look!' Mary gasped, dragging Marita to a halt at the door. 'And Mei-Lee usually so — so reserved.'

Now Mei-Lee was talking vivaciously to a knot of boys and girls, and they were listening, protesting, agreeing.

'I say a Jap is a Jap,' Bud France said with finality.

'Then why do you not also say, A German is a German? Or, An Italian is an Italian?' Mei-Lee inquired in her quaintly spaced and accented English. 'Surely if I can associate with these — these Americans of Japanese descent' — she spread slim hands in a dramatic gesture — 'I, who have been driven from my home ——' She hurried on to cover the break in her voice, 'And Missimo — Madame Chiang, what does she say about giving them justice and mercy?'

Then she caught sight of Mary, standing poised at the door with her mouth ajar, and she lifted her hand in a small silencing wave. The knot of girls and boys turned toward Mary and Marita, smiling a bit sheepishly or staring curiously, before they drifted apart.

'Let's talk to Carolina, too,' Marita proposed, her eyes glistening with purpose.

'It isn't any of it going to do any good,' Mary muttered. 'You can talk your head off to people, and nothing happens.'

This time, however, something did happen. Even the next week saw a trickle of Negroes, of Spanish-Americans, back into Friendship House; and a small Chinese brother and sister, besides. The following week one or two more returned. The week after that, when Father and Mother tabulated the records and found no further gain, Mary's throat tightened with anxiety. Then Thanksgiving week showed a half-dozen additions.

The staff of volunteer helpers increased, also. Six East High students came the first week to offer their services. Two of them were Girl Reserves and one was Gordon Pitcairn. Those three did not surprise Mary, but there were two who did. They were Day Kapps and Patsy Benton.

Day explained that she was supposed to interview a career woman, as an assignment in Social Science. So she telephoned Mother for an appointment. Patsy came with her and, since it was Thursday, they walked home with the Sisters.

'There's Mrs. Locke now,' Marita observed as they drew near Friendship House, 'leaning over the back fence talking to the push-cart man.'

'Mr. Abernethy,' Mary corrected. She knew him well; small and warped, his hair falling on his ragged collar, and on chilly days like this one his feet and legs wrapped in gunny-sacks.

'I never knew he had a name,' Marita said amusedly.

'Is he selling something?' Patsy chirped.

Mary shook her head, ashamed of her momentary embarrassment. 'He pushes that cart around — an old baby buggy from the Year One, with a box nailed on — and rummages the trash heaps. I think he reminds Mother of old Suta on the mesa. She mothered Suta for years, and she misses him. She's always running out with hot cookies and things for Mr. Abernethy.'

'And then I suppose he comes to your settlement house?' Day inquired with interest.

Mary laughed. 'No, and neither did Suta. You get used to that. — Oh, speaking of Hopiland,' she interrupted herself, 'I had an extra long letter from Shouting Luke. Whatever do you think? He'd seen our names in the Denver *Post*!'

'Oh. Oh, dear,' Mei-Lee moaned softly.

They had reached the door of Friendship, which Father had just thrown open. Standing firm amid the flood of impetuous children, he smiled at the girls. Mother, too, hurrying through from a back door, met them graciously. Mother looked nice, and not too simple, Mary thought thankfully, even if she had been carrying on a chummy conversation with a ragpicker.

'Mary,' Mother said, 'if you and your gang will take over the Club this afternoon, I'll show Day and Patsy the plant.'

Compliantly the Marys went to the clubroom. But in her mind Mary Locke was following Day and Patsy and viewing the place through their eyes. Rather absent-mindedly she took the roll and helped to start the afternoon's work. Mentally she was with Day, Patsy, and Mother, inspecting the makeshift Clinic room, divided into two with muslin curtains, and equipped with secondhand chests of drawers and chairs which the Lockes had laboriously painted white.

Helping a little Japanese girl choose an embroidery pattern, with the other half of her mind Mary was tracking the trio to the game room. When they reached it, the wild yells became mere hearty shouting and laughter. And Patsy and Day would be thinking that it was a very dreary place, except for the gaiety of flying arms and legs, of shining eyes, of tossing mops of hair.

Next on the tour of inspection would be Father's woodcraft class. There the shriek of rending boards indicated what was happening: orange crates from the grocery were being broken up to get precious wood for door-stops, for book-ends.

Next the trio would go upstairs and visit Rusty's band, since this was band day. Thus far Rusty had assembled a ragged assortment of boys, girls, and instruments. Benjy and his violin were really good. There was a drum which had hidden under Friendship's attic eaves, and which now rumbled beneath the rhythmic sticks of a small Negro sway-backed with pride. There were two trumpets, Rusty's flute, and the piano.

The resultant music had been swelling wildly through the building. When it ended in abrupt silence, Mary knew that Mother and the girls had gone into the chapel. Then a pirouette of piano notes danced through all the unrelated noises of Friendship, and wound up in a solo, brief but spirited and true.

Mary was leaning over a table, helping the little Japanese girl hold her length of unbleached muslin steady while she traced on it the embroidery design they had selected. Both palms flat on the cloth, Mary looked across at Marita and Mei-Lee, her winged brows flying upward in question.

'It's Patsy,' said Marita. 'Didn't you know she was a super-duper at the piano?' She returned to the blouse pattern brought by one of her Spanish friends whom she had herded back to Friendship House. 'You see,' she instructed, 'this piece is the sleeve ——'

Mary sighed with itching curiosity. She did so want to know how Day and Patsy were taking it all, the bleakness, the shabbiness. She so wanted to know what Rusty thought of the two girls, and they of him. Through ceiling and intervening rooms she could picture Patsy glancing demurely from under luscious lashes at a bemused Rusty, making him feel tall and stalwart by her crystal tininess. Mother and the girls evidently stayed with the band some time, for the piano kept threading firmly through the tentative sounds of other instruments.

It was not until the hour was over and the club girls were reluctantly putting away their things that Mother, Father, and the two girls came in. Day was frowning down at her open notebook, pushing it up against the wall to make another entry. Patsy danced in, bright-cheeked and eager, with both Father and Mother smiling at her benevolently.

'I'm going to play in your brother's band!' Patsy announced. 'And for Sunday Vespers. Oh, hello, Caro. Hello, Yoshi.'

Day blinked thoughtfully at her notes. 'That gives me material for a swell report, Mrs. Locke,' she said. 'Thank you so much. But I do wonder about one thing: Why couldn't we get up a Hi-Y committee and sort of fix up the game room? The girls could make cheerful-looking curtains, and they could paint things. And the fellows could make toy cabinets. They could make them out of orange crates,' she hastened, as if anticipating an objection. 'I know a nursery where they did that, and even made cute little chairs for the kids, and painted them in rainbow colors.'

'Then you've visited settlement houses before?' Mary asked feebly.

'Didn't you know Day was head of the State Youth Council?' Patsy asked.

Mary gaped at them both.

The early winter dusk had fallen, and now, as Friendship House emptied out its young hordes, the shouts and laughter fading into the distance had a curiously muffled sound. Mary ran and pushed aside a curtain.

'Snow!' she cried. 'I didn't know it was snowing.'

'"It snows!" cries the schoolboy, "Hurrah!"' Father quoted, as he always did, and he glanced at his watch. 'Mother,' he said, 'how about asking Mary's friends to stay and have supper with us? Then I could ride them home. Or Rusty could.'

Mother looked as if she were taken off balance, but she made a quick come-back. 'It will be pot luck. Will you stay, girls? And Mei-Lee and Marita, of course.'

Marita said, 'Thank you. It is my evening off.'

The other three said they would love to, and could they please telephone home? Rusty came in breathless at that moment, looking as if he had slid down the banister the minute the last uncertain note had died out in the chapel. He and Father fished nickels from their pockets, because the telephone was the pay kind, and the three girls went off to confer with their elders.

The family held a council while they were gone. Mother said, 'Rus, you don't seem to realize it, but there are times when it is next to impossible to feed four extra people at the drop of a hat.'

Father said comfortably, 'Oh, you always manage to make it a feast, Mother.'

And Rusty offered eagerly, 'I can do any errands you want done, Mom. It ought to be extra special ——'

Mary and Mother silenced him with a glance. This was the last day of the month; both Little Boys had gone through their shoes so thoroughly that there was not enough left to hold patches, and the last cash had had to be used for replacements. And Father refused to run bills.

'I have a huge baking pan of *garbanzos*,' Mother said, 'with very scrappy bits of yesterday's ham-end. There's a head of lettuce, thank goodness, and by using every leftover in the refrigerator we can make a big tossed salad. And we can bake plenty of johnny-cake. But dessert? I don't know ——'

'Is there dry bread? Is there cheese?' Marita asked briskly. '*Sopa* would go well with those Mexican peas.'

'*Sopa?*' they asked in chorus.

'It is a kind of Spanish bread pudding. It is even better if there's stale cake for it, or cookies or doughnuts.'

'Stale cake, with these devouring locusts?' Mother exclaimed. 'Wait a minute, though. This time there is some. I hid a dozen cinnamon rolls — so as to keep them for breakfast — and forgot all about them. I found them today, as hard as rocks.'

'Fine,' said Marita. 'Now if I may please wash my hands ——'

Everything had been planned before the three girls came back from the telephone, the Little Boys devotedly attending them.

Jick jumped up and down excitedly before Mother. 'I want to show them my room!' he cried.

'My room,' Bitsy corrected, pulling at Jick's shirt.

'My and your room,' Jick responded impatiently. 'I want to show the girls the pictures I make.'

Mary looked despairingly at Mother, and Mother was evidently framing a refusal, when Patsy fluttered her lashes at Rusty and cooed, 'Oh, Bitsy, we'd love to see your room, honey man.'

Mother wore an in-turned expression, as if she were trying to recall whether the beds were all made, and whether Father had left his clothes in their usual procession across the floor. But she only said, 'Well, Marita and I will be starting dinner, and Mary and Mei-Lee can display our camping quarters.'

'Put on your coats, then,' Mary said grimly. 'It's like a trip to the North Pole, these days.'

'I'll rush ahead,' Rusty offered in a great hurry, 'and light the gas heaters to take the chill off.'

'We can't leave the heaters on,' Mother explained, 'because they would exhaust too much oxygen, even in that great barn.'

'And because Biffin would raise a howl about the extra gas,' Mary mentally added.

She thought resentfully that Day and Patsy were as curious and delighted as if they were on a slumming expedition. The attic rooms, with the small gas heaters feebly fighting the sharp chill, with the snow whispering against the windows, with the dangling light bulbs softened by miscellaneous bright shades, with the gay baskets and rugs — the rooms were quaintly cheerful. Yet there was no denying that they were definitely cold, and definitely attic, and definitely queer.

'This is Bro's room,' Jick announced, holding aside a curtain.

Rusty turned a scarlet face to the visitors, smoothed back his tousled auburn hair, and uttered a forced laugh. Their too early arrival had caught him hurriedly thrusting odds and ends out of sight under his bed.

'Rusty ab-so-lutely won't pick up his things,' Jick informed the girls importantly.

'As-po-looply,' Bitsy echoed, and dropped plumply on his stomach to peer under the concealing spread. 'Things,' he said rebukingly. 'Dust.'

Dinnertime came. The small dining room could hardly have squeezed in another person. The living-room table had had to be added to the dining table, and the two slightly different heights draped with the longest dinner cloth. Inevitably, Bitsy set his glass of milk at the exact place where the two tables joined; and of course it tipped over, sending out a river of white. Inevitably Jick commented that they used paper napkins for every day, because these cloth ones were wearing out too fast.

Nevertheless, dinner was fun.

If there could have been any ice in that close little room, with everyone hungry and the good hot smells of *garbanzos* with just enough garlic and johnny-cake with a popcorn tang — if there could have been any ice, it would have been broken when Marita asked, 'Mary, wouldn't you all talk in rhyme, the way you do sometimes?'

And Mary laughed till her eyes were almost shut, it seemed suddenly so funny to her that she should be airing even their oddities before Day, and said:

> 'Dad, Rita wants the girls to see
> How very silly we can be.'

Father responded,

> 'Alas, dear child, she does not know
> How fast and far the Lockes can go!'

Rusty continued with

> 'But really, Pop, it seems to me
> For every Locke there is a key!'

Rusty immediately flamed red, knowing that he
left himself wide open for Mother's attack, which c
with prompt gaiety:

> 'Yes, beauty, wit, and music still
> Can turn the Rustiest Locke at will!'

The table could not have rocked with more deligl
laughter if the verse and the wit had been really su
Rusty and Patsy glanced at each other and then drop
their eyes to Marita's *sopa*, which everyone begar
taste with curiosity.

> 'And this confection: what's its name?'

Father inquired, pausing to savor it and gain time
his next line:

> 'For it deserves a lasting fame.
> Hm! Sugar, spice, and all things nice ——'

Here Rusty, still flushed, took the verse away f
him:

> 'And here tongue savors and eye sees
> The crunch of nuts, the gold of cheese!
> It is bread pudding, I would guess,
> Raised to the heights of blessedness!'

arita turned to Day and Patsy with a gently pro-
ary pride. 'See?' she said. 'Aren't they wonder-

ere was more laughter at that, and Jick, exhilarated
he fun and wanting to add to his family's fame,
ed shrilly into the conversation: 'And my Pop's
ng!' he bragged. 'Gosh, can he spank hard! And
he got so mad at us boys that he ——'
ome, come, that will do, son,' Father ordered
ly.
k subsided, though he still bubbled with scattered
ds and phrases: 'Well, Father, you did — took
y, wham! by the coat and ——'
spite of the Little Boys, Mary had to admit that
, as well as the moonstruck Patsy, seemed to relish
evening. Day's good-night thanks to Mother lacked
ose and slickness.
haven't had such a good time in ages,' she said.
s she went to sleep curled up under her Hopi blanket
night, Mary was thinking, Why, they even liked
margarine on the johnny-cake. Reminds me of
n we used to visit the minister's children down at
Railroad. Ten of them. And much poorer than we
were. But I loved it, even the threadbare carpets.
I thought their dinners were delicious; bread with
gravy ——

16

The Difficult Mr. Fong

PATSY BENTON surprised the Marys by her faithfulness to Friendship House as the days and weeks went by; or perhaps it was Friendship's Rusty Locke that inspired her. As for Day, she bullied Girl Reserves and Hi-Y's into carrying through the game-room project. They made the place gayer and more convenient, as Day had envisioned it, with bright curtains, and with cabinets and funny little fat chairs made from orange crates, and with new tables for which the group raised money. After the game room had been revamped, some of the young people had such a sense of ownership that they kept coming, to help with the younger groups. Gordon Pitcairn had continued to help Mr. Locke with craft classes, and he and Mary, Rusty and Patsy and Day, took turns seeing home some of the youngsters through the early winter dusk, children like Serafina and Asuncion, who must be safely locked into their clean, crowded room before their escorts left them.

For Mary all this interchange had altered the face of East High. Its resounding corridor canyons no longer flowed with heartless rivers of indifferent faces. Girls called to the Assorted Sisters as they lugged their books from class to class. Boys grinned at them companionably.

And still the Sisters held together, attended Recreation Nights together — and came home from them together, with Rusty calling for them in the station wagon and delivering them at their own front doors. It was when they were making their plans for a mid-year dance that the familiar pattern began to shift.

In the first place, Patsy had invited Rusty to the dance. He would not be free to see the Sisters home.

'This once,' Mei-Lee said, 'I think I will ask Doctor Lau to call for us.'

With absorbed interest Marita contemplated the long, crimson ovals of her finger-nails. 'Don't bother about me,' she said lightly. 'I was just going to tell you. Ammie asked to take me, and I don't know but it's my duty to encourage him once in a while. Reward of virtue.'

'Ammie?' Mei-Lee asked incredulously. 'I thought it was that Cris Maes.'

Marita's nostrils dilated. 'Cristobal Maes and I — we are entirely washed up.' Airily she dusted him from her hands.

'Well, isn't this awfully sudden?' Mary asked blankly, shifting her books from one arm to the other as she tramped sturdily along the hall. 'Not that I'm sorry.'

Marita squinted into the mirror of her compact and pushed a loose lock into place. 'I might as well tell all,' she said. 'Things sort of came to a head when Cris took me to the skating rink one night last week.'

So she really had been dating, as they suspected! Mary frowned at her as at a loved but faithless sister.

Marita was too engrossed in her own story to n[...]
the glare. A thunderstorm was gathering behind[...]
dark oval of her face, and she stopped still in the mi[...]
of the current of boys and girls. 'They wouldn't l[...]
in!' she burst out, her eyes flashing. 'Was I furi[...]
Wouldn't let us in because we were Spanish!'[...]
stamped an indignant foot, scowled at the worl[...]
general, and then suddenly grew calm, and let he[...]
be led onward. 'Well, I thought, I've been here be[...]
and I never was turned away. And no one would [...]
take me for anything but Spanish. Even Cris look[...]
more so than I do. So then I sort of took stock of [...]
I mean, the way the skating-rink people might ha[...]

She paused. They had reached their locker, which[...]
three of them now shared, after making more or [...]
legal adjustments to that end. Mary twirled the [...]
bination, her brows knitted with question as to [...]
Marita was getting at. All three had plumped t[...]
things inside and got their coats before Marita contin[...]

'I never did pay much attention to how sort [...]
extreme his hair was. Why, it's so long it keeps[...]
collar soiled.' Marita lowered her voice and hurrie[...]
without looking at Mary and Mei-Lee, as if it [...]
almost more than she could do to admit that [...]
Marita, was ever mistaken about anything or anyb[...]
'And his finger-nails — oh, my soul! And he [...]
talking so loud — And you can't blame anyone for[...]
having nice clothes; but when they're flashy and [...]
too clean ——

'Well, that's why I said O.K. when Ammie asked [...]
she finished abruptly.

m awfully glad you're done with Cris,' Mary said.
oh dear!'

h dear what?' Marita demanded, as if coming back
her own thoughts.

ow Ammie will turn out to be a Boy Friend,' Mary
curling her lips as if the words tasted bitter. She
ied at her own dramatic intonation, yet she felt
yed all the same.

rita smiled indulgently, again superior in her
er maturity. 'Oh, well. Next year it will be you
That lieutenant of yours, Mei-Lee. And Gordon
irn isn't half bad since he's begun to grow up.
eing you, kids. I'm in a hurry now.'

e was off, just as Gordon Pitcairn came racing up
em, sliding the last six feet as if to show Mary
he could be a pretty dashing fellow.

h, Mei-Lee,' he said, 'I thought maybe I'd find you
'

le?' Mei-Lee raised questioning brows.

'hen I was in the office just now the principal was
g if anyone knew where to find you before you got
. There's a gentleman looking for you.'

gentleman?'

Chinese gentleman.'

i-Lee moistened her lips, her face paling. 'A
ese gentleman — Thank you, Gordon — A Chinese
eman,' she repeated. 'Oh, Mary, please come
me. I'm — frightened.'

ry trotted along soberly, Mei-Lee's concern weigh-
lown her spirits. 'What are you afraid of?' she
l anxiously.

Mei-Lee only shook her head absently and hastened her steps.

The Chinese gentleman was sitting very erect in the principal's office when the two girls entered.

'This is Mei-Lee, Mr. Fong,' the principal said, rising from his desk chair. 'And Mary Locke, her constant companion. And now, if you will excuse me, I will leave you to talk with your young compatriot.' And he strode into the outer office.

Mr. Fong bowed to Mr. Graham, bowed to Mei-Lee, bowed to Mary. He was smiling, but when his smile reached Mary, she thought she had never seen one with so many teeth and so little warmth. She felt that she had been weighed and found wanting.

'You are looking well,' Mr. Fong said politely to Mei-Lee. 'I observe that you call yourself still Mei-Lee. I think the precaution is no longer necessary.'

'It is awkward to change here at school, sir. — Oh, Mr. Fong, do you bring me word of my father and mother?'

Mary's heart plunged as he shook his head gravely. 'But they are still finding — prisoners — hidden and unsuspected.'

Mei-Lee's blanched face was more than ever like new ivory. 'Then they are not at our home in Pei-ping? They really are not?'

He ran the point of his tongue around his reluctant lips. 'Of that we can be very sure,' he said sorrowfully, 'for the home itself is gone. And from the little news we have had, no one knows — anything. But you must take courage. Many survive imprisonment and exile. Our people have courage and toughness to endure.'

Mary edged closer to Mei-Lee on the small settle. You did not caress Mei-Lee. You did not throw your arms around her or kiss her; not any more than you would Marita; not any more than you would Carrie Kate; they all repelled caresses. But Mary felt sure Mei-Lee would like to feel the warm nearness of her friend in this bleak moment.

Mary's throat was aching with sympathy. Mei-Lee must be picturing the old home — the moon gate — the pool — the plum trees — all bathed in the eternal sunshine of memory. She must be picturing the present reality: ashes and rubble. And her family?

After a painful silence Mr. Fong said: 'Some moneys reached me; arrangements your father made long ago. I have used them to reimburse Doctor Lau. Have you found it needful to incur obligations in the meanwhile?'

Wordlessly Mei-Lee shook her head. Wordlessly still, she lifted the necklace of gray-green beads, pulled the cylinder into view. Mary had not noticed the necklace for some time, and now she saw with surprise that half the lacy carved beads were gone. Then her attention was distracted from the necklace. With an oblique glance of cool apology, Mr. Fong drew from his billfold a clipping, waved it toward Mei-Lee, and spoke rapidly and protestingly in Chinese.

That clipping! Mary recognized it, for she had scrutinized the same item repeatedly, to see what hidden suggestions could be gleaned from it by the unsympathetic. It was, of course, the story of the Marys and their vindication of Gordon Pitcairn. The *Post* must have grounds for its claim that it went everywhere.

Shouting Luke in Arizona, Mr. Fong in the Eastern or Central States ——

Mr. Fong abruptly turned off the faucet of his speech, and waited for Mei-Lee to reply. Mei-Lee had listened with the tight lips and lowered eyes of resistance, her hands folded in her lap. She answered in English, as if purposely to include Mary.

'You ask about the man who was injured. He is making a complete recovery. — As for leaving Denver, I cannot think my father and mother would wish it.' She sat very straight, not inclining toward Mary nor touching her. 'I cannot think they would wish you to take me away from the refuge, the friendship, I have found.'

Mr. Fong sat silent, darting quick glances from one girl to the other, without change of expression unless you could call the stiffening of his face a change of expression. At length he spoke again, accenting his remarks with a slowly moving forefinger which Mary found herself following as if mesmerized.

Mary heard 'Friendship House,' with the end of the title questioningly turned up; and Mei-Lee's rush of Chinese words in reply, including the name 'Hull House.' Clearly Mr. Fong had asked what sort of place Friendship House might be — did he think it a hotel, perhaps? — and Mei-Lee had explained that it resembled the famous center in Chicago. Mr. Fong's face seemed to soften slightly at that, but he still shook a dubious head as question and answer flowed on.

Mei-Lee turned resolutely to Mary. 'Mary,' she asked, 'can we take Mr. Fong to meet your father and mother?'

'Why, Mei-Lee, of course. — Mr. Fong, my parents would be delighted to meet a friend of Mei-Lee's family.'

'I thank you,' Mr. Fong said coldly, rising to make a courtly bow from the hips. He turned to Mei-Lee. 'You will inform Mrs. Lau? I trust you are not accustomed to accepting invitations without consulting her?'

'Certainly not, Mr. Fong.' Mei-Lee's voice was as cold as his. 'I will telephone her at once. — Will you come with me, Mary?'

'Will I come with you?' Mary muttered in soft explosions as she trotted at Mei-Lee's side. 'I wouldn't have stayed there without you for any money. He petrifies me. Oh, Mei-Lee, what on earth was he saying?'

Mei-Lee was breathing gustily through her aristocratic nostrils. She didn't even see Patsy and Day when they approached, and they veered away, looking awestruck and puzzled. 'Mr. Fong — Mr. Fong is a stuffed shirt!' Mei-Lee declared vehemently. 'He thinks he should have me under closer supervision. In this Cleveland, Ohio, of his — I won't be but a minute phoning, Mary.'

Mary's mouth popped open, but she closed it, swallowing her questions. If Mei-Lee chose to be evasive ——

Mary was glad that Mr. Fong had a taxi waiting at the school entrance. She had been wondering how she could endure trying to make polite conversation throughout the walk or bus-ride; or maybe not even talking, but tagging forlornly on the edges of Mr. Fong's lecture to Mei-Lee in Chinese. The taxi would shorten the ordeal.

When they arrived at Friendship House, Mary could

see Mr. Fong's quick glance appraising the cold exterior even while he was paying the driver. And when they pushed through the crowd of youngsters matted, as always, around the door, she was certain that his nostrils quivered as if he were protesting, 'This scum! These Japanese! This rabble!'

When she opened the door with her latch-key, the Friendship House atmosphere engulfed them: its present echoing emptiness; its stubborn old-building odor and the contending smell of waxed linoleum and the antiseptic effluvium rising from the Clinic.

'Would you care to look at the Clinic and meet my father and mother at once?' Mary asked. 'They will be helping the doctor and the dentist.'

Mr. Fong jerked a quick bow and followed the girls down the shabby stairs. The Clinic looked more makeshift, more poverty-stricken than ever to Mary, with Mr. Fong surveying it over her shoulder. And the people: some of them were neatly dressed working people; and no one could be tidier than Serafina and Asuncion, waiting primly for the doctor. But there were others whose desolate look always turned Mary's heart upside down. There was Old Nina, eyes red-rimmed under a frizzled topknot that arrested the glance because it had been dyed a violent rose color. There was a little girl mother in a funny costume topped by a broad-brimmed summer hat, her thin child legs blue with cold above her spike-heeled pumps.

Mother, in spotless white, smiled across the scales where she was weighing the little girl's wizened baby. Father's head poked up over the curtain on the men's side and he boomed a welcome. Mary felt better as she made the introductions. For all his business suit and topcoat, Mr. Fong had the air of an ambassador; but Father's and Mother's poise equaled his own, and their graciousness was not even slightly tarnished by their surroundings.

Mother asked hopefully, 'And is there any word ——?' Her face sobered when Mr. Fong shook a brusque head. 'Mr. Fong,' she suggested hospitably as a basement door opened and more patients came in, 'perhaps you'd rather go on up to the apartment until we can get away. Two of our volunteer helpers seem to have been detained, so I cannot tell how soon we shall be free.'

'Why not stay and have dinner with us, Mr. Fong?' Father called persuasively. 'Dinnertime is the Lockes' visiting time.'

'Yes, do, Mr. Fong,' Mother seconded him. 'I trust you won't mind a very casual meal.'

'Please, Mr. Fong,' said Mei-Lee.

Bowing and smiling, Mr. Fong accepted, and the three climbed the two flights of stairs, meeting the wide-eyed gaze of Day and Patsy, on their breathless way to their posts in chapel and game room.

Again Mary seemed to sense Mr. Fong's reaction as they entered the crowded living room. Mother had not had time yet to lighten its stuffy drabness. She had made the merest beginning by clearing one wall of miscellaneous pictures and mottoes and hanging in their place a group of family miniatures. Great-grandfather, Great-grandmother, and a pair of great-grandaunts gazed serenely on their new setting.

'If you care to read,' Mary said politely, 'you may
find something of interest here or in the dining-room
bookcases across the hall. Most of our books are upstairs in Father's study. And if you will excuse us ——?
I am the cook when Mother is busy.'

The two girls escaped to the kitchen and closed the
door between. Mary swung open the refrigerator and
clucked apprehensively at its meager shelves.

Mei-Lei said, 'Mr. Fong is from North China. Those
North China dumplings ——'

'Might soften his hard heart! Oh, Mei-Lee, you be
making the dough, and I'll dash to the store for meat
and greens.'

Twenty minutes later, when Mary came pelting upstairs again, panting with haste, she stopped aghast.
The living room was empty, and from the bathroom
came voices and the sound of splashing. Mary peered in
the bathroom door above her double armload of grocer-
ies. The bathroom was crowded, with Mei-Lee, Jick,
Bitsy, and a round dot of a Negro boy. And Mr. Fong.

Mr. Fong was holding the squirming colored child
while Mei-Lee washed his bared arm with abundance of
soapy water which was turning pink in the lavatory.
Jick stood with the spread feet and penetrating gaze of
an expert, and Bitsy had pushed in between Mr. Fong's
legs and was squatting there to peer up at the operation.

'Now the mer-thi-o-late,' Jick ordered. 'On the top
shelf so Bitsy can't get it again to make red lips like Mary.'

What would Mr. Fong be thinking of all this?

'Why didn't Lancelot go down to the Clinic?' Mary
asked.

All five faces jerked round.

'Jick brought him up here,' Mei-Lee explained. 'And he was howling so.'

'Well,' Mary said resignedly, 'as soon as you've finished, the Little Boys must take him back where they found him.'

'In the game room,' said Jick.

'Lots-a-lants slided off the slide into a gurrul,' Bitsy explained solemnly. 'And scraped all his arm off on the floor. The germy floor.'

Mary reluctantly left the nursing corps to complete its task and went back to dinner preparations. She put the best Chinese tablecloth on the table, and managed to piece out nearly a service of unchipped dishes: ten-cent-store china, but pretty. Mei-Lee soon joined her, and they worked to the usual Friendship House accompaniment of muffled sound. Loud blasts of the trumpet, tattoo of the drum, and gusts of laughter eddied upward. Feet pounded up the stairs, down the stairs. The steady hum of voices behind closed classroom doors sharpened whenever the doors were opened for a moment. At last came the finale: a thunderous clatter, a repeated echoing bang of the front door, the storming entrance of the Little Boys, Mother's light, quick step and Father's heavier one, the smell of lysol from their hands.

'Dinner is served,' said Mary.

In the crowded dining room Father drew out Mother's chair, an attention he occasionally remembered but oftener forgot; and Mr. Fong drew out Mary's; and Rusty, coming just in time, placed Mei-Lee with a flourish. Father matter-of-factly bowed his head and

began their favorite family blessing, and Mei-Lee joined
in with a sure voice. Though her head was decorously
lowered, Mary watched Mr. Fong through her thick
lashes. His eyes went first to Mei-Lee repeating the
words with the family, and then, with an interested
gleam, to the dumplings.

Those dumplings were a success. Mr. Fong looked at
his plateful, moistened his lips, tasted the dainties, and
asked, 'Surely this is not an American dish, Mrs. Locke?'

'Oh, no,' Mother answered. 'I think these must be
in compliment to you, Mr. Fong. Mei-Lee introduced
us to them. She made them for us once before.'

Mr. Fong surveyed them fondly, and made a little
bow to Mei-Lee. 'It is long since I have tasted them,
but these are almost exactly as I remember them,' he
said. 'So few North China restaurants in United States.
Most of them Cantonese. My wife also is Cantonese.'

'There were North China students in my university,'
Father said sociably, eating dumplings with relish. He
named an Eastern school.

Mr. Fong's answering laugh held more warmth than
he had shown before. 'My school also,' he said. 'Class
of 1922.'

'Well, this narrow world!' Father replied, chuckling.
'My class was 1924. You remember Johnnie Skipps, the
sensational forward in twenty-two? He was my room-
mate. And Jim Farrell ——'

Mary tried to catch Mei-Lee's eye. Men were such
unaccountable creatures, this discovery might be enough
to soften Mr. Fong. But Mei-Lee was staring somberly
into her plate. Mr. Fong must have expressed a settled

intention of taking her away from Denver, Mary thought, and her own heart sank.

Jick and Bitsy had bargained, as usual, for seats on each side of Mei-Lee, and they, too, seemed to sense something unnatural about her. They would not be pried loose from her when the company withdrew into the living room after dinner.

Mary and Rusty were last out of the dining room.

'Why would you have cheese, of all things?' Rusty hissed.

She frowned at him indignantly. 'Everybody knows blue cheese and crackers and coffee make a very sophisticated dessert.'

'Lin Yutang says there are two foods the Chinese never learn to like. They're oysters and cheese,' Rusty said witheringly.

Still more depressed, Mary pushed into the packed living room, sitting in a corner on the hassock. Father and Mr. Fong talked about their undergraduate days. They skirted the edges of Nationalist and Communist parties in China, warily, since Father did not know Mr. Fong's politics. And Mr. Fong politely asked about Friendship House and how the Lockes liked Denver.

Mei-Lee had been forced down on the davenport by the Little Boys. There Bitsy had taken advantage of the undeniable shortage of space by sitting on her lap, while Jick edged in beside her with a strangle-hold on her neck. Mei-Lee was deep in Little Boys, whose eyes grew heavier and heavier with sleep.

Yet Mr. Fong not only made no mention of the business which had brought him to Denver; he even appeared to avoid looking at Mei-Lee. It took Bitsy to draw his aloof eyes to that end of the davenport. Bitsy's arm also clasped Mei-Lee and he glared defiantly across her at his brother. With his red cheek pressed against Mei-Lee's ivory one, Bitsy suddenly barked a resounding croupy cough.

Mother was on her feet at once, and lifting him from Mei-Lee's crumpled lap. 'My patience,' she scolded anxiously, 'you've picked up a germ, Bitsy. You're hot as a little stove. And here we've let you sit in Mei-Lee's lap, practically in her mouth. Mei-Lee, run to the bathroom, dear — Get her a clean tumbler, Mary, and fix some chlorazene and salt and soda. Gargle it well, Mei-Lee, and use some of the nose-drops. We can't have you getting a cold.'

Mei-Lee went docilely while Bitsy reached after her with sleepy arms, muttering hoarsely that he wanted a 'brace, and that there was a fish in his stummick. Mary, hurrying with a tumbler from the kitchen, wondered whether Mr. Fong's dignity was offended by all this informal scramble. Mr. Fong seemed sunk in deep thought.

And still he had said nothing about his plans when the taxi took Mei-Lee and him away from Friendship House.

17

Hovering Cloud

WHEN MARY TRUDGED soberly into school next morning, Day was waiting for her, peering expectantly over the bobbing heads in the lobby.

'Mary,' she demanded, 'was that really a Chinese ambassador? Though I don't suppose there's a bit of truth in what the kids are saying.'

'What are the kids saying?'

'That Mei-Lee is a Manchu princess.'

'What do they know about Manchu princesses?' Mary scoffed. 'What do they know about anything but jive and hep talk?'

'Oh, come, now,' Day remonstrated, 'I guess you didn't read the morning papers. One of the editors gave a talk before our International Relations Club, and he said it kept him on his toes, the kids knew so much about UN and UNRRA and the rest. That's probably going to extremes, but there's a happy medium. Is Mei-Lee a princess, Mary?'

'Not that I ever heard of.'

Day, striding along beside Mary, sighed disappointedly. 'Oh, well,' she said paradoxically, 'she doesn't need to be a princess, because she is one anyway. Mary, will you be mad if I ask you something?'

'Probably,' Mary answered dryly. 'If it's anything that could possibly make me mad, it probably will. I'm in a mood to be mad if anybody points a finger at me.'

'Well, it's Pep Club. We wish you'd join. Your record makes you eligible, all right, and we all want you.'

Mary stopped short and rolled astonished, frowning eyes at Day.

'If the girls all came to you and begged you? The girls who ——'

'The girls who snubbed us? Just me, do they mean? Or the Assorted Sisters?'

'All three of you, of course.'

'Because Mei-Lee might be a Manchu princess?' Mary inquired stingingly.

'Oh, Mary! Because you're fun. You aren't bored with life or pretending to be, like some of the kids. I always did take to you, Mary. From the first day I did. With your funny little voice and everything. Even the way you sit, with your toes turned straight in.'

'Oh, yeah?' Mary retorted. 'You may think now that you liked me then. And you might leave my voice out of it. I can't help it if it's funny,' she complained in a soft squeak, which broke off as she recalled Day's final words. 'My toes. You said my toes — Do I honestly turn them straight in, Day?'

Day threw back her head and laughed, shortening her long gait to Mary's trot as they walked on toward the Sisters' locker.

'And what about my consorting with people like Caro?' Mary asked. 'I warn you I'll walk down Six-

teenth with Caro and her friends whenever it happens
that way. I think it's simply idiotic not to. How will
you feel about that?'

'How would I feel about it? Good grief, Mary, you
know perfectly well that I'm president of the State
Youth Council.'

'What's that got to do with it?'

'Why, race friendship is one of the things we're supposed to be working for.'

Mary stopped short, her mouth sagging open. 'Why
didn't you say so?' she demanded.

'You had your ideas all fixed. About East High kids.
About me. Is it all right, then, Mary? And can you
persuade Mei-Lee and Marita?'

Mary's face had indicated her changing moods: worried, petulant, astonished, sheepish. Now it dropped
into lines of worry again. 'About Mei-Lee,' she said,
'I may not have any chance. Your Chinese ambassador
came to take her away from Denver.'

'There she is now,' Day said. 'I must say she looks
darned happy to be leaving us. If she is leaving us.'

Mei-Lee was sparkling, and Mary awaited her with a
thrill of hope. 'Did he ——?' she quavered.

Mei-Lee said politely, 'Good morning, Day. Mary,
how is Bitsy's cold today?'

'Well, it's a cold,' Mary admitted. 'But, Mei-Lee, do
come to the point. Did Mr. Fong ——?'

'Mr. Fong is flying back to Cleveland. And I am
here,' Mei-Lee replied demurely. Nodding and smiling
at Day, she slid an arm through Mary's and drew her
onward toward their locker.

Day blinked and stared, shrugged resignedly and went her way.

'Poor Mr. Fong,' Mei-Lee said, amusement fluting her voice, 'he really believed — you don't mind, Mary? — that I had got involved with modern youth of the kind you see in the movies. I don't think anything could have convinced him that I was not lowering myself, except your own home and family.'

'But what on earth convinced him there?' Bewilderedly Mary sought for an explanation. Mother and Dad were wonderful, but the Little Boys — and Mary herself had simply no air at all. The living room and dining room were completely undistinguished. And Mr. Fong had certainly turned up his nose at the dirty little kids, and at Old Nina with her toes coming through her shoes; you couldn't fool Mary about that. As she recalled Mr. Fong's expression, her curly little face straightened itself till only the faintest fold of smile was left under her gray eyes.

'The books had something to do with it,' Mei-Lee said. 'And your great-great-great-great-grandparents, with the whole wall to themselves. We Chinese still reverence ancestors and books and learning.

'But there were other things, too. Mr. Fong isn't so cold and stiff as he appears, I guess. And he has sons and daughters. I think he liked the way I was — well, was just — there, in your house, as if I belonged. Maybe he was surprised at my making dumplings in your kitchen; but he has doubtless acquired enough American ideas to like it more than he was startled by it' — Mei-Lee smiled to herself. 'I think he was most impressed,

though, by your mother's sending me off to gargle before she even did anything for Bitsy. As if I were a
daughter,' she added wistfully.

'Mother really does feel very — very motherly toward you,' Mary said gravely. 'Know what she said?
She said if only we had more room she'd want to ask
you to come and live with us. . . . And now,' she recalled with deep satisfaction, 'the Pep girls want us to
join Pep Club, if you and Marita will.'

They walked on, in a brooding, happy silence that was
only underscored by the frequent exchange of greetings.
There was something about 'belonging.' You could
think you were strong and independent and capable of
sheltering yourself in your trio and caring nothing about
the rest; but it was not true. Just as the Hopis needed
to belong to the tribe and were only half-people if
they didn't, so you needed to belong to the whole group.

At school everything was better, and it promised to be
better still. At home conditions were less happy. It
was not the Friendship House program which was at
fault. The work was gathering momentum. Once the
Spanish-Americans and the Negroes and the plain white
Americans really got acquainted with the Japanese-
Americans, they found them agreeable, and the boycott
was gradually forgotten.

The Japanese-Americans were especially willing to
work and to cooperate. They were in the majority
when the women met weekly to mend and make-over
the garments collected for overseas clothing drives.
They were among the first to respond when Father and
Mother started a Home Relations Clinic, mainly to dis-

cuss parents' problems. Mr. Locke brought in qualified
speakers from university, churches, welfare boards, but
at first there were sessions that were attended by Mr.
and Mrs. Locke and the speaker, and by no other soul.
Then Yoshi had got her father and mother to come to a
session, and they had brought friends, and the Home
Relations Clinic had begun to grow. Occasionally it
broke up in a social hour which the parents seemed to
enjoy as much as if they had been children. They reminded Mary of the Hopis when the Mission had put on
picnics, and the roundest, most ungainly old Hopi
woman would laugh the loudest when she tried the
sack race or attempted to push peanuts with her nose.

No, Friendship's program marched on gallantly. It
was Friendship's attic that was giving trouble.

Bitsy's cold dragged on through all the miserable
stages common to colds. From Bitsy it passed to Jick,
and from Jick to Mother, who of course took care of
both Little Boys. The attic bedroom was all right while
the children were really sick and could be kept flat in
bed with their arms under the covers; though even then
Mother had to give all her time to imprisoning them
there. The gas heaters, burning day and night in the
Little Boys' cubicle, had small effect except in making
the drafts noticeable and the air flat and breathless.
Mother finally muffled her impatients in their skimpy
outgrown robes and ensconced them on the davenport.
By that time her own cold had swooped hoarsely
downward.

Mary felt of Mother's neck just as Mother always felt
of Mary's when she suspected fever and the Little Boys

had done away with the family's own thermometers. Finding Mother hot and dry, Mary borrowed a thermometer from the Clinic and put Mother to bed on the strength of its report.

Nor was that the end of the siege. Before the Little Boys were well, Father was barking tremendously; and by the time Mother was creeping around the apartment again and Father had wrestled through the worst of his infection, the Little Boys had been reinfected, and cried all night with earache. The Clinic doctor termed theirs a low-grade infection, and said that it kept flaring up in spite of the new 'miracle drugs.'

'The truth is,' Father croaked one evening at dinner, 'this is no place to live.'

'Oh, Father, I'm getting to love Denver!' Mary cried.

'I don't mean Denver. I mean this apartment. I mean our attic.'

'I like our attic, too,' Mary protested.

'To look at, maybe. Not to live in. Not to do any studying or writing in, either.'

'But this is January. Winter will soon be over,' Mary pleaded. Though she spoke stoutly, she was remembering what Day and Patsy had told her, that the slow, uncertain springs were the single flaw in Colorado's climate-character.

Father shook his head. He ate the popover Mother had made to cheer them up, not even pausing over its light and puffy crustiness, nor over the melting richness of the Hopi peach sauce inside. 'Did you ever realize,' he asked, 'that if it's open to every wandering breeze in cold weather, it's going to be awfully hot when summer comes?'

Jick had sat staring at Father, his face reddening and puffing out with restrained anguish. Now he burst into tears. 'I like my room,' he hicupped. 'I like to have it so I can make my own pictures on the wall of it.'

And Bitsy bounced up and down in his chair, roaring, till it slid out from under him and banged him down on the floor, where he added to his own sound effects by bumping his head and kicking his heels and going into a violent coughing fit.

'Out of this room!' Father thundered. 'Out of the room this instant!'

Howling, the Littles ran out, drawing in their small behinds to avoid a possible spank as they passed Father.

In the comparative quiet Mary asked dolefully, 'But, Father, what can we do about it?'

Glancing at Mother, Father took a letter from his pocket. Rusty and Mary looked askance at the letter as if they expected it to coil and strike like a sidewinder.

'You may not have known,' said Father, 'but immediately after the famous November Board Meeting I put out some feelers. At that time our situation looked none too secure, and it seemed prudent to begin looking around. While we have had several replies, there had been nothing that promised much improvement. Till yesterday. As you know, we must have a good climate and a suitable home for our family — our quiet little family.' Father gestured toward the door, where the Little Boys stood puffing and glowering, lips stuck out and eyes wet.

'Go away,' said Father, 'unless you're ready to sit still and finish your suppers like — like Christians.'

The Little Boys stalked in, chins down, eyes rolling self-consciously.

Rusty asked, 'Well, Dad? You were saying ——?'

Father flattened out the letter and read it aloud. It was an offer from a settlement house in an Arizona city, near the Mexican border. While the salary was not really adequate, the living quarters, as described in the letter, seemed more nearly so.

'How do you all feel about it?' Father asked, looking up at them. 'The Little Boys need not answer,' he added, as Jick's brow puckered and his mouth popped open.

Jick clapped his mouth shut, glaring mutinously.

'We're just getting established here,' Mother said hoarsely. 'I doubt if any of us would choose to leave. And it always has a suspicious look when you change so soon; as if you couldn't get along with the people. That's what most folks would think.'

Rusty said: 'I sure go for Denver. The university and all. And our band is really getting ready to go places. Dad, if you have to leave, couldn't I get a part-time job and stay?'

Mary summed up his remarks with sisterly scorn and one word: 'Patsy!'

'Tck, tck,' said Father. 'And how do you feel about it, Sis?'

Mary crowded the floor with her feet. 'Oh, awful!' Her voice was at its deepest, and shaken with misery. 'I never had a friend as close as Mei-Lee; and there's Marita; and Day, too. And now, when I've just begun to fit in ——'

Soberly Father replaced the letter in his pocket. 'But it's not right to stay, with things as they are. Not right for your mother. Even the stairs. Do you young ones realize how many times a day she goes up and down three long flights?'

They looked at Mother. She had been pleasantly plump when they came to Friendship House. Now even her comfortable suggestion of a double chin was missing.

'You see. It is really necessary for us to consider this offer,' Father concluded gravely.

18

The House

THE PROPOSED CHANGE was a heavier blow to Mei-Lee than to any of the Lockes. When Mary told her about it, she was silent for a long moment. Then she caught her breath desolately and said, 'Sometimes it is as if one could not take anything more.'

Looking at Mei-Lee's face, where the mask had slipped, Mary felt her own heart tighten. Yes, she thought, I can imagine, though I can't do more than imagine. I can imagine that when you've been beaten and beaten, there comes a time when one more blow would be too much.

For Mei-Lee had been beaten and beaten. Every day that passed without word from her family was a fresh hurt. And winter was passing, with no news at all. Even in late January, when an airmail letter came to Mei-Lee, with two hundred and seventy dollars in postage to carry it, it brought her no information.

The letter came from Lieutenant Hsu, and at the same time a delayed Christmas package had come from him, addressed to Doctor and Mrs. Lau.

Mei-Lee brought to school the letter, the customs declaration that had come with the package, the thirty-seven hundred dollars in postage that had carried it, and her own present. The other Sisters — and Day and Patsy — looked incredulously from the customs tag to the letter portfolio, Mei-Lee's gift. It was a folder covered with elaborate embroidery and containing blotters and stationery pockets; and the declaration listed its value as five thousand dollars. The other articles were an evening bag for Mrs. Lau, at five thousand dollars, and a handkerchief for Doctor Lau at one thousand.

'Some handkerchief,' Marita marveled.

'No. Very ordinary,' Mei-Lee said. 'It could have been purchased for fifty cents before the war.'

'Runaway inflation,' Day said competently.

Mei-Lee nodded, looking dreamily at her portfolio.

'Ho-ho!' cried Patsy. 'A man sent you that!'

Mei-Lee shook off the dreaminess. 'I like Lieutenant Hsu,' she said with some reserve. 'But I'd feel this way about anything that had come straight from my country. The lining of this portfolio — it is silk from Szechuan. I know, because that is the only section where they weave this particular kind.'

'But the letter — was there any news?' Mary asked.

'No news.'

The girls were eyeing the letter curiously, but when Mei-Lee opened it out they had to swallow their curiosity. Its vertical rows of beautifully penned characters told them nothing.

Patsy said, on a respectful indrawn breath, 'Well, naturally I knew Chinese wrote like that, but somehow you don't think of a guy's letters to a girl ——'

'But, Mei-Lee ——' Mary pursued her own query — 'didn't Lieutenant Hsu inquire?'

'He found my aunt and my cousins in Shanghai. The ones who fled from our home taking my little sister,' she explained to Day and Patsy. 'But Aunt could tell him nothing. That is how he puts it here: "She could tell me nothing." It makes me wonder whether they are not all hiding something from me. Mary,' she added under her breath, not looking at Mary, but down at the letter, 'I think I cannot stand it if you go away from here.'

The five of them stood in a miserable little group, not knowing what to say. Patsy broke the silence.

'You mean it's just living quarters that would make you leave Denver, Mary? Well, then, why doesn't your family get a house near Friendship?'

'Just like that,' Day said dryly, snapping her fingers.

'Did you ever hear of a housing shortage?' Marita asked.

'Or that welfare workers don't run to important money?' Mary put in.

'I suppose the Board wouldn't want you to leave the apartment at Friendship House empty,' Mei-Lee meditated. 'For fear the building would be broken into when nobody was there.'

'Oh, that is one thing that wouldn't bother,' Mary said. 'Our janitor has just one wife and baby. He'd be tickled pink to use our doll-house apartment. But that's beside the point.'

Mei-Lee was not willing to drop the subject. 'Why can't we see if there aren't some good houses within reach of the Center? Grown people don't always see the possibilities. Sometimes it takes the young folks to.'

'How American you're getting!' Mary said, her eyes hiding themselves and her lips curling in their wide smile. 'All right, let's go house-hunting. This is Club day, but we can look on the way home.'

Anything to make Mei-Lee feel a little better, she was thinking. Anything to soften the stricken look in her dark eyes. Even anything so senseless as looking for houses when prices had zoomed out of reach, and hadn't yet come back near normal.

For a little while they thought Mei-Lee was right about the superior initiative of youth. Almost at once they found a big FOR SALE sign tacked to the fancy wooden railing of an old-fashioned Denver house. Eagerly they rang the doorbell.

The place had been turned into an apartment house, and the caretaker shuffled to the door in ragged mules. She looked doubtfully at the motley group — Mary, Mei-Lee, Marita, Patsy, Day, and Carolina. But she let them into the hall and slid open the door of the front apartment to show them.

'What gorgeous carving!' Mary said politely. 'And look at the tall mirror over the fireplace.'

'Fireplace don't burn worth shucks,' the woman said. 'And between you and I and the gatepost the drains is bad. That's why they's such a sight of sickness here.'

The girls trooped out, their faces definitely sobered.

'That's what you'll run into in most places that are for sale around here now,' Marita said. 'I could have told you that.'

The other Marys were reluctant to let go of this first faint hope.

'Of course that caretaker did not want it sold,' said Mei-Lee.

'If it had new plumbing — Did you see the lavatory that opened on the hall?' Mary asked, shuddering. 'And it smelled as if the place had been steeped in odors for a hundred years.'

'It couldn't have been,' Patsy said practically. 'Denver isn't that old yet.'

'Smarty! But wouldn't new plumbing ——?'

'It takes ages, these days, to get a place replumbed, or whatever you call it,' Marita instructed them. 'Even if you succeed in getting the priorities you have to have.'

'It's a pity,' said Carolina, 'that the big house next door to us isn't some other place than where it is.'

Mary asked, 'How do you mean, Caro?'

'It's a bargain,' Caro answered, 'in a day when you don't expect bargains. The people had built it when they were young. They just wouldn't give it up, even when — when the district got to be entirely colored. They had money, too, and they kept up the property. I don't mean they had anything to do with the neighbors. They didn't. They were pretty offish. But they lived there and died there, the old man just last month. And now it's for sale, and Papa says they're not asking much more than it's really worth.'

Mary's mouth had curled delightedly open. She stopped short and let out a joyous little yelp. 'Hey! Lead us to it, Caro! Why were you holding out on us?'

Day and Patsy gasped slightly. Marita smiled silkily in an irritating way she had. Caro simply stared.

Finally she moistened her lips, swallowed, said:

'Weren't you listening, Mary? It's in the heart of
Denver's Black Belt. It's next door to us.'

Staring back at Caro, Mary flushed hotly. 'I think it
would be fun to live next door to you, Caro,' she said
angrily. 'Is it too far to go and see it now?'

Day, her arm linked with Mary's, pressed it warningly. Patsy turned her wrist to consult her watch,
and said, 'We're already almost late.'

'Then we'll go and look at it tomorrow,' Mary declared.

Carolina gave her a long, steady gaze of appraisal.
'If you are serious about this, you better telephone the
real-estate company and get an appointment,' she said.

Next afternoon the girls set out to inspect the old
house. Even the neighborhood impressed Mary favor-
ably.

'It's nice, isn't it?' she said in a pleased tone. 'So
neat and quiet.'

It was a pleasant block: comfortable houses built forty
to sixty years ago, brickwork well-pointed, woodwork
well-painted, shrubbery well-trimmed. Neatly dressed,
healthy-looking children roller-skated along the cement
walks, and boys and girls coming from school exchanged
greetings with Carolina and glanced curiously at her
companions.

'This one on the corner,' said Carolina. 'This is it.'

'Lots of snow to shovel: such a big corner. And how
very Victorian!' Day's manner was elaborately casual,
but it was clear that she was trying to pile up objections
which could not be attributed to race prejudice.

'Mother would love the Victorianism,' Mary cried.

'Mother is a little bit Victorian herself. In a nice way. Oh, look at the perfectly adorable brick tower! I always longed to live in a tower.'

'You certainly did not exaggerate when you said it had been well kept up,' Mei-Lee said to Caro as they mounted the porch steps.

'Painted every few years,' Caro agreed; 'reroofed just before the war, and new gutters, Papa says. Mr. Heinz wouldn't leave so much as a broken spindle overnight.'

A hatted and gloved woman had answered the doorbell and stood surveying the youthful group in surprise.

'Good afternoon,' Mary said, in a breathless little voice. 'We are the party that arranged to see the house. For my parents.'

The woman stood back and let them in. 'For investment?' she asked. 'For rental property, I suppose?'

'No, ma'am. For us to live in.'

The woman stopped, her eyes edging away from Caro. 'You understand that this district has become entirely colored?'

'That is all right with us,' Mary said sturdily.

The woman scrutinized her more closely. To see if I'm a very light mulatto, Mary thought, peering impatiently over the agent's shoulder. 'It's all furnished,' she exclaimed. 'Is it to be sold furnished?'

'It is,' the agent answered.

Carolina interpolated, 'The Heinzes didn't have a soul to leave their stuff to.'

'Isn't it too funny and quaint for words?' Patsy gurgled.

Mary said, 'I think it's wonderful. Don't you think it's wonderful, kids?'

'Well, you wouldn't have any trouble selling the stuff you didn't want,' Marita answered practically.

'Yes, I'd really want to keep my little blue bed' — Mary leaped far ahead in her planning. 'But Mother would simply go crazy. Oh, she wouldn't leave it just the way it is. She'd change a few things, and put away most of the plush and fringe, and keep just a sort of Victorian basis ——'

'It is good, solid furniture,' the agent said, taking her cue from Mary's delight. 'I suppose you've noticed the Empire sofa. But it was all good taste in its day. And it's remarkably well preserved.'

The black walnut had no scratches, the chair rungs were unscuffed, the upholstery wore protective covers, tidily tucked in.

'No little boys grew up on that furniture,' Mary thought aloud. 'May we see the whole place, please?'

They saw it from the starkly clean cement cellar to the attic, which smelled of leather trunks and old garments and moth-balls. Mary's eyes shone brighter and brighter, and it was plain that the other five were impressed, willingly or not.

'Imagine a wedding procession down this grand stair,' Patsy murmured.

'And the parties you could have in this parlor and sitting room, with the folding doors open between,' said Day, rounding her long eyes and pursing her lips.

Patsy spoke again. 'And the candy you could make in this huge kitchen,' she said. Mary looked at her with half-scornful amusement. Patsy's rosebud face was flushed to deep pink inside its pale gold halo. Un-

doubtedly she was imagining Rusty helping to beat
fudge at the broad work tables glossily enameled white,
or to stir it at the big electric range which was one of
the unexpectedly modern features of the house. Un-
doubtedly she had imagined herself trailing white satin
skirts down the broad stair ——

When they had at length worked back to the front
door again, Mary stood and sniffed the untainted air,
which held no smell more threatening than those of old
draperies and furniture polish and clean age. 'Will you
please give me all the figures?' she asked solemnly.
'Will you tell me just how we could buy it without
paying cash?'

Mother was busy with a class of junior-high girls
when the house-hunters trooped in. Mary opened the
door of the classroom a few inches and poked in a pleading face. 'Mother,' she begged, when Mrs. Locke
looked up from the attendance chart, 'could you let us
speak to you just a minute? You'd think I just dreamed
it up if I didn't have the other girls for witnesses.
We've found a house.'

'Mrs. Locke,' said Carolina, 'you ought to know right
away that it's next door to us. It's in the colored district.'

Mary sensed that all eyes were on Mother's face,
watching for her reaction. 'The nicest, neatest block,'
said Mary.

'I suppose we'd have to talk over any location, but I
can't see any real objection to its being colored,' Mrs.
Locke said, blinking thoughtfully. 'If people are

prejudiced — well, there are times when you have to
let them think what they please. But, Mary, after
all ——! Whatever put it into your head that we could
buy a house?'

'Mother, this one is a bargain. It would be a good
buy even in ordinary times, I bet. And now, when
houses are still way out of sight — and it could be managed with a thousand dollars down.'

'A thousand dollars down!' Even Mother, who
didn't like to advertise the Locke poverty, laughed irrepressibly at that. 'Why, Sis, your dream house might
as well cost a million and be done with it!'

19

Plots?

'Oh, but Mother!' Mary wailed. 'You'd love it! You'd simply die when you saw it!'

Yet even while she protested, Mary recognized that a thousand dollars was an impossible hurdle for the Lockes. People didn't go into Father's profession to make money; and the plain, simple business of filling six stomachs and shoeing six pairs of feet, with all the other necessaries that went with food and shoes, had kept Father from any savings except the regular payment to the pension fund. Even that payment had cost much contriving and doing without.

'But, Mrs. Locke, wouldn't you and Mr. Locke look at this house? Only look at it?'

If it had not been Mei-Lee who asked, Mrs. Locke would doubtless have replied with a definite negative, and so ended the whole adventure, in spite of her fondness for houses. But Mei-Lee's usually impassive oval face was now genuinely pleading, and her almond-shaped eyes were accented by violet shadows. Mei-Lee was too much for Mrs. Locke. She hesitated with one hand on the partly closed door, behind which wild young giggles were rising.

'Oh, Mei-Lee,' Mrs. Locke protested, 'don't look like that! We'll go and see it, but it can't possibly do any good, dear; you know it can't.'

The giggles boiled up anew. 'I've got to get back to my little monkeys,' Mother said decisively. 'But I've had the best news today,' she added, turning back once more to the deputation in the hall. 'Though there's some that's sad, too.'

'Oh, Mom, what?'

'There's a visiting surgeon here from the East: a heart specialist. And he's going to do that spectacular new operation on Rosa's little Mary Consuelo!'

Then the sparkle in her eyes dimmed with regret. 'Rosa brought one of those little girls with her to the Clinic, Marita, again. Asuncion. She hadn't been well enough to go to school, and she came along to help Rosa with the baby. The Clinic doctor made some tests with Asuncion, and he wasn't a bit encouraging.'

The girls' knitted brows mirrored Mrs. Locke's own look of anxiety.

'He says she needs — oh, almost everything different from the way she has it now: more nourishing food; and lots of outdoor air; and cross-ventilation where she sleeps. And right now she needs a steel brace for her back.'

'But doesn't the Chest take care of such things?' Mary demanded.

'Asuncion and her family haven't lived here a year,' Marita explained competently. 'They aren't eligible for aid yet.'

'But haven't we a fund here at Friendship?'

Mother sighed as she opened the door. 'It's all been used for other needs. I can't see the fifty dollars for that brace anywhere.'

Mary stared thoughtfully at the closed door after Mother had gone in. She nibbled her lower lip. 'I've got a war bond,' she said, 'but of course it's the smallest kind.' Her eyes dropped to her wrist and crinkled almost shut with her relieved smile. 'Polemana's bracelet!' she said. 'I can sell Polemana's bracelet. She wouldn't mind if she knew why. I bet it would finish out the fifty dollars. Really good Indian stuff is higher than it's ever been, and this is really good.'

Marita was tapping a dainty toe. 'Well, now, listen, Mary,' she protested, 'you have no call to do a thing like that ——'

Mary twirled around gaily. 'Goodness! That bond means nothing in my young life. And the bracelet — well, I got along without it for fifteen years. I guess I can get along without it again. Doctor wouldn't have said Asuncion needed that brace if she didn't.'

Inspecting the old house next day, Father and Mother kindled to its possibilities as enthusiastically as Mary could have hoped. 'I like everything about it,' Mother declared.

'But the district? You really wouldn't mind living in the colored section?' Marita asked, with unusual hesitancy. Caro was not with the party, only Mei-Lee and Marita accompanying the Lockes today.

'Well, of course, Marita, that's only an academic question,' Mother said in a practical tone. 'There isn't a chance of our getting such a house, in the colored district or out of it.'

'But would you live here if you could?' Marita persisted.

'I don't know why not. Mr. Locke and I have talked about it, and both of us think it would be sound sense. After all, it would be real proof of what we believe, Marita, and without our saying much about it, either. And it wouldn't seem too forced, too unnatural, since we are directing a settlement.'

'As you say,' Father warned, 'the discussion is entirely academic. I wish it weren't. This house is better built than those that are put up nowadays. Copper pipes, imagine! And the cellar walls as dry as a bone, which indicates ——'

'A big, big coat closet,' Mother said wistfully, 'and a broom closet and bedding and linen closets. And the kitchen ——'

'I thought those drygoods-box affairs like the one in our apartment were supposed to be the last word in kitchens,' Father observed.

'I'm just not the small-kitchen type, I guess. And look: plenty of room by these kitchen windows for a breakfast table and benches big enough for the whole Locke tribe — and Mei-Lee and Marita.'

'Oh, why torment yourself, Mother? You know very well the thing is out of our reach.' Father blustered in the tone he always used when he must disappoint Mother and could hardly bear to.

'Father,' Mary quavered, 'couldn't you ask the Board?'

'No use,' Father said brusquely. 'They should put their money into workers before they put it into buildings. Men count more.'

Mei-Lee had kept a complete silence. Now she spoke.

'If you did have a large house,' she asked huskily, 'might it be that you would consider taking me in to — to board with you? The way you have said before?'

More than ever since Lieutenant Hsu's letter had come, with the no news which seemed such bad news, Mr. and Mrs. Locke had both been tender with Mei-Lee. 'Why, surest thing you know,' Father said, with a gentle look at her. 'If we had room anywhere you can bet your bottom dollar there'd be a place for you.'

'I'd have a sister at last,' Mary said solemnly. 'Oh, Mei-Lee, that tower room! We could have a screen for times when we wanted to be alone — And Marita could stop overnight whenever there was a chance. And ——'

'Don't excite yourself, Sis,' Father advised impatiently. 'You know perfectly well you're only building castles in Spain.'

'But you aren't planning to give the Arizona people your answer yet?' Mei-Lee's voice was tremulous but determined. She had never before ventured to argue with Mr. Locke. 'Wouldn't you wait, sir — oh, just a little while! — to see if something might not work out?'

Mr. Locke said gruffly, but still with that parent look gentling his eyes, 'Well, as a matter of fact, we have talked of holding off till the next Board Meeting.

That's — let's see' — he consulted a pocket calendar —
'on Lincoln's Birthday, it happens.'

'Two weeks.   You'll surely wait two weeks?' Mei-
Lee begged.

'Well, as I say, we thought we'd lay the Arizona
matter before the Board at the regular meeting.   Only
don't get your hopes up, Mei-Lee,' he said, with the
tender indulgence Bitsy would have called forth.   'The
Board's not going to do a thing except say that it's
sorry, but it can't see its way clear — and so forth and
so on.   You'll see.'

Father and Mother had a call to make in another direction, so the three girls walked together to the bus-
stop.   Mei-Lee was unusually silent, and Marita kept
darting speculative glances at her.   They looked lovely,
there in the sun, Mary thought, looking at them as if
they were already lost to her.   Everything was lovely.
A sycamore's bare white limbs drew milky lines across
the deep blue of the sky, and the cottonwoods wove a
copper web, as if spring were already warming their
wintry bark.   Oh, Colorado was a glorious place to
live, with friends like these!

'You've got something up your sleeve,' Marita burst
out, flashing lustrous eyes at Mei-Lee.

'Up my sleeve?'

'Oh — more American slang.   You've got some
scheme or other.'

'Well, I wouldn't say it was up my sleeve, exactly,'
Mei-Lee answered, as if she were enjoying a private
joke.

Mary blinked back a sudden moisture.   'Mei-Lee, I

can guess what you've got on your mind. You think
somehow the Board could be made to see the light and
buy that house for a sort of distant Friendship Annex.
But, honey, it's an awfully slim chance, with Biffin the
Board president.'

In spite of her own warning, Mary's pulse quickened
at the remote possibility. It would be so wonderful.

'Well, the thing I see,' Marita put in with cool common sense, 'is that they won't hold that house any two
weeks on the chance of the Board's wanting it. Heavens!
what with the housing shortage and the labor shortage
and the shortage of supplies, and the new strikes always
bobbing up — well, you just have to face it: that house
may be snapped up the next half-hour.'

'But I thought — I thought it's being in the colored
district ——' Mei-Lee's voice rose in startled question.

'Oh, it won't be snapped up by white people, except
for a rental investment. But there are plenty of colored
people who would jump at it,' Marita said instructively.

Mary's little voice assented reluctantly. 'Father says
they've come in fast since the beginning of the war:
there were about eight thousand, five years ago, and
maybe fourteen thousand now.'

'But do they have the money?' Mei-Lee asked hopefully.

Marita nodded vigorously and then tossed back her
heavy bangs. 'You'd be surprised. Mr. Parks is in real
estate, and he says they make their payments better than
white people, on an average. Some of them would buy
a place like that and rent out rooms. And some who are
well-fixed would get it for an investment. So there you
are.' She snapped expressive fingers.

'But, Marita,' Mary exclaimed, 'don't people take options on things? Seems as if I've heard them say, "He paid a hundred dollars for a month's option ——" '

Marita nodded again. 'Yes, of course they do.'

Mary jiggled on her toes. 'Well, then! Why don't Bro and Sis Locke take an option? Bro has a few bonds. And he wants to stay in Denver bad enough. I do believe we could scrape up a hundred dollars together!'

'But you say yourself there isn't much chance the Board would do anything,' Marita reminded her. 'And then you'd lose your bonds. And your bracelet.'

Mary continued to jiggle. 'Nothing ventured, nothing won! And I got along without this bracelet for fifteen years ——' She stopped uneasily. Those were the same words she had spoken only yesterday.

The other Marys must be remembering, too. 'It's a better gamble than putting it into a brace for Asuncion, if you ask my honest opinion,' Marita said, studying her finger-nails. 'That wouldn't get you anything. They'd take it, and not even appreciate what you were doing for them ——'

Mary's two oxfords stood planted flatly on the sidewalk. 'I'm a pig,' she squeaked. 'And I've got fewer brains than a — than a peanut. I've already spent my bracelet and my bond.'

Marita lifted her brows. 'My, but you were in a rush! I don't see how you managed so much business overnight.'

'Oh, I haven't actually,' Mary rumbled in a husky little voice, 'but I really have — in my mind. I couldn't possibly take the brace away from Asuncion to — to option the house. And then like as not lose it. I'm not quite that mean.'

'Oh, you're nuts,' said Marita.

And, 'Here's our bus,' said Mei-Lee.

In the bus that swerved to the curb for them, they found themselves so separated by the crowd that they could talk no more about houses and Boards, options and braces. Mary swallowed a lump in her throat and thought, 'Well, I'm no worse off than I was before.'

And the other two girls clung to seat-corners and swayed with the swaying of the bus, and seemed to stare ahead of them into space, as if forgetting all about Mary.

Time and again, during the next days and weeks, Mary found Marita and Mei-Lee absent-minded. Time and again they broke away from the trio entirely, and Mary would be alone, watching rather blankly as the other two chattered to Day or Patsy or Gordon Pitcairn. And when they were walking home from school to Friendship on Club afternoons, the girls had a surprising number of errands which excluded Mary.

One day it was Marita who departed without cere-mony, darting into a Spanish café that they were passing. She murmured something sketchy about finding out whether she could buy some tortillas there to take home. She did not overtake Mei-Lee and Mary till they were at the door of Friendship House.

Another day Mei-Lee stopped suddenly in front of a Chinese laundry, exclaiming that she must ask the pro-prietor a question. All three girls went into the laundry, with its smell of steam and hot irons and clean hot cloth, but Mary might as well have stayed outside. Mei-Lee said politely, 'Please excuse me, girls,' and launched into an animated conversation in Chinese. The proprietor rested his wrinkled old hands on the counter and listened smilingly, glancing now and again at Mary. Finally he answered. He spoke at some length, jerking his head toward the back of the shop, blinking, nodding, evidently asking a question. Mei-Lee responded briefly, and spoke a sentence with its end turned more interrogatively upward than most of her remarks seemed to be. The proprietor nodded.

'Have you been having laundry done here?' Mary asked suspiciously as they went out.

'Yes. All Doctor Lau's shirts,' Mei-Lee answered, beaming.

'A lot of talk over a mess of shirts,' Mary grumbled.

Marita giggled to herself.

Mei-Lee and Marita were not the only ones of Mary's friends to develop surprising new activity. Passing the Cosmopolitan Branch Library another afternoon the Sisters could see Caro inside, her chair drawn up to the librarian's desk and the two talking, nodding, shaking their heads, as in a pantomime. And Yoshi came bolting out of the Japanese restaurant and almost collided with the Marys. 'Pretty good,' she murmured to Mei-Lee and Marita. She added indulgently to Mary, who was glaring with irritated patience, 'Don't you think it would be fun to have dinner there sometimes, the whole Home Ec Club? As I said, the menu is pretty good.'

At that everyone laughed, even Mary.

It was on that same afternoon that the girls saw a

familiar figure swing out of Mr. Abramson's secondhand store, a tall man at her side, and climb into the roadster parked in front. 'Funny!' Mary commented, one winged brow up and one down, like her father's. 'That was certainly Day and her dad. What would they be doing at Abramson's?'

Obviously, all this had something to do with the House; but what? How? When? It was like seeing a large, exciting tissue-wrapped package under the Christmas tree and having to wait weeks instead of hours to find out what was in it; and all the while pretending you didn't even see it, though everyone knew you did.

Besides, there was a shade of anxiety in Mary's hopefulness.

'Marita,' she said one day when Mei-Lee had darted off and left them walking alone, 'you kids, you wouldn't be planning anything that would ——? I mean, you know how Father is, sort of quick on the trigger. And Mother, she cares a lot about what folks will say. I mean, things do have to be sort of dignified.'

Marita said: 'Good grief, can you imagine Mei-Lee in on anything undignified? Or indelicate? My soul, Mary, she is such a complete lady. Not the clinging-vine type, though, the way I always supposed Chinese girls would be. You know that nothing can really scare me. I can make almost anybody stand off. But Mei-Lee beats me about getting out and going where she intends to go.'

'Well, is that a good example of changing the subject, or isn't it?' Mary demanded.

'Maybe not as much as I meant it to be,' Marita said, laughing and sliding a quick, calculating glance at Mary.

'Remember, Mary, even Mei-Lee could bite off more than she could chew. More than all of us together can chew. After all, we're nothing but a mess of girls.' She made a disdainful little face at the phrase, as if she despised the people who underrated girls, or despised being a girl: Mary wasn't sure which.

Almost every day Mary managed to pass the House, and always her eyes flew ahead of her to the sale sign on the porch railing. And always she began to breathe freely again when she saw the sign still there, and without the additional little board with the bold letters: SOLD. The House had become not only a desirable home, but a symbol of life in Denver. It had become a symbol not only of Denver, but of the Assorted Sisters.

Nor was that all: it had become a symbol of East High. East High seemed to Mary a very special sort of school. Its history reached back into Denver's early days and sparkled with illustrious names. It had always stood high in athletics, as well as in scholarship. This year, as often, it had led the state in football, and was setting high hopes on its track. And this lofty East had become a companionable place, which would be even friendlier next year, when the Sisters would be juniors. Even this spring, though, there was Pep Club. Right now Mary, Mei-Lee, and Marita were making their own jaunty Pep Club uniforms as a Home Ec Club project. Presently, out at the Hilltop Stadium, in the glistening Colorado sunshine, the Sisters would be helping to cheer their team to victory. And when they were seniors they might even be chosen Seraph Sisters.

Yes, the House became very precious.

Somehow the endless two weeks limped almost to their end. Friday, February 8, arrived. Still Marita and Mei-Lee had reported nothing. They were still busy. During the whole of the school year Mary had never felt so divorced from them. Their withdrawal, their preoccupation, might mean they were winding up what they had undertaken. Yet it seemed to Mary that they lacked the proper air of triumph.

'See you all Sunday?' she inquired, trying to be casual while she searched their faces for some sign, as they casually bade her good-bye that Friday afternoon.

Marita and Mei-Lee exchanged glances. 'I — hope so,' Mei-Lee said. 'And you, Marita?'

Marita patted a vastly indifferent yawn. 'If I can make it,' she said. 'But I'm dead. Studying for a stiff exam.'

For Mary, that yawn was like a match set to a fuse. So that was how it was! They let her, Mary, believe they were going to work wonders, and then, after torturing her with suspense for almost two weeks, they ——

The old, hot love of battle surged up in Mary as it had seldom done of late. It began, as always, with that queer tingling just above her knees; then the blood raced upward to her forehead, and she was ready for anything.

In another minute she would burst out at them and tell them just to drop the whole thing. She hadn't asked them to do it, had she? They could just scrap their old plan for Friendship House, whatever it might be ——

Mei-Lee was standing perfectly still. Mei-Lee ——

Mary gripped herself. It was like pulling yourself up by your own bootstraps, she thought. But don't let go, Mary. Don't let go.

Slowly, slowly, the hot blood ebbed away from her face.

'Well, come if you can,' she said in a small voice. 'I'd miss you if you didn't. No matter what.'

20

Such Things Don't Happen

'I DON'T KNOW when anything's surprised me more. What do you suppose got into them?' Father rumbled. 'But couldn't you steer them away from Board Meeting night? It does seem as if, with all the other nights there are ——'

'I was too much surprised myself,' Mother said defensively. 'The grown-ups never do start anything, and this Parents' group hasn't been especially lively.'

'Mother, what are you talking about?' Mary demanded with hope jumping in her heart. 'What is going to happen on Board Meeting night?'

'A party! Believe it or not, Sis, a party planned and to be carried out by the Parents. You could have knocked me over with a feather.'

Parents! Mary's hope grew limp like a balloon with the air leaking out. 'What parents?' she asked.

'Well, it was Mrs. Collins who came to me' — the balloon puffed out a trifle at the name — 'Carolina's mother. She's an attractive woman, isn't she? She said she knew she had been very inactive; that she and Mr. Collins had come to Parents' Clinic a few times; but that Friendship House had meant a lot to Carolina, and so

she thought it might be nice to put on a social that we
hadn't had to do a thing about.'

Mary stood winking her eyes rapidly. Did this mean
something? Or didn't it?

'But why not some other night?' Father fussed.

'I was so taken by surprise,' Mother admitted. 'It's
such a remarkable thing to have them show a little initiative. But I did tell her about the Board Meeting. And
she said, oh, yes, they knew about the Board Meeting,
because Carolina had mentioned it. But it seemed such
a pity not to have the party on Lincoln's Birthday. So
she — or someone, I'm not sure who — talked to someone on the Board, and they said it would be all right.
This Board member even said she thought the Board
could join in the fun for an hour. So what more could
I say?'

'I only hope Biffin was consulted,' Father said.

Seven-thirty on the evening of February 12. For once
there was a full meeting of the Board, except for two
members who sent word that they were down with flu.
Mary's heart was stifling her, just as it used to on Christmas Eve, as it still did when report cards were handed
out, or when she had tried out for the Wolcott Reading
Contest this year. She hadn't much hope. Neither
Mei-Lee nor Marita had come to Home Ec Club this
afternoon, and their excuses had been unsatisfactory.
Probably they were staying away from her because their
wild plans had failed.

Feeling deserted, Mary got the Little Boys off to bed,
reading to them impatiently and leaving them discon-
tented and thrashing wildly in their bunks. She had

tidied her hair hastily, and then, with Rusty, slipped into a back seat in the chapel. Father would put the Arizona offer before the Board tonight. What would come of it?

Arizona was not to be brought up at once. When Mr. Biffin had called the meeting to order, he cleared his throat fussily, and said, 'This, as you all, no doubt, have had called to your attention repeatedly, is the natal day of Abraham Lincoln, the Great Emancipator. If Abraham Lincoln were in our midst tonight ——'

He paused impressively, and Rusty whispered irreverently to Mary, 'If he were, he'd be a pretty dry old specimen.'

Mr. Biffin went on: 'If he were in our midst, I feel, without the peradventure of a doubt, that he would approve the interracial amity which we have attained here at our beloved Center.'

'Butter wouldn't melt in his mouth,' Rusty commented, his blue eyes glinting dangerously blue like Father's. 'Fat lot you had to do with that amity, Biff, old boy.'

'Hush,' Mary said listlessly, keeping her eyes on Mr. Biffin.

'Hence I think it is in keeping with the spirit of this illustrious day,' Mr. Biffin droned on, dizzily twirling his spectacles, 'that we accept the invitation of the Home Relations Clinic, and adjourn temporarily to their social gathering in the game room. We can return to our business after we have partaken of the collation so graciously prepared, and have enjoyed a brief program which I understand they have arranged.'

Father, frowning anxiously, was on his feet. 'Mr. Chairman, I rise to a point of order.'

'Brother Locke,' Mr. Biffin acknowledged, still beaming and still twirling his spectacles.

'Mr. Chairman, may we not transact some really important business before going in to the social?'

'It will wait. The business will wait,' Mr. Biffin said blandly. 'We stand adjourned for the present.'

The game-room doors were closed when the Board and the family came in sight of them, and when Mr. Biffin threw a pair of them open no light flowed out. The Lockes quickened their steps, puzzled, Mary's heart alternately soaring and swooping. Just as they entered, the lights flashed on, and there was a multitudinous rustle and titter, and then laughter and hand-clapping.

The Lockes stood blinking. The greater part of the game room was packed with rows of chairs, and the chairs were packed with people. In the open space kindergarten tables had been set end to end, decorated with a combined Lincoln's Birthday and Valentine motif, and with plates and bowls of food. Another group of chairs had been left vacant for the Board and the Lockes.

Hardly were they seated, taken aback but smiling, when Mrs. Collins addressed the gathering.

'We have met here together,' she said, her lustrous eyes smiling as warmly as her lips, 'to do honor to Past and Present; to the great martyred President, and to a family in our midst. I don't know if you've noticed,' she put in, her voice creamy with laughter, 'but there's a resemblance. If Mr. Locke were just twice as tall as

he is — and half as handsome — and if his eyes weren't
blue and his hair didn't verge toward auburn — why, I
declare if he wouldn't be the spit and image of Honest
Abe!'

Mrs. Collins waited in poised and beaming silence till
the laughter and clapping had died away. 'This little
party,' she said, 'is really to express our appreciation of
Mr. and Mrs. Locke and their family — the Family at
Friendship, we like to call them.' As she spoke her
eyes were searching the room, and now she broke off
informally. 'My land, didn't anybody think to bring
down those little boys?'

'Tck, tck,' said Father.

'They've been asleep for an hour now,' Mother was
saying, when she was interrupted by a pleased voice
from the doorway.

'We're here already,' it announced. Jick and Bitsy
padded into the assemblage in pajamas, skimpy robes and
slippers. Jick came head up, surveying the roomful with
an ingratiating smile. Bitsy stumped after him, stomach
in advance, chin tucked down, eyes solemnly watchful
under his lashes.

'Well, that's all right then,' said Caro's mother,
chuckling, when the Little Boys had climbed into the
chairs next their parents. 'Now we can go on. You
see, Reverend Locke and young people and children,
it is this way: it seems like your place had been waiting
for you. And if you should go away — well, I know
they say there's always someone to take the place of
those that go; but "it ain't necessarily true." If you
should go, I don't see how your place could be filled. So

we wanted to give you a little idea of how much we
think of you by having a birthday party. And what
better birthday could we choose than this one?'

Mary thought: 'This hasn't a thing to do with the
House. Marita and Mei-Lee aren't here, even. This
just happened to be tonight.'

Caro's mother went on. 'But mainly we have gathered to say our say.' She nodded toward the door and
at the signal a procession of children came in, evidently
propelled by adults outside.

'Hi, Lancelot!' Jick shouted irrepressibly.

'Hi, Lotsalants,' Bitsy echoed deeply, and then hid
his face in his mother's lap at the laughter.

Lancelot showed dazzling white teeth and deep
dimples as he pranced in, carrying against his breast a
placard with the big red letters, WE. After him sidled
Artemisia, head on one side and eyes lowered, shying
like a startled colt. Her placard rather puzzlingly said
BREAD, until Mrs. Collins, unruffled, stretched out a
long arm and turned the card over to reveal the word
WANT. Next trotted Haruko Furumoto, not a wrinkle
in her smocked dress, not a quiver in her serious doll
face, her placard held mathematically straight and
shouting THE. Finally a small boy as tow-headed as
Jick came sauntering in, his placard tilting this way and
that as his big blue eyes wandered interestedly over the
throng. His word was LOCKES. The four children
grouped themselves raggedly before Mrs. Collins, who
managed to capture Lancelot and turn Artemisia around
to face the terrifying audience, and settle Tod in his key
position.

'Now!' prompted Mrs. Collins.

Stragglingly the four piped and whispered and shouted their words with her. Stragglingly the rest of the company joined in as Mrs. Collins beat time with a compelling hand. By the third repetition the chorus was really impressive: 'We want the Lockes! We want the Lockes!' And someone added, in a shrill treble, 'We want the Family at Friendship!'

The Lockes sat in stunned silence. Mary, with chills of excitement washing upward from her feet, stole a glance at Father to see how he was taking it. He was clenching his jaw ferociously to keep his face from melting. Mother's neat features were untidily soft with emotion, and she was frankly wiping her eyes. Rusty's arms were folded across his chest and he was smiling incredulously.

Mary felt incredulous, too. Such things, she argued to herself, didn't happen. They simply didn't happen. Except in stories. You did your work the best you could, and some people liked it and some people didn't. But demonstrations like this didn't happen.

She stopped her internal arguing. Close on the heels of the chant two more people came into the room: Mei-Lee, carrying a bulky object, and Marita following her. Mei-Lee set the bulky object on the table, amid the dishes of food.

Mrs. Collins was addressing the assembly again. 'You might call this a Valentine box,' waving a hand toward the box while the four children in front of her squirmed and stared and stood on the insides of their feet and then on the outsides. 'Or you might call it a birthday cake.

Or you might call it a Locke box. But I guess "Hope Chest" is the best name for it, because we do hope, with all our hearts, that it will keep you with us.

'Now Reverend Locke and his family don't even know what it's for, folks, but the rest of us do. Some of you have already helped to fill it — rattle it, please, Mei-Lee and Marita — and those who haven't — well, I hope you came prepared. Checks will do nicely, ladies and gentlemen,' she added, laughing her creamy laugh in the direction of the Board members. 'And now, for you who don't know already, this is a house for the Family at Friendship, so they won't wear themselves out climbing up to their attic, or just plain drip away with colds.'

Everybody laughed at that, for by this time the Lockes were all, except the Little Boys, blowing their noses or dabbing their eyes. Mary stared moistly at the 'Hope Chest.' It was a box, painted to represent the House. It even had a tower, with a plastic tunnel topping it for a cupola. It had besides a padlock, both useful and symbolic, and a roof shingled with scarlet hearts.

'And now' — Mrs. Collins's voice was rich with satisfaction — 'I turn the meeting over to you all. The young ladies will help you to refreshments. And don't forget the Hope Chest.'

Marita and Mei-Lee were joined by Carolina, by Yoshi, by Day and Patsy, by Gordon and Ammie. Chairs scraped and feet scuffed as the guests helped themselves at the tables, or refreshments were carried to some of the shyer and less acquainted fathers and mothers, who appeared to be glued to their places.

The refreshments themselves seemed symbolic. The Spanish-Americans had brought *enchiladas*, because even the queerest *Americanos* usually liked *enchiladas*; the stuffed tortilla rolls, topped with cheese and chopped greens, nestled invitingly in hot baking dishes. With them went three-cornered *empañadas*, turnovers with crimped edges; and *frijoles*, beans, in green chili sauce. Jick, holding up his plate with his most angelically confident smile, received abundance of green chili, took a large, burning mouthful, leaped up frantically, spilling half his refreshments on the floor in his hurry to get a quenching drink of water.

The Japanese had brought fish in paper-thin slices, and rice cakes, and bright, firm jelly made from seaweed. The Chinese contribution was almond cookies and confections in green and magenta. The Negroes and the 'plain white Americans' were represented by fruit punch and plates of cake and cookies. The guests ate unfamiliar delicacies with considering eyes and gingerly tongues, and there was much laughter.

The company was as heterogeneous as the food. Here were people Mary had never before seen in Friendship House, and others who had come only to the Clinic.

There were Rosa and her young husband, only recently home from overseas service. They looked shyly happy, for Mary Consuelo was no longer a blue baby. She was in the hospital, well on her way to normal health after her operation. With them were Serafina and Asuncion, her neat print frock faintly showing the outline of the brace she wore.

There were Mr. and Mrs. Abramson. Mother had
been crowding in an hour's English lesson at the Abram-
sons' each week, and when Mrs. Abramson accepted a
plate of refreshments from Mary tonight, she said,
'Goot morning!' with something like a smile on her
gaunt face. In a corner of the room Benjy was playing
softly on his violin, his eyes always following Rusty.

There was a tiny old Spanish woman in a long black
skirt and high black shoes, a bright red blouse, a bright
yellow sweater, a bright blue necklace. Mrs. Montez
thirsted for color, and when there was something especially pretty and gay in a box which had been sent to
Friendship House, Mother often ran over to Mrs.
Montez's lonely single room with it.

There was Mr. Gallegos. There was the Chinese
laundryman. There was Old Nina. Old Nina went
slapping along the streets in loose-soled shoes and trailing skirts, the eyes below her frizzed pink hair haunted.
Old Nina stopped in at the Catholic church to genuflect
and cross herself and kneel for long minutes before the
statue of Mary. She went into Salvation Army meetings
and sat on a back seat, her face frozen. She went into
the Buddhist Temple, to see if there she might find what
she lacked. Never before had she come to Friendship
House except to the Clinic.

There was even Mr. Abernethy, the push-cart man.
Tonight Mr. Abernethy's clothes were clean and whole,
though Mary thought his trousers looked as if Mrs.
Abernethy had made them for a much larger man, and
then Mr. Abernethy had climbed into them backward by
mistake. Mrs. Abernethy was with him tonight, a dot

of a woman with tight-drawn gray hair and bright little
raisin eyes, respectably dressed in the garments of a
past day.

Meantime, the Locke box, the Hope Chest, was not
being forgotten. Some of the Board members backed up
in corners and wrote checks, holding their checkbooks
down on a vacant chair seat or up against the wall.
Some of the company dropped in coins with a cheerful
clatter, as if to say, 'Come on! Don't do less than we
do!' Out of an inner pocket the push-cart man pulled
a little bag, a tobacco sack, it seemed to be. Smiling
and nodding at his wife, who smiled and nodded back,
he approached the box with it. Mei-Lee unlocked the
house and opened it to receive the fat little sack, too
chubby to go through the slit. Mary's heart swelled
at the thought that the Abernethys had given all those
toilsomely earned pennies. And why? Were there so
few people in this world to whom he was Mr. Abernethy,
and not just the push-cart man?

At length Mr. Biffin set down his emptied plate and
bowed largely to the roomful. Father and Mother stood
beside the table and said thank you and good night with
words that halted and eyes that shone.

Mrs. Collins said, 'But this is part of the party, Reverend Locke!' and handed him the house from the center
of the table.

Rusty scooped up the Little Boys, Bitsy fast asleep in
a corner, both hands full of crushed cookies. The Board
and Father and Mother went upstairs for the postponed
meeting. The guests began to scatter.

Mary said breathlessly, 'Let's go up and see what's

going on in the Board Meeting, Caro, Day, all you kids.'

'No,' said Caro, 'we'll stay and help clear things up. You three go along. After all, it was you who started it, and we can't all peek through the service window.'

In the kitchen the Sisters stealthily inched up the service window.

Without turning his head, Mr. Adams said, 'Come in, young ladies, come in. Who has a greater right to join the deliberations?'

Giggling uncontrollably, the three tiptoed out of the kitchen and in through the chapel door.

Mr. Biffin stood, making a peaked roof of his two hands and declaimed: 'As I was saying, this youthful delegation approached me and laid the situation before me some two weeks ago. I must congratulate them on their acumen. I have inspected the house with care, and it is an excellent purchase. I may say that, with real-estate values still ridiculously inflated, it is an exceptional purchase.'

'You went to *Biff*?' Mary whispered to her companions.

'Elementary, my dear Watson,' Marita patronized her. 'We had to let him think he was in on it, even if he wouldn't do anything, the old tightwad. This way he can claim the credit of backing a worthy project — if we put it over.'

'Hush, you two,' said Mei-Lee.

'Unfortunately, Friendship House is only now getting on its feet, so to speak. Since we have no organization backing us, we had not the requisite funds for the down payment of a thousand dollars. Especially since we plan to increase the staff of workers as soon as it is possible to find the right individuals to help take the burden from our esteemed superintendent and his good wife.

'Unfortunately, therefore, we could not say, "Go ahead, young ladies! We will underwrite your magnificent venture!"' He paused, removed his glasses, tapped his teeth with them for emphasis. 'However, the young ladies persevered. With admirable initiative they secured an option, being aware that so excellent a property would not long wait for a buyer ——'

'Did you do that, Mei-Lee?' Mary's fine, high squeak was audible beyond the back row, and Marita pinched her warningly.

'Fortunate we did. Someone else offered the agent spot cash the same day. And we suspect,' Marita muttered, 'that it was Biffin.'

Mary's mouth popped open in soundless laughter.

'And now,' Mr. Biffin continued, 'we are about to learn whether the young ladies attained their goal: whether the Hope Chest, as our friend playfully called it, contains the requisite nine hundred dollars.'

All this time there had been a subdued clink and rattle at one side of the room. With chairs drawn up to the table, two of the motherly members were counting a heterogeneous mass of money. One of them said, 'We're about through, Mr. Chairman, and I'm afraid we're running a little short — just a little short.'

She was untying a small muslin bag as she spoke, and she interrupted herself with an exclamation of pleasure. 'I thought this was pennies, but it's dimes.' Quickly they attacked the dimes, everyone in the room watching tensely.

'Three hundred dimes!' the chief counter announced.

'But that was the push-cart man!' Mary whispered. 'Goodness, but he must have saved a long time to get that many dimes.'

One of the motherly women put down a figure, added, her soft pencil taps perceptible in the waiting hush, erased, added again. 'It comes to $826.75,' she said.

Marita drew a deep breath. 'And that last fifty dollars was the dickens to get. We got it since Friday, and we certainly had to plug.'

Since Friday! That was the day when Mary's patience had come near exploding. She felt herself shrink smaller and smaller with the humiliation of the thought. Thank fortune she had got hold of herself before it was too late!

Mei-Lee was on her feet. 'I have an additional pledge of seventy-five dollars, just received,' she said.

The storm of applause was deafening, and fully half of it came from outside the room. Mary jerked around and looked into Caro's face. She and Yoshi and Patsy peered in from the door, with Day and Gordon and Mrs. Collins smiling over their heads, and still others massed behind them.

Mr. Biffin nibbled his glasses, smiling benignantly.

'I think even Biff is sort of glad,' Mary murmured.

'O yeah?' scoffed Marita.

'Well, if he did try to buy it, maybe it was because he didn't think you kids could put it over ——'

'Softy,' said Marita.

'I would suggest,' Mr. Biffin continued, 'that Friendship House take over the burden of taxes and payment and upkeep ——'

'See?' Mary accused Marita.

'Sure I see,' Marita said wrathfully, 'and have the title in Friendship House's name. Oh, no, you don't, brother.'

She was in the act of springing to her feet when Mr. Adams took the floor.

'Why not instead increase our director's salary by an adequate rental?' he asked. 'Then he can take care of the payments himself, as I am sure was the understanding of the initiators of the project. We can house the new worker, or the caretaker and his family, in the present Friendship House apartment. I make this a motion, Mr. Chairman; that the director's salary be increased by the amount of an adequate rental.'

Mr. Locke had risen. 'In that case,' he said, 'Mrs. Locke and I could manage to repay into the work of Friendship House this initial thousand dollars. The repayment would have to be extended over a period of years, I am afraid. But only so could we accept the touching generosity of our good friends.'

'There is a motion before the house, Brother Locke,' Mr. Biffin interrupted. 'You have heard the motion. Are you ready for the question?'

With the motion unanimously carried, the meeting adjourned to an impromptu reception. The Board, the Lockes, the Sisters, Yoshi and Day, Caro and Patsy, Gordon and Ammie, Mrs. Collins and some of her helpers, wove around and around the crowded room, all congratulating each other and themselves.

When everyone else had departed in a satisfied glow, the family and the two extra Marys went up into the living room, Mr. Locke bearing the Hope Chest before him like a royal coffer. He set the miniature house on the table and threw back its heart-shingled roof. While the others bumped heads in their eager curiosity, he riffled through the checks.

'Is there one from Biff?' Mary squeaked.

Father pursed amused lips. 'No, Sis. But here's one that's — that's a stunner.' He detached it from the rest. 'One hundred dollars. From whom do you suppose? Abram Abramson.'

'Little Benjy's papa, my goodness!' Mary cried.

Mother tucked her head down on Father's shoulder and sniffled. Father said, huskily: 'There, there, Felicity, I know. I feel the same way. Humble. Humble as all get out. And happy. Because it does look as if we'd made a little start toward helping, or they wouldn't want to help us.'

Mother's reply followed Mary's own thoughts: 'Russell, people can feel kindly, but they don't do things like this. These girls' — she blew her nose and smiled shakily over the handkerchief at Mei-Lee and Marita — 'I simply can't see how they ——'

> ' "Three together riding,
>   Can win new worlds at their will," '

Marita quoted, and then hurried away from sentiment. 'I do wonder, though, about that seventy-five-dollar gift Mei-Lee fished out of her sleeve. Just in the nick of time. You hadn't reported any seventy-five-dollar pledge, Mei-Lee.'

'Biff!' Mary exploded excitedly.

'Incorrigible optimist,' Father said.

'Where did you fish it from, Mei-Lee?' Marita pursued relentlessly.

'Fished up,' Mei-Lee murmured, looking for once highly uncomfortable. 'You keep saying "fished up," and "up my sleeve." And that is very funny. You see I had to have a part in this. It means more to me, I think, than to any other one person in the world.'

'She says a part in it!' Mary hooted. 'When you've worked like a Trojan ——'

'And paid the option herself,' Marita put in.

'Oh, hush,' Mei-Lee interrupted, scarlet and self-conscious. 'I am trying to tell you that for me it is not giving anything; not anything.'

Father looked at her with troubled eyes. 'But, Mei-Lee, it seems out of proportion. Could you — that is, should you?'

Mei-Lee pulled at the silk cord around her neck, 'fishing up' the hidden necklace, from which, Mary saw, still more of the beads were missing. 'I'll really be glad to be through wearing this,' she assured them. 'The rest of these beads will pay my little pledge.'

'Those beads will? Why, what are they?' Mother asked, while they all crowded round to stare with dubious respect at the lacy gray-green spheres.

Mei-Lee doubled her little chin to look at them too. 'They are very old carved jade,' she said. 'They were stolen from the tomb of the Empress Dowager. How they reached my father I do not know; but he had many treasures of jade. Jade, and bronzes, and scroll paintings, those were what my father liked best to collect, though most of them he had lost in the decline of our fortunes. And when it came time to send me away, he and my mother discussed what small thing I could carry with me, of his treasures that remained. They wanted it to be something that would escape notice, and yet which I could sell to collectors in this country. The bronzes —' She waved eloquent hands, smiling at the thought of concealing the heavy bronzes on her small person.

'And the scrolls would be spoiled by the garbage,' Rusty said practically.

'Only this, which they call a sleeve scroll,' Mei-Lee answered, tapping the silken cylinder pendent from the cord.

'A scroll?'

'That tiny thing?'

'Yes. It is a painting by a famous artist of the Chou period. All along it has been handed down in our family. Now Mr. Fong has found a buyer for it, and I am to send it to him at once, by registered first-class mail.'

'Oh, let us see it before it goes,' Mary begged. 'All these months I've wondered about it — a live mystery hanging round the neck of — of my Assorted Sister.'

'Why, certainly,' assented Mei-Lee, and turned so that Mary could unclasp the cord.

Rusty took his penknife from his pocket and handed it to Mei-Lee with a flourishing bow, so that she might cut the stitches which held the tightly sewed oiled silk, the tightly sewed brocade.

At last she had the cylinder open. She unrolled it, a long, narrow strip, on the living-room table beside the

Hope Chest, pressing it flat with both hands as it started to curl like a released spring. The family pressed close and peered at its minute lines, fine as spider silk, its sweep of soft color. Across a deathless landscape a water-buffalo plodded eternally, a boy upon its back.

Mary's forefinger hovered over the boy. 'It should be three,' she said.

'Why three?' Father inquired, peering near-sightedly.

Mary giggled. 'It's our own poem,' she explained, '"Three together riding can make the planets sing!"'

'Three together riding can do most anything,' Mei-Lee improvised.

'Only it was two. I didn't do any of it,' Mary grieved.

'Oh, no?' drawled Marita. 'Don't you know it really got started when you bought a brace?'

'Only think of it — a home!' Mary cried, changing the subject. 'A home for all of us — you, too, of course, whenever you want it, Marita.'

Rusty grunted at the feminine foolishness. 'Mei-Lee,' he demanded, 'do you mean this scroll will bring anything much?'

'It will bring — quite a big much,' Mei-Lee assured him.

Mary's curled lip suddenly quivered. 'But to give up everything you brought from home, Mei-Lee!'

'No, I shall save one bead. I shall have it set in a ring and wear it forever.'

Father returned to his earlier question, cocking a mildly astonished eye at the sleeve scroll as if he could not find an answer there. 'Mei-Lee, I must get this straight: you mean this little painting will bring enough to take care of you in case ——?'

'But I may, even yet, have good news. I have not ceased hoping. And now I have a home; and a nest-egg. And I suppose some day ——' Mei-Lee left the sentence unfinished except by a blush and downcast eyes.

'Some day, that lieutenant,' said Marita.

'Captain,' Mei-Lee corrected her faintly.

'A home; a home' — Mary crooned the words as if they were the sweetest of all songs; 'a home in Denver. A home for all of us. We really have a home.'

'Sure we got a home,' Jick complained from the door-way. 'Why does Mary have to say it over and over? Mother tells us we got to go to sleep, and then you talk and laugh and pound around and sing. How do you expect I and Bitsy to get our proper rest?'

He staggered over to his mother, his flower face indignant, his thistledown hair on end. Bitsy stumbled after him, a limp gray lamb under his arm, his thumb in his mouth. He pattered on one slipper and padded on one bare foot. The combination was strikingly familiar. It jerked Mary's mind back to the family's entrance into Friendship House, a scant six months before, when everything was so much the same and yet so deeply different.

Mary's happiness swelled until it was too big for her. It overflowed. She dropped on her knees and hugged the Little Boys tight, and after a moment's instinctive resistance, they gave back moist, sleepy kisses.

'Yet everything's so different,' Mary said shakily. 'And it's all owing to my Assorted Sisters.'

THE END